CW01032913

LOST BROTHER

An absolutely gripping crime mystery full of twists

GRETTA MULROONEY

Tyrone Swift Book 10

Joffe Books, London
www.joffebooks.com

First published in Great Britain in 2022

Cover art by Nick Castle

ISBN: 978-1-80405-533-5

For Brian, our dear friend through the years,
with love and affection always.

CHAPTER ONE

'Tyrone Swift? Thank goodness you're there! I'm so upset — frantic. I've been wondering what to do. It's like my life's been turned inside out and upside down. One of my customers suggested I try a private investigator. I found you online, saw you had good reviews, decided to go for it.'

The caller had launched straight in, gabbling at Swift as soon as he'd answered his phone at seven in the morning. He'd just made coffee and was inhaling that wonderful aroma of an early morning brew.

'Who is this?'

'Sorry?'

'What's your name?'

'Steve. Steve Buckley.' An embarrassed laugh. 'Sorry, I must sound, dunno, cracked or something. Bit of a panic attack. My heart's racing.' He caught a ragged breath. 'This might be a complete waste of your time. I woke up at half four and I've been waiting hours to make this call. Time dragged by so slowly!'

It sounded as if the man needed to ring the NHS helpline, not a private detective. 'Has something happened?' Swift poured the coffee and reached to the fridge for some milk.

'Yeah, it's my brother — oh God, I can hear my heart pounding in my ears right now. I've hardly slept for a week. I can't eat. It's hard to explain on the phone. It's so complicated and unexpected. Been worrying I'm gonna go mad.'

Swift wasn't an emergency service provider and he'd been planning an early row on the Thames on this mellow, sunlit morning. There was little breeze and the flow would be easy. In his mind's eye, he was already out there, sculling gently, his heart pumping steadily, the oars swishing rhythmically as they cleaved the water. But Steve Buckley sounded at his wit's end.

'This seems like a deeply personal matter. Why don't I come and see you?'

'I wasn't really expecting you were gonna . . . Would you do that?'

'You need help, and I can tell you if I'm the right person for the job.'

'Thanks. Thanks *so* much. Lifesaver. Can you come this morning?'

* * *

Buckley had a second-floor studio flat in Fulham, not far from Swift's home. The scent of warm, fresh linen filled the crowded room. An iron perched on its stand in front of the window, ticking quietly as it cooled. Shirts and trousers hung in ranks on a portable rail, next to a tiny table with a tower of folded sheets and pillowcases that steepled halfway up the curtains. A pair of jeans lay across the ironing table, ready to be pressed. The kitchen was in a tiny alcove with a door leading off, presumably to the bathroom. One narrow armchair holding a stack of T-shirts stood near the single divan bed, which was smothered by mammoth checked laundry bags. Two mismatching rugs covered the floorboards. The door of the built-in cupboard was hanging by one hinge, and a set of shelves were crammed with magazines, books and electrical equipment.

2

There was so much going on in this claustrophobic space, Swift wasn't surprised that Steve Buckley's head was buzzing. Every action would mean bumping into something or moving an object out of the way. If he had to live here, he'd need tranquillisers.

Steve removed the T-shirts from the armchair and balanced them on top of the ironing board. He seemed a little calmer, reassured now that help might be at hand, although the room fizzed with angst. Swift had once worked with a colleague who experienced synaesthesia. She'd perceived others' anxiety as flashes of bright colour. If she was here now, she'd be dazzled.

Swift sat wedged in the pinching chair, wondering if he'd ever be able to extricate himself, while Steve heaved a laundry bag onto the floor and sat on the bed with his legs resting on top of it. The mattress dipped and sloped away beneath him. He had a thin face, tapering to a pointed chin, and his skin was smooth, with a tiny trace of acne scars on his forehead. His faded black jeans were fashionably ripped with a red skull print down the seams. He tugged his blue T-shirt down over his slender waist, fingering the leaf motif around the neck.

'The ironing has been keeping me sane,' he explained. 'The routine and predictability. I'm amazed at the things people send me.' He'd made coffee and placed a mug on the floor by Swift with a trembling hand. 'One woman gives me her tea towels. I mean, who irons those? She needs her head examining. Not that I'm complaining — it pays my bills.'

'Do you enjoy your work?'

His voice was edgy, rough. 'Love it, especially compared to what I was doing before. I used to be a receptionist at the council, but I got fed up of the regular abuse. I understood customers being upset about their council tax and delayed repairs, but it was as if they reckoned I was personally responsible for their leaking loos and damp walls. I decided to stop being a punchbag. The job was just about absorbing non-stop moaning and the odd threat. Whenever someone said, *I don't mean to be rude, but* . . . I knew I was gonna get an earful. One morning, a man brought a dustbin bag in and emptied it over the front desk. It was disgusting. The smell hung around for days. That evening, I came home and decided I couldn't stand it any longer.' The memory of his unbearable job was making him jittery again.

'I can understand that,' Swift soothed.

Steve tapped his fingers together. 'I read an article about people in London searching for ironing services and there weren't enough around, a real gap in the market. So I set myself up, reckoned a man doing it would be different, attract attention. Call my business *Iron Man* — get it?'

'I do. Clever pun.'

'Yeah. I definitely attract the pink pound — lots of gay men among my customers. I've been doing it a couple of years now. Some people react oddly, like it's a strange job for a guy, but very few. I'm my own boss, no one ranting at me. I like the peace and quiet. Turning wrinkles sleek and smooth, listening to music.'

'Ironing's one of my least favourite things.' Swift tasted his coffee. It had a hint of artificial sweetness, something caramel.

He understood the 'own boss' part. That's why he'd become a private investigator. At times, it was a tad solitary, but overall, he preferred answering only to himself.

Steve had an intense smile, the kind that doesn't match the topic of conversation. He finished many of his sentences on a nervous laugh and with his hand over his mouth. 'No offence, but it's obvious you don't iron much. You're sort of crumpled. I'm itching to press your clothes.'

Swift regarded his creased shirt and chinos, regretting not hanging them up the night before. 'Scruffy's my middle name. My cousin calls me a hippie.' He was crumpled in more ways than one, he reflected. He was missing his daughter, Branna, now she was living in Guernsey. He'd been prepared for the move, understood that it would be hard, but he hadn't realised that he'd feel as if the air had been sucked from his lungs. Some days, he walked around half awake. If

4

only Steve could iron his life as expertly as he did the laundry. Swift pictured handing it to him and receiving it back, all evened out and fragrant. Some hope.

He gestured at the ranks of clothes. 'Business looks to be thriving.'

'I'm turning clients away at the moment, got a waiting list.'

There'd been enough ice-breaking. Swift crossed his long legs to give himself a bit more room on the seat, taking care not to kick Steve's knee. 'So, tell me what's causing you such anxiety.'

Steve sprang up from the bed and took a couple of steps across the room, with a kind of lurching grace, to take a photograph from a shelf. 'Here. This is what started all of this off and made me call you.'

Swift scrutinised a framed photo of two men in cricket whites, posed on grass in a sunny field. They were flanked by a picnic basket, knee pads and bats. One had his legs stretched out while the other knelt beside him, a hand on his shoulder. They looked sun-bronzed, happy. 'Who are they?'

'The guy sitting is Tom, the one kneeling is his boyfriend, Sergei Sebold. I'm Sergei's ironer-in-chief. He showed me the photograph when I delivered his laundry recently. He was telling me what a great day they'd had at a charity cricket match. When I saw it, I couldn't believe my eyes. Sergei had to give me a brandy for the shock.'

'Why does this photo of these two men upset you?'

He shook his head, a flick of hair waving by his ear. 'Not them. Look at the man behind them, carrying a glass of beer.'

Swift refocused. The man was walking towards the camera face-on, wearing denim shorts and a T-shirt. Tallish, fair hair with a side parting. 'What about him?'

Steve came and stood behind him, bent down, thumbs hooked in his jean pockets. 'See his left hand?'

It was the hand hanging by the man's side. Swift tilted his head. 'His little finger is missing and the other fingers are stubby.'

'Hold that thought.' Steve bent and pulled out a drawer from under his bed. It snagged on the runners and he had to jerk it sharply. He lifted out a photo album, opened it at a page and handed it to Swift. 'That's my brother, Zac — well, half-brother. We had different birth mums.'

A toddler, straw-haired, perched on his toy scooter, both hands on the handlebars. 'The fingers on his left hand are short and the little finger is also missing.'

Steve's cheeks were flushed, his expression tense. 'It's called symbrachydactyly. It's a congenital anomaly. Zac was born with it. Also, look at his front right thigh. There's a large red mark, like a squashed fruit.'

'Yes, I see.'

'Now go back to the man again, below the hem of his shorts. You can just make it out.' He reached down again, into the drawer. 'Here's a magnifying glass.'

Swift held the glass over the image. On the right thigh he could see a reddish mark — larger, but the same shape.

'It was Zac's birthmark. We called it his strawberry. I was fascinated by it, wanted to touch it. I used to lick it when he was a baby, convinced it would have a strawberry taste. I was sure it would come off. My dad laughed at me and told me Zac would always have it, it was part of him.' Steve linked his fingers, pressed them on his knees. 'The man in that photo is Zac. I can tell you, when I saw him there in the background, I was reeling.'

Swift compared the photos: the missing finger, the birthmark. There were other points of likeness between the boy and man — similar skin tone, round eyes and a cowlick at the front of the hair. 'I grant you, there's a strong similarity, although it's hard to be certain. But why would this cause you such shock?'

Steve had a drink of coffee, balanced the mug on his knee. His voice shook. 'Because Zac died when I was four.'

Swift frowned. 'Then how can this be him?'

'Dunno. But it is, it must be. The finger and the birthmark. Sergei let me borrow the photo. I spent a week staring at it and going through my pictures of Zac before I rang you. I've been waking at night and examining it. I'm so confused, Mr Swift.'

'Please, call me Ty.'

'Thing is, symbrachydactyly is rare. That's my adult brother. I'm not a fanciful person or a daydreamer. I've turned this over and over. Sod it, I'm right.'

His eyes were brimming with tears. The air was heavy with his torment. Grief can last for life and make you yearn for the impossible. Time to take careful, slow steps. 'Let's start with the obvious. What do your parents say?'

'My stepmum — although I always called her Mum — died seven years ago. My dad died when Zac was one.'

'What about your birth mother?'

'She died when I was born.'

It was warm in the room. Swift pushed up his sleeves. 'Do you have other siblings, a partner?'

'No, just me. I was with someone but it didn't work out. Skye said I made mountains out of molehills. I expect she's right, I can be a pain. We're still friends. I talked to her about this, but I could see she reckoned I was making too much of it. I have an Aunt Tilly, Mum's sister.' Steve brushed his fingers across his eyes.

'Have you told her about this?'

'Not yet. We're not that close. It's going to upset her, so I wanted to sound you out first.'

He'd had no one else to truly share the story with — share the burden and the possibilities of this photo. The iron ticked once. Swift placed the tip of an index finger on both pictures.

'How old was your brother when he died?'

'Two, just.'

'What age would he be now?'

'Twenty-four.'

'And have you asked Tom and Sergei if they recognise this guy in the background?'

'They've no idea. He was just walking there when the photo was taken. There were quite a few spectators at the match. This was after it ended and people started milling around, getting refreshments.'

'I see.'

Steve locked his gaze on Swift. 'Would you be able to find him?'

'Possibly. A random stranger caught in someone's lens. It'd be difficult.'

'There's a chance, though, yes?' He made fists, rubbed his thumb knuckles together. 'I mean, it's what you do. Your sort of thing.'

'There's always a chance.'

'Oh. You don't sound hopeful.'

Swift flexed his leg muscles. The restricting chair was causing creeping paralysis. 'Tell me about the circumstances of your brother's death.'

Steve spoke fast, stumbling now and then. Swift guessed that he'd been rehearsing it in his head, building up to this visit, looking forward to the unburdening.

'It's hazy, because I was little. I have flashes of what happened, things I was told. It was Easter 1999. I'd gone to stay at my aunt's in Durham for a couple of days. While I was there, my mum — Corinne — phoned her and said that Zac had died suddenly of sepsis. He'd had a cut on his leg. It had become infected, and by the time she got him to hospital, he was seriously ill. He died within hours.'

'Your mum was on her own with Zac?'

'That's right. I'd just woken up that morning. Aunt Tilly came and sat on my bed and told me. I cried. Funny, I remember the salty taste in my throat. I'm not sure I understood what she was saying. My cousins were really nice to me and Tilly bought me a new glove puppet, a giraffe. I stayed with them a while longer and then my mum came and fetched me after the funeral.'

'Your aunt didn't attend the funeral?'

'No.'

'Wasn't that unusual?'

'I suppose, yeah, but Tilly had four children, and her husband was a firefighter, on shifts. Durham was hundreds of miles away, it would have been difficult.'

Still peculiar, in Swift's opinion. 'What about your dad's family?'

'He was from Falmouth, had a lovely Cornish accent. All I know is that he was an only child and his parents were dead. Mum never spoke about him having any relatives. I got the impression there weren't any.'

'And your birth mother, was she from Falmouth?'

'Dunno. I never knew anything about her, except that she died.'

Swift gazed at him. Families were as odd as they were diverse. Many people treated death as if it was something to be promptly tidied away. 'It must have been very strange and shocking for you, your brother vanishing from your life while you were on holiday.'

'It was like a weird dream, but in all honesty, I don't recall that much about it. I did get weepy at times, wanting my mum, longing to go home, but Tilly was very good at distracting me. And by the time I got back, Mum had cleared out a lot of Zac's things. She hardly ever talked about him. I'm sure I must have asked questions.'

'Did you visit Zac's grave with her?'

'There isn't one. Mum told me that she'd scattered his ashes in the local park, near the see-saw he loved to play on.'

Swift was sniffing something off here. It was such a neat story. 'That must have been hard for you, if your mum didn't help you grieve.'

Steve cleared his throat, rubbed his neck. 'I could see she was upset sometimes. Her eyes would be red or she'd be blowing her nose. Then she'd cuddle me and say, "Just got to keep jogging on." Maybe she'd been traumatised by what happened. At least, that's what I always believed. Until now, because . . .' He covered his mouth and leaned sideways against a laundry bag. It crackled and sighed as if affected by his sad tale.

Swift tapped the borrowed photo, trying to comprehend what he'd heard. 'Because if this is Zac, then he didn't die, and your mother told the most awful lie.'

Steve murmured, glanced away.

'Steve, this is painful, but do you think your mother could have been capable of such a lie? Why would she have deceived you? What reason would she have had for pretending such a thing?'

The man pulled himself up and hunched, bracketed his eyes with his hands. 'She always seemed like a truthful person. I suppose all children believe that about their parents. I trusted her completely.' He plucked at a seam on his jeans. 'She was kind to me. But now . . . this photo . . . it's too much of a coincidence. Put it this way — if it's not Zac, it's his doppelganger.'

'Do you have Zac's death certificate?'

He gestured at a filing case on a shelf. 'Since I saw the photo, I've been trawling through the stuff I kept after Mum died, but I can't find one. There's my dad's death certificate and I've put Mum's with that. Zac's definitely isn't there. I can get a duplicate, can't I?'

Swift couldn't imagine the circumstances when a mother wouldn't hang on to her child's death certificate. 'Leave it to me. I'll need to check the records. If I can find this man and he turns out not to be Zac, what will you have accomplished? Apart from parting with your money to me.' He could guess Steve's reply. It was the one he would make in similar circumstances.

'Peace of mind,' he said with no hesitation.

'Right, but consider it from another angle. If I can find him and he is Zac, that's going to make you review your life and who your mother was. Everything will change. So maybe you'll achieve the opposite of peace of mind. It will throw a grenade into Zac's life as well.'

Steve's brow creased. 'How do you mean?'

'If for some reason his life altered completely at two years old, he must have been deceived as well, and it will be traumatic. He'll discover that his mother fabricated his death.'

Steve picked up the photo, traced a finger across it. 'Yeah. Sorry, that was dim of me. I hadn't considered it from his point of view. It's so hard to untangle it all. My head keeps spinning, I get kind of hot and cold chills. Like a bad flu. I've been overwhelmed at the idea that I might get my brother back. Excited too.'

Careful what you wish for. 'Whatever the outcome, it's a hill to climb.' And of course, Steve wouldn't get his brother back, even if this man was him. That person was long gone. He'd meet someone who was both his brother and a stranger.

Steve sounded downcast, tetchy. 'You're trying to put me off. I didn't expect that.'

Swift recalled the rage, anguish and devastation that some of his clients had experienced when he'd presented them with the answers they'd employed him to seek out. 'Not "put you off" — I'm trying to make sure you've weighed up the consequences. I have to, given that there could be a lot of pain in store. It's impossible to guess where something like this might lead. You should definitely talk to your aunt about it.'

Steve picked his way to the window and pressed his forehead to it, the shirts jangling on their hangers as he brushed against them. The early September light was misty. Outside, a street cleaning lorry was thudding along the gutters. Tall plane trees swayed, some of their leaves amber already.

Swift had pins and needles in his right calf. He used the moment to escape the chair, get his blood flowing. With a hand on the back of the chair, he lifted his leg up by the ankle, pulling it behind him, stretching the muscles. As he did so, he watched Steve. There was a lack of confidence about him that made him seem younger than his years. Something missing, an absence that was hard to pin down. Swift wanted to ask more about his childhood, but realised that he'd have to go easy with him, let him talk more another time.

The lid was already off the box regarding Zac. It would be hard to slam it back down. Finding the man in question would be a challenge, but he had an appetite for the task. It would take his mind off pining for Branna, ease the ache.

He picked up the photo album and leafed through. The first half featured Zac at parties, in gardens, by Christmas trees, on a beach, Steve perched on a sofa and cuddling him on his lap, the proud big brother. Some of the children with their father, a chunky man with a thick neck, holding baby Zac in one arm, the other circling Steve. There were the two children with their mother, taken presumably by their father, as Zac was still a baby. She was slim, dark, with a quiet smile and soft hazel eyes. Then the father disappeared from the photos — and, a couple of pages later, Zac too.

Why would Corinne Buckley have concocted a terrible lie and broken up her remaining family?

Steve turned, his expression plaintive. 'I can't bear suspecting that my brother might be alive in this world. I want to do this. I have to, don't you see? I've been lonely since Mum died. I'm used to just getting on with life, but I might not be alone after all. I might even be an uncle.'

'Yes, I understand.' Swift had been caught up in barbed family dynamics a number of times. He'd learned the hard way to draw firm boundaries. 'I need to make something clear though. If I track down this man and he is Zac, that's where my involvement ends. Job done. I'm not approaching him about you. I'll give you his contact information and you'll have to deal with it from there. I'm not a mediator.'

'I get it.'

'Fine.' Swift took out his notepad and resigned himself to spending a bit longer in the torture chair. 'Now, let's make a list. And I'd like to make copies of some of these old photos, including those of your mother.'

CHAPTER TWO

'This soup's wonderful, the pear is so delicate.' Mary Adair waved her spoon. 'How's your avocado thingy?'

'Fresh, great.'

'Can't abide avocado myself. Tastes and looks like soap.'

Swift was with his cousin, the person he was most at ease with in life. They'd been friends since childhood and had both joined the Met, she having since risen to heights he'd never aspired to. They were eating lunch in a restaurant terrace above the Thames at Blackfriars. Swift didn't often get to see Mary alone now that she had her son Louis, so he was making the most of this opportunity. He found Mary's wife, Simone, brittle and opinionated. There was always an underlying tension when they met. With his cousin on her own, he could relax.

Over their starter, they'd discussed Swift's ex and Branna's mother, Ruth. She had thrown them into confusion last spring by inviting Mary's family and Joyce, Swift's step-mother, to her wedding to Marcel. Mary had never forgiven Ruth for ending her engagement to Swift and had been loath to attend. (*'She broke your heart and I really don't want to stick a smile on and watch her prance down the aisle.'*) There'd been dip-lomatic negotiations, and Joyce had attended with Louis, an

13

arrangement that had satisfied all parties. After the marriage, Branna had moved with Ruth and Marcel to Fermain Bay in Guernsey.

'Branna had a terrific time in her swanky outfit,' Swift said. 'She's still talking about it.'

Mary glanced up at him. 'And how's it going with her?'

'I visited Guernsey and Branna came to stay with me in August. We have online chats several times a week. She loves it there. Why wouldn't she? It's a stunning spot.'

Branna now lived in a house with a view of the sea, a quick run down to the glorious sandy beach. She'd settled so well, he experienced pangs of despondency. He was glad that she had taken to her new home — it was best for her — but there were gloomy times when he felt left behind. He missed collecting her from school, being able to arrange ad hoc outings. Now everything had to be planned, organised, scheduled.

'Tough for you though, Ty.'

'At times. It's happened. I have to make the best of it.' Steve's mother's words came back to him — *just got to keep jogging on*. He didn't want to dwell on it, pick at the scab. He caught Mary's perceptive glance when he switched the subject. 'Have you had any more discussions about moving into training?' he asked her. She was an assistant commissioner and had been mulling over a career sidestep.

'I'm still unsure. I've done a few days here and there, which have been fine, and I've enjoyed them, but I'm not convinced I have the talent for it full-time. The patience, mainly. I consider it, then forget about it again, which must mean I'm not that keen.'

'I can't see you at police college, somehow. Those green, fresh-faced cadets might not hold your interest.'

'We were fresh-faced once.'

'So long ago, I can't remember. And I learned more on the streets than I ever picked up at college.'

Their main courses arrived and they watched the river traffic for a few moments. Swift tracked the sunlight on the fast-flowing water. To him, the Thames was like a constant, rewarding lover: he lived near it, rowed his boat regularly on its tides, was soothed and comforted by its currents, read its moods, couldn't imagine life without it. He didn't express this to Mary, who'd likely comment that it was just as well he had the Thames as a companion, given that he didn't have much luck with women.

She had an unnerving talent for picking up on his thoughts. 'How's it going with Sofia Weber?'

'We've got together a couple of times. It's a friendship.' He'd met Sofia in Wales, liked her a lot, and had wondered if it might go somewhere.

'Oh, nothing more?'

'No, no spark to develop. You can tell when it's never going to progress past a certain level. The miles between don't help.'

'Live to fight another day.'

'Exactly.'

'Speaking of battles . . . Joyce wants to host a get-to-gether this Boxing Day.' Mary twirled pasta on her fork, mimicking Joyce's fluting tones. '*It's ages since we had a big meet-up and we really should all celebrate together.*'

'It's September! No one's talking about Christmas!'

Mischief played on Mary's face. 'Joyce is. She's making lists, planning a menu, in major campaign mode. She'll be in touch soon, so be warned.'

He groaned inwardly. His overwhelming stepmother was hard going, and any social event she organised was full-on bells and whistles. She'd insist on carols around the piano, and there'd be enough food to feed an army. 'I might be in Guernsey,' he hedged. 'I haven't decided yet.'

'Oh yes?' Mary narrowed her eyes. 'Christmas chez Marcel and Ruth? I can't imagine you fancying that, being third wheel. There'd be a dollop of indigestion with the turkey.'

'Not *with* them, obviously. I might stay in a hotel nearby, have Branna for parts of it.' Truth was, he hadn't broached it yet with Ruth. He'd been letting the dust settle after the move, or so he told himself.

'Doesn't sound such a good idea to me.'

'For who? It'll be good for Branna.'

'Maybe. Could just confuse her and make her feel divided loyalties. I'd keep it simple. Might be better to have her in turns at Christmas.'

She was rubbing a sore spot. 'I'll consider that.'

'Well, if you're not away from London, don't think you're getting out of Joyce's bash.'

'And I was convinced you loved me unconditionally.'

'Big mistake. On this issue, my affection is entirely conditional.'

'I do owe Joyce for navigating Ruth's wedding and taking the heat off everyone,' he admitted.

'Exactly. Payback time.' Mary shifted and had a sip of her mineral water. 'Um, Ty, there's something else. I wasn't sure if I should mention it.'

'What?' It was unlike Mary to be reticent.

She put her fork down, linked her fingers. 'I heard something on the Met grapevine about Nora. You might still be mad at her and not want to give her headspace.'

He speared a baby potato. He'd met DI Nora Morrow during an investigation. They'd been close for a while, until she'd left him for Fitz Blackmore, a colleague in another force. 'I was hurt when Nora went off with Fitz, but not for long. Once I'd licked my wounds, my main reaction was relief. Nora was hard work, she was moody and she didn't hit it off with Branna. We weren't right for each other.'

'I agree with you about that. I reckoned Fitz had done you a favour.'

'So. What have you heard?'

'Not good news. Nora is having treatment for breast cancer.'

He swallowed, sat back. 'That's sad. Did they catch it early? Is she very ill? What's the prognosis?'

'I don't have details. She's been off work.'

'Hope Fitz is helping her.'

'That's the thing. I've been told he backed off after the diagnosis and he's not around now.'

'That's crappy, but can't say I'm surprised.'

'Yeah, he's the hit-and-run type. More fool her for falling for him. Was it right to tell you?'

'Why shouldn't you have?'

Mary busied herself with a mushroom. 'Good. It's just . . . Nora hasn't any family in London, has she?'

'They're in Dublin. I expect Nora has her support sorted, she's a good manager.'

'Sure, and she'll have colleagues to lend a hand.' Mary reached a finger out, touched his temple. 'Your silver streak is spreading. I do like it.'

'Evidence of my great wisdom. How come you've no such signs of the passing years?' Her brunette waves were gleaming richly.

'"Warm chestnut", applied regularly by my hairdresser — you know, Ty, those useful shops where you don't take your custom often enough.' She grimaced at his wayward curls.

'I'm worried that if I have my locks snipped, it'll sap my strength. And I'm not going anywhere near hair dye. As they'd say in the tabloids, I'm rocking my black-and-silver look. Branna says with great sympathy, "Are you very old, Daddy?"'

Mary laughed. 'I've no room for pud. How about you?'

'Just coffee. I can hear the bells of St Paul's. Listen!'

* * *

After he kissed Mary goodbye, Swift walked a mile south along the glittering river to Sergei Sebold's flat. He felt content after being in his cousin's company. She had the knack of making the world seem a more benign place.

The clement afternoon sun stroked his face. He stopped for a few moments and watched a heron on the riverbank. His mind strayed to Nora and the shock of cancer. Mary's news had made him catch his breath. Nora had always glowed with health, kept fit with an admirable dedication. She had often been snappy and unpredictable, but the good times with her had been very good and he'd enjoyed her intellect and vigour. She was a skilled rower too, a good companion on the water. Time in Nora's company had never been humdrum. She was fond of her personal space, so approaching her in light of this illness would be thorny. It was a random disease and she'd been unlucky.

He glanced at his watch. Best get a move on.

Sergei Sebold's flat was on the twentieth floor of an ex-council block. It was built of unlovely seventies concrete, but the views were stunning and Sebold's living room was an ode to chrome and black leather. They sat outside on the balcony, enjoying the light breeze. The boats ploughing up and down beneath resembled toys.

'I was alarmed about Steve when he saw the guy in that photograph,' Sebold told him. 'I was worried he might collapse or I'd have to call an ambulance. One minute we were chatting about when I'd need my next batch of laundry ironed, the next he was as pale as one of the shirts he'd handed over. I had to make him sit down.'

'It's had quite an effect on him.'

Sebold scratched at his close-cropped dark hair, smoothed it down again. 'Too right. Steve explained how he thinks it's his brother, although he's supposed to be dead. That would mess with your head. Seems unbelievable. I had to sit down and have a stiff drink myself when he told me.'

'You and your partner have no idea who he is?'

'Afraid not. He just happened to be walking by. Steve was disappointed when he found that out.' He put an ankle up on the balcony railing. 'I printed and framed that photo because I liked it so much. It captured a relaxed, happy day. Never realised it would cause so much mayhem.'

Swift altered position on the hard metal chair, which had no lumbar support. One of the penalties of being so tall was his twinging back. 'Tell me about the day the photo was taken. Where were you?'

'The cricket match was a friendly, to raise funds for dialysis machines in London hospitals. My brother has renal problems, so there's a personal connection. We played it in West Ham Park. It was a beautiful, cloudless day and there was a fair crowd. Afterwards, we sat around, relaxed, chatted, had wine and a picnic. There was a refreshments tent and a bouncy castle for kids — it was a kind of party, great atmosphere.' He smiled broadly at the memory.

'So, the man in the background could have been associated with a player or just a random spectator.'

'Exactly. It's a good-sized park, he might have been a passer-by idling away an afternoon who decided to join in the fun. "Needle in a haystack" comes to mind if you're going to try and find him. And by the way, I've asked the friend who took the photo on my phone and she doesn't recognise the guy either.'

'Who organised the match?'

'A renal community nurse, Barry Harte. He's outreach for the Colne Dialysis Unit in Leytonstone. The teams were made up of hospital staff and friends and family of dialysis patients. I suppose Barry might be able to tell you more. Worth a try.'

At the door, Sebold added, 'I hope this works out for Steve. I hate to see him so upset. He's such a nice guy, quite shy and nervy. His emotions always play near the surface and he's quickly knocked back. It takes a while to put him at ease, although once you do, he's incredibly friendly. He's a demon with the iron and I admire him for leaving his crap job at the council, setting up on his own and making a go of it.'

Swift took the stairs down, to get his back moving. Picasso prints adorned the landing walls, and he stopped to admire *Les Trois Danseuses* before building up speed to the ground floor.

CHAPTER THREE

Andy Fanning, the trumpeter who lived next door, was practising in his converted loft. He'd had it sound-proofed, but the faint strains of 'My Buddy' snaked down to Swift, who was sitting in his dressing gown, eating breakfast. It made a change from Elvis, who Chand Malla, his top-floor tenant, liked to play, although the King was mainly silent at present. Chand had married, and now stayed at his wife's most of the time. He'd told Swift that they'd bought a larger place together and he'd be moving out in a couple of weeks.

Swift wasn't sure if he'd rent the top flat out again. He appreciated his good fortune. His great-aunt Lily had left him the house in Hammersmith, affording him a mortgage-free life close to the Thames. (Although he did grow tired of people pointing out how lucky he had been with his inheritance.) He was making a reasonable income and toying with the idea of turning the top floor into an area for Branna. Then, when she was older, she'd have her own quarters. Not that he was seeking ways of luring her to London. Truth was, he still missed his dear dead friend Cedric, who'd lived upstairs for many years. Lily had bequeathed Cedric to him as a sitting tenant. He'd been a true companion, a wonderful jam maker and a wise counsel. Wouldn't it be amazing, he thought, if he spotted Cedric in the background of a photograph, found him, and heard him say, '*It's all been a silly misunderstanding, dear boy.*' Swift shook himself from the delightful fantasy as Fanning segued seamlessly into 'A Night in Tunisia'.

He ate his toast and continued his online search for Zachary Buckley's death certificate. He scanned the results, checked them again, referred back to the details Steve had given him. There was no record of the death. He drank his cooling coffee, a ripple of excitement in his stomach, and then rang the number for Steve's aunt, Tilly Western. There was only the faintest trace of an accent, despite all the years she must have lived in Durham.

'I was expecting your call,' she said in a robust voice. 'Steve rang and explained about this photograph. He emailed me a copy of it. I can see why he's beside himself. I can't work out what to make of it. The man does have the same unusual characteristics as Zac.'

'It's a strange occurrence.'

'Can you find this chap?'

'I'll try. It'd be a real help if you could explain what happened back in 1999, when Steve stayed with you. He's given me his version, but his memory of it is patchy.' The connection wasn't great. He turned and the signal strengthened.

'I've been going over it all, as you do when something triggers it like this. Long time ago now. To be honest, I was put out that Corinne wanted me to have Steve over that Easter holiday. She'd never invited any of my kids to stay with her.'

'You resented that?'

'A bit. We didn't see that much of each other. I moved up here when I got married, and neither of us were that well off, so we couldn't afford many journeys. We chatted on the phone now and then. My second eldest had broken his leg just before that Easter, and I had a lot on my plate — four kids aged five to eleven. My husband was working nights, so I needed to try and keep them quiet during the day. I told

Corinne it wasn't convenient, but she was persistent. Now I think of it, it was a bit funny, the way she wouldn't take no for an answer. She wasn't usually the pushy sort.'

This sounded like fertile ground. 'Any idea why Corinne was so keen?'

'She went on about being dead tired and needing a break.' A dry laugh. 'Who doesn't need a break from young kids? I could have done with one myself, back then. These days, I sometimes wonder where I found the energy. Youth, I suppose! I gave in because Kev, Corinne's husband, had died not that long before and I supposed she was worn out. Anyway, she brought Steve here on the Good Friday, for a week. Turned into much longer, of course. Corinne went back to London that evening.'

'Was Zac with them?'

'No. He was at a friend's.'

'Who was this friend?' Swift walked to the window, watched sparrows dive-bombing the honeysuckle in the small back garden. Nigel, next-door's cat, was lying beneath it, chin on his paws, observing them. He wouldn't expend any energy trying to catch one. He was too well fed.

'I can't say, not after all this time. Not sure Corinne mentioned it.'

'How did she seem that Good Friday?'

'It's so many years back . . . bit tired from the long drive, I should imagine, and keeping Steve amused in the car. I'm sure I invited her to stay the night, but she needed to get back for Zac.'

'Tell me about what happened to him.'

'Corinne rang me early morning, the Wednesday after Easter. She was sobbing. I remember *that* as if it was yesterday, because the forecast was fair after a miserable, rainy few days and I'd planned to take the kids to Seaham Beach for the day. They'd been cooped up in the wet weather, getting scratchy with one another, so I was hoping the sea air would exhaust them. I was preparing sandwiches, making the most of the calm before they were all up and about, when the phone rang. Corinne said that Zac had cut his leg when he fell off his scooter on the previous Saturday. On the Monday, he was lethargic and he had a rash on his leg. He was admitted to hospital on the Tuesday and died shortly before she called me. The shock was awful, but I couldn't break down because I had to tell Steve. That was terrible, because he was only four, he couldn't take it in.'

Swift checked that date with her, crossed back to the table and made a note. 'And you didn't attend the funeral?'

'We discussed that during other calls, but Corinne told me that she'd be OK, she couldn't bear any fuss and she'd rather just deal with it herself. She said that she'd only just held Kev's funeral and she couldn't believe she was having to arrange her son's. I was relieved, because my husband couldn't get time off work and I didn't fancy having to travel all that way with five children, one on crutches. She asked if I'd keep Steve until she was able to come and collect him, and I agreed. That seemed the most useful thing I could do in the circumstances, and the best thing for Steve. He really missed her, of course, and was upset that he had to wait to go home. At least he had the other kids to distract him here.'

Swift could see how that would have worked for Steve, but given the absence of a death certificate, Corinne's actions appeared to have been geared to secrecy. 'Where did the funeral take place? Were there other friends or family there?'

'I was the only family. Our parents were dead — we were late arrivals, they were in their forties when we came along. Corinne was too upset to invite any friends, said she couldn't face it, although I suppose there might have been someone there to support her. She arranged a cremation.'

'Can you recall any of her friends back then?'

There was a sound like a pen tapping. 'Corinne became a solitary kind of person after Kev died. His death really knocked her back. She took up a hobby, stone painting. Got a bit obsessed with it, I'd say. She'd send us them for birthdays, and it got so we'd groan when another one arrived. She was good at it, created intricate designs, but there are only so many decorated stones you want in the house. Let's just say the local charity shops benefited from them. Corinne didn't socialise much, or she didn't mention it when we talked. I remember her referring to an Alys, she might have worked with her.'

'What hospital was Zac in when he died?'

'I assume it was the Connaught, her nearest hospital in Wembley.' Tilly added a tad defensively, 'It's so long ago, and I was trying to talk to Corinne with a house full of kids marauding about.'

Swift decided not to mention the absence of a death certificate. He wanted to contact the hospital and Steve had a right to be the first to know.

'It would be helpful if you could tell me a bit about your sister and her family set-up.'

'Oh . . . let's see . . . Corinne worked at Royal Victoria, a posh boarding school in Essex, after she left school and before she got married. She wasn't sure what she wanted to do and pretty much applied for the job because she was at a loose end, but it worked out for her. She lived in and really liked it there, had a fair bit of fun from the sound of it. From her description, it was a friendly place, lots of money splashing around, and the students sounded well-mannered. She left when she married Kev, a Cornish chap, and moved to London. He was nice enough, worked as a glazier. Not much get-up-and-go, but they suited each other. Did Steve tell you that Corinne wasn't his birth mum?'

'He did. Said his mother died when he was born. Was Steve living with Kevin when he and Corinne met?'

'No, he was being cared for by someone in Cornwall and Kev used to visit him. I was never told the details. Then Kev and Corinne brought him to live with them once they were settled in Wembley. Corinne was thrilled with him, really got stuck into homemaking. She seemed happy not to work. I was surprised about that, but Kev was very keen on her being a stay-at-home mum. He had old-fashioned views on that score, and Corinne went along with him. Then they had Zac, so she had plenty to keep her busy. As I said, Kev's death really affected her, she sort of withdrew. A while after Zac died, she found a job in a department store a couple of days a week, mainly on kitchen goods. Steve was at school, so she fitted the hours around him. I was glad. It meant she got out of the house. The money was handy too, of course.'

'What did her husband die of?'

'Stroke. He'd left for work after breakfast one morning and was unlocking his van when he collapsed. Died on the spot. That was tough, leaving Corinne with young kids.'

'Did you see much of Corinne and Steve over the years?'

A tired laugh from Tilly. 'No, but not for want of trying. I issued lots of invitations, offered to visit, but Corinne usually turned me down or vaguely agreed and then cancelled. It was mainly phone contact. You can only try so much with people, can't you?'

'And Corinne died a while ago?'

'Yes, from ovarian cancer. It was very quick, just months after the diagnosis. They say that it can be a silent killer and hard to detect.'

Swift went to the kitchen, poured fresh coffee. 'Did Corinne mention Zac when you spoke over the years?'

'Sometimes, if it was around his birthday, say, but that was it really. I guess she found the subject too difficult.'

But possibly not for the reason you thought. 'Steve told me that there's no grave.'

'That's right. Corinne scattered his ashes, said she found children's graves too upsetting. I got that, it's heartbreaking when you see them, so small and sad, dotted with teddy bears and toys.' Her voice went quiet. 'This is all a bit bewildering. How on earth can the man in the photo be Zac?'

'I agree it's hard to take in.'

'I'm in a daze, so Steve must be bowled over. He's a bit of an introvert, always been one to take things to heart, and working on his own at home these days, he's quite isolated.'

'It's hard for me to tell, because I've met him only once, but he did seem disturbed by the discovery.'

'I always wondered what his childhood was like after Zac died, on his own there with Corinne, and her not engaging much with the world. Must have been lonely at times. I've quite a lot on my plate here with family stuff, but I told him I'll come down to see him soon, talk it over properly.'

'That sounds a good idea. I'm sure he'd appreciate the support.'

Swift stepped into the garden when he finished the call. The day was still, under a clear canopy of sky. A lawnmower coughed into life a few doors up.

Nigel stretched, wandered over and twined around his legs.

'Bad cat, hiding and watching the birds.'

Nigel looked up balefully, leaped up on the wall and disappeared.

Tilly had been helpful, to a point. The sisters had been distanced, and not just by miles. They didn't seem that involved in each other's lives.

He crouched down by the pink tea rose where he'd buried Cedric's ashes. *It makes sense in a way, old friend. It all adds up at face value as a sad story of a child's sudden death and a mother's grief — until you can't trace the death certificate. Something's not right here. Sounds to me as if Corinne planned to get Steve well away from home at Easter 1999. What happened?*

He put a hand on the warm earth. A ladybird drifted onto his thumb, then away again. He recalled his aunt Maura in Connemara telling him that the insects were once called 'Our Lady's bird' because the Virgin Mary had often been depicted wearing a red cloak. The seven-spot ladybird was said to symbolise her seven joys and seven sorrows. He must pass that story on to Branna, although he could hear the questions it would provoke. *What's a virgin? Why did she wear a red cloak? Why seven joys and sorrows?* With her relentless grilling, she'd make a good detective one day.

* * *

26

He picked up his phone to call the Connaught Hospital, hesitated, stared at the screen, and rang Nora instead.

'Hi,' she said, sounding flat, 'didn't expect to hear from you. I'm surprised you haven't deleted my number. I would've.'

'I have letting-go issues.'

She snorted. 'How're you?'

'Fine.'

'Good. Been out in the boat recently?'

'Lovely row to Hampton Court last weekend. The river was calm, smooth.'

'Grand. Why the call? No, let me guess, the doom-spreaders have been in touch with you.'

'Sort of. I heard that you have breast cancer.'

'Correct. People love to share bad news. Bet you heard that Fitz has binned me as well.'

'Yep.'

'Bastard. Still, rather he showed a clean pair of heels than hang around out of duty or martyrdom.'

'*No comment*, as the suspect says in interview.'

She laughed again, coughed. 'What d'you want, then?'

He was pacing up and down the living room. *Why am I so bloody nervous?* 'Can I come and see you?'

'You really want to?'

'Yes.'

'I don't deserve it after I walked.'

'That's for me to decide.'

'Want to visit and twist the knife, load a guilt trip?'

'I'd have done that before now if I'd been in a punishing mood.'

'Fair point.'

'Are you at home?'

'Yes. Skiving off work. Hold on, you've taken me by surprise, I need to regroup.'

He waited, ate a plum. Nora had always brought fresh fruit when they went out in his boat. He pictured her chucking an apple or banana to him, her grey-green eyes dancing.

'You can visit. But only on condition that you don't express any sympathy or ask questions. No "how am I dealing with it", or significant glances and meaningful sighs. And *absolutely* no reference to making the most of every day. No pity party.'

'Wilco.'

'I don't want flowers either, or chocolates. I'm awash with the bloody things.'

'Right, I'm up to speed with the prohibitions. Is there anything you *do* want me to bring?'

'Get me mango or pineapple slices, thanks.'

'Tomorrow evening, then?'

'Can you make it late afternoon? I get a bit knackered by evening.'

'See you around three.'

'See you.'

She vanished. He expelled a deep breath of relief. That had gone reasonably well. Conversing with Nora often reminded him of coastal rowing: the currents could be unpredictable, and the wind and waves could take you by surprise and send you veering in an unplanned direction.

He rang the Connaught Hospital and was connected to patient liaison, then put on hold. After a couple of minutes, he was informed that the relative of the deceased would have to ring or visit in person and provide ID. Swift phoned Steve, left a message on his voicemail and set out to keep his appointment with Barry Harte.

CHAPTER FOUR

'We made about two thousand pounds from that cricket jamboree.' Barry Harte sat with a baby strapped to his chest in a bright blue sling. She was called Rosie, and now and again he cradled her head.

'Must take a lot of work to organise something like that.'

'Yes and no. I've heaps of contacts, so once I press the right buttons, things start coming together.' Harte radiated quiet competence with his steady, deep voice and calm manner.

Swift moved his foot to avoid kicking a changing mat. The small living room was stuffed with Rosie's paraphernalia.

'Sergei's great, we can always rely on him to give us loads of support,' Harte said. 'Why d'you want to find out who the guy in shorts is?'

'My client believes that he looks uncannily like his dead brother and he'd like me to identify him.'

'That's an interesting one and a bit of a puzzler. I'm trying to work out if I can help you. The match was widely publicised and we made sure it was child-friendly, so it attracted as many people as possible, not just those directly interested in the renal unit. That's not what you want to hear, is it?'

'No,' Swift admitted. 'Presumably you have or could get hold of the names of the team players? That would be a start.'

The baby made a soft mewing sound. Harte rocked her. 'I do have an email list. I needed it for arrangements.'

The doorbell sounded. Harte frowned at his watch.

'That's a new sofa bed being delivered. They're early, but better than not turning up at all. Sorry.'

'No problem. Go ahead, I can wait.'

Harte answered the door, spoke to the delivery crew, came back. 'Would you hold Rosie while I sort this out? They might need a hand up the stairs.'

'Happy to.'

Harte slipped the sling off, extricated Rosie and passed her over. Swift cradled her in the crook of his arm. She slept on, her translucent eyelids quivering. She was so light. It seemed ages since he'd sat like this, holding Branna, sniffing her milky scent. A hand squeezed at his heart. He stroked the baby's downy hair with a finger. They rested in a peaceful bubble while thumps and bumps rocked the ceiling. 'To your left, tilt it, now to my right. That's it!'

Footsteps on the stairs, then Harte closed the front door and reappeared. 'Thanks so much. You had enough of her now?' He rested his hands on his hips and smiled down at his daughter.

'I'm fine here. Don't want to wake her up.'

'She's a good baby, sleeps like a dream. I'm glad that bed's sorted. My mother-in-law's coming next weekend and we couldn't have put her in the creaking old frame we had in the spare room. Have to stay in her good books, she's generous with her time and money. So, where were we?'

'You mentioned that you have a list of team members. Could you send all the people on it a copy of the photo, ask them if they recognise the man? And if they could show it to anyone they attended with on the day. If you add my contact details, they can come to me if they have information. I don't want to increase your workload.'

'Can do. It's a strange story. How can this be your client's brother if he died?'

'That's a question I have to try and answer.'

'Nightmare.' Harte leaned over and kissed the top of Rosie's head. 'I can't begin to imagine the confusion the man must be in.' He sat back. 'I'll send the photo around anyone else who was there that Saturday. It might bring some info.'

'Thanks. I'd better hand your baby back now. There's a sudden warmth on my lap that indicates a nappy change.'

Harte reached for Rosie, sniffed her. 'Nature takes its course. Ah, Rosie-posy, I envy you so. You have the simple life: feeding, sleeping and pooing.'

* * *

Branna was on his iPad screen, wearing scarlet pyjamas. She bounced up and down while they talked, so that her head kept disappearing.

'Hey, keep still, you're making me seasick,' he told her.

'Ha! I'm by the sea, not you!'

'How was school today?'

'Sort of nice.'

'What were the nice bits?'

'I taught the class some sign language.'

'Excellent. What did you teach them?'

She made the signs for *Hello*, *Thank you* and *My name is Branna*. 'Hang on, just getting an apple.'

He waited, hearing noises off. Branna had been born with profound hearing loss. She'd worn hearing aids and used sign language. Now she had cochlear implants, which were a huge help, and mainly used spoken language, but she still preferred to sign at times.

She was back, holding up a red apple with a bite taken from it for him to see.

'That's like the apple the Wicked Queen gave to Snow White.'

Branna twirled it around by the stem. 'Silly Daddy.'

'That's me. I'm babysitting Louis next weekend.'

'He's *so* boring.'

Privately, Swift agreed. 'Don't be rude about your cousin.'

'He can't hear me. Want to see the sea?'

Before he could reply, she'd run to the window and was angling her screen so that he could see sky and pale grey waves.

'It's lovely, but I'd rather see you.'

She yanked the screen close and pulled a face. 'When you coming here? I want to show you a new rock pool. I found a little crab in it.'

'I'm coming to fetch you at the end of October, not long now. We can check out the rock pool before we head back to London.'

'Yeah, yeah. Got to go brush my teeth.'

'Talk to you soon. Big hug from—'

She'd ended the call. He rested his head back against the sofa. She'd grown, and in a matter of weeks her face had changed subtly, thinned out. This was how it was now, with him observing his daughter's development across the miles.

He reached for a cushion and hugged it to his chest.

* * *

Swift drove to Steve's flat the next morning. It had rained heavily overnight. The roads were greasy, thronged and noisy, troubled clouds racing across a watery sky. The first mile of the journey was stop-start. Swift diverted on side roads when he could.

Steve had been angry and weepy when he heard that there was definitely no death certificate for Zac. Swift had offered to take him to the Connaught Hospital, realising he'd need support.

A woman in her twenties opened Steve's front door. She was compact, olive-skinned, with hair braided and pinned.

'Hi, I'm Skye. Come on in.' She chewed her gum.

'Hello, I'm Ty. You're a friend of Steve's?'

'Yeah. We used to be together. Tea, coffee?'

'No thanks.'

'Take a seat.' She indicated the vicious armchair. 'Steve's still getting ready, he won't be long.'

Swift saw that the bed was clear today. 'D'you mind if I sit on the bed? The chair's a little tight for my frame.'

'Sure. You are super tall.'

Swift sank into the yielding, thin mattress, his back to the wall. It was almost as uncomfortable as the killer armchair, but at least he could move his legs and arms. He could hear a shower running and was glad he'd left plenty of time. Skye sat in the armchair. A scent of coconut wafted from her. Her eyes were dull, sincere.

'I'm glad we've got a minute,' she whispered. 'Steve's not handling this too well. He's quite a neurotic person, gets ever so strung out.' She linked her fingers, her nail varnish sparkling in the light.

'I got some inkling of that. He's dealing with a difficult problem.'

The shower stopped. Skye tilted an ear. A fan started and she continued, keeping her voice low.

'He's not strong mentally. I met him at the council, when we both worked there. He struggled with meeting the public. They sacked him because he was so irritable with customers. If people had too many questions, or presented him with difficult problems, he'd get tetchy. There were loads of complaints about him being rude.'

So Steve had lied to him about why he'd left his job, presumably to save face. 'Has he ever tried getting help?'

'No. I wish he would — I'm sure there's things that'd help him. I'd say his weird childhood messed him up. It sounds as if his mum was pretty neurotic in her own way, and now he's found this out about his brother . . .'

'Did you finish the relationship with him?'

She nodded and moved her chewing gum around her mouth with a sucking sound. 'I'm fond of him, but I couldn't take any more of his being needy and whiny, always complaining about how I washed up or made a sandwich. The least little thing can upset him for the whole day — breaking a fingernail, burning toast. It got me down.'

'Sounds exhausting. It was probably the right decision.'

'I dithered for too long. He gets envious too . . . jealous. If I was going to see friends, he'd try to sabotage me, say he was ill so I'd stay with him. My parents invited me on a holiday last year and he rang me every day I was in Spain, saying he was anxious or poorly. My dad was livid, said Steve was draining me. That's when I decided to end it. I did it when I came home.'

'Yet you've stayed friends.'

'Yeah.' She tucked her hands under her thighs, sounding resigned. 'He's a sweet man a lot of the time and I'm the only friend he's got.'

Maybe Skye was needy in her own way, wanting to be a rescuer. Swift gestured at the ironing board. 'The work he does now must suit him better.'

'You're right, although it gives him a lot of time to dwell on stuff, get things out of proportion.'

'I appreciate you telling me all this. I'm not sure what my investigation into Zac will mean for Steve. I have tried to warn him, but he's fairly blinkered.'

'I just . . . dunno . . . wanted you to have the whole picture, understand what you're coping with. He can be unpredictable, so be careful how you tell him things.'

A door banged. Steve came through and stood beside Skye. He was dressed in a grey suit that was on the large side and smelled of charity shops. It lent him a waifish air. His damp hair was flattened and he had a tiny shaving nick on his chin.

His voice trembled. 'Hi, thanks for waiting. I got a tad dizzy, had to sit on the floor for a couple of minutes after I'd showered.' His skin was sallow, and he had an unhealthy sheen on his forehead, as if he had a temperature and should have stayed in bed.

'Are you sure you're up for this?' Swift asked. 'We can do it another day.'

'I want to get on with it, make progress.'

Swift found his car keys. 'We need to get a move on, then. Traffic's pretty heavy.'

'Right. Am I OK?'

Skye touched his shoulder. 'You're very smart. Don't fret, you've got Ty to look out for you.'

'You'll call me tomorrow?'

'Yeah, like I promised.'

They went down to the car. Steve's lace-up shoes squeaked on the stairs. Swift might have been a parent in charge of an adult child, taking Steve to apply for a job or a college place.

* * *

The hospital administrator's office at the Connaught was airy, with frosted windows and an array of bright houseplants on a shelf. Ms Dudley had a dry tone and a formal manner, but at least she didn't seem like a jobsworth. Sitting beside Swift, Steve was a bag of nerves, unable to keep still. He kept jiggling his leg and adjusting his tie at the collar.

Ms Dudley sat poised, hands resting on the arms of her chair, while Swift outlined the nature of their enquiry. Her growing frown was the only sign of her surprise.

'This is unusual,' she commented. 'I haven't dealt with such circumstances before.'

'I should hope not,' Steve snapped. 'I suppose people don't generally lie about their children dying in hospital.'

'Quite, although we need to check the facts first, if we can.' She raised an eyebrow, scrutinised Steve's driving licence and Swift's ID. 'It must be terribly upsetting for you.' Her voice softened as she addressed Steve.

'I'm all at sea, don't know if I'm coming or going. Can you help?'

'I'll try. It might be difficult.'

'What's the problem? Hospitals have to keep records, and you must be able to search them.'

'Yes, but I can only search what's there.'

Steve's voice was shrill. 'Bloody hell. If Zac was admitted here, it'll be logged. It's not rocket science.'

Ms Dudley's expression shifted from mild concern to unease. 'I'll do what I can for you.'

'Says you. I hope you're not going to hide behind bureaucracy and confidentiality crap. I saw how that worked at the council, when they wanted to give bland responses and fob people off. They calculated that if they created enough fog, people would go away. This is my life being messed up here and I won't be bamboozled. I need answers.'

Ms Dudley went to speak, paused. 'Mr Buckley, I appreciate that this is painful, but it's best if we try to stay respectful and cooperate in the process. If you can't do that, I'll have to ask you to leave.'

Swift was wishing that he'd been able to do this on his own. 'It's a difficult, emotional time, isn't it, Steve?'

'Yeah. Sorry for sounding off. I'm just . . .' He tugged at his tie, moving his chin from side to side.

'Anything you can tell us would be helpful,' Swift assured Ms Dudley.

She gave him a curious glance. 'From the address you've given me for that time, this would have been Ms Buckley's local A & E. I assume that Zachary would have been admitted here in the circumstances you've described and with symptoms that serious. That department closed here in 2004. We now deal only with surgical cases.'

'Have you got access to records from 1999?' Swift asked.

She hesitated. 'Our records were computerised, but not very expertly. It was a hit-and-miss affair and some information was lost. I am happy to search for you, but I must stress that it's not one-hundred-per-cent reliable.'

Steve glanced at Swift. His mouth was twisted. He folded his long jacket cuffs back, worrying at them. 'Just like the bloody council,' he mumbled.

'We understand,' Swift said.

'Then let's consult the oracle.' Ms Dudley turned to her screen and tapped her keyboard.

Steve jiggled a foot and sniffed. Swift smiled at him, but he didn't appear comforted. Ms Dudley sighed, hit a key, tapped again. She glanced at Steve, turned the screen to face him.

'As you can see for yourself, there is no result for that name, date of birth and address on the system.'

The screen displayed: *NO RESULT. PLEASE TRY WITH DIFFERENT CRITERIA.*

Steve squinted. 'So Zac wasn't here.'

'It appears not. But as I said, transfer of records wasn't foolproof. Unfortunately, it was carried out by incompetent youths who should still have been at school. Paper records for that time have now been destroyed. I will just check the separate database of deaths.'

Behind her, the window was pelted with rain blown sideways by sudden gusts of wind. Ms Dudley gave a little shiver, turned the screen back, tapped. 'No, I'm sorry, same result.' She showed Steve the message.

'Is it possible that Zac could have been taken to another A & E?' Swift said.

Ms Dudley nodded. 'Possible, yes, but unlikely. The nearest hospitals besides this one would have been St Mary's and Ashfield. Ashfield was closed in 2001, with their records transferred to St Mary's.'

Steve put his hands over his eyes and groaned. Ms Dudley pushed a box of tissues in front of him with a wary expression.

Swift decided to trade on the fact that a considerate woman was on the other side of the desk. 'Like you, I've never come across this kind of worrying conundrum before. It would be very distressing for Steve to have to contact another hospital and go through all this again, but it needs to be done, to ensure that we have the facts.' He held Ms Dudley's gaze. 'If you'd be willing to help by speaking to St Mary's, it would be much easier and spare Steve the upset.'

She regarded Steve again, pulled her chair in, nodded and picked up her phone, speaking quickly. Swift could see her realising that the sooner she dealt with this, the sooner she'd get shot of this strange duo.

* * *

Half an hour later, Swift and Steve were in a café nearby, sharing a pot of tea. The rain had stopped as suddenly as it had begun, just a few soft drops still falling. The air smelled of damp and dust. A child had drawn a huge round face with a turned-up mouth and square eyes on the misted window beside them.

The query at St Mary's had drawn a blank.

Steve added a sachet of sugar to his cup. 'There's no death certificate and no record of Zac being in hospital.'

'No.'

'This is incredible. What does it mean?'

In Steve's company, Swift had a sense of someone who, despite his outward truculence, could be easily influenced. If his mother had been of a similar disposition, had she been leaned on by someone, coerced? Enough to fake her child's death?

'Steve, can you recall that Good Friday when your mum drove you to Durham?'

'Sort of. Dimly. We stopped at a service station and she bought Easter eggs for my cousins. She let me choose my own egg. I picked one shaped like a rabbit.'

'Who did Zac stay with that day?'

'Oh . . .' He stared through the window. 'I can't tell you. I expect he might have been with Alys Tice. She and mum were friendly.' He fiddled with the clasp of his watch strap. 'I've been going back over the years. Mum was hit hard by Dad's death, she was very low. She started a hobby, decorating stones and pebbles. Then she really changed after Zac died . . . or whatever did happen to him. A bit of

38

her was closed off, as if her mind was often elsewhere. She turned Zac's room into a studio with a table, lamps and boxes of paints and spent hours in there on her hobby. The door was always closed and she didn't like me interrupting her. The house used to be full of those stones. I resented them. It was as if they stole her away from me. Does that sound stupid?'

'No, it makes sense.' Now that Steve was talking more freely, Swift wanted to encourage him. 'It sounds as if she found refuge and relief in her pastime, but that was hard for you. You must have been lonely.'

'Yeah. I was a solitary kind of child. Mum never made an effort to help me socialise. She didn't invite kids to the flat or arrange outings. I spent far too much time watching telly. I've never really worked out the knack of being with people.' He methodically flexed each finger, cracking the knuckles. 'There were times when I wondered if . . . well, if she was fed up, being stuck with me. I mean, I wasn't actually her son. Zac was, and she lost him. Maybe she wished that I was the one who'd vanished.'

There was no possible reply to that. Steve might have had a point, though.

'I gave away most of the stones after she died,' he continued. 'They reminded me of loneliness, hers and mine. How could she have lied to me like that about Zac? What kind of woman was she?'

'Only your mother could tell you her point of view, and that's never going to happen now. If the man in the photo is Zac and I find him, he or the person who cared for him from age two will be able to give you a version.'

Steve blinked, reached into his pocket. 'I nearly forgot. I was going through Mum's things again. I keep doing that now, wondering if I might find something I've missed. I found a condolence card she got sent about Dad. I've never heard of this person, so he must be from Dad's side of the family. It might be of some help to you.'

The card was a simple photo with a spray of white roses, and inside a brief printed message with a signed comment beneath:

Another shining star has joined the heavens
I am very sorry for your loss
From Dan Buckley

'Have you asked your aunt if she's heard of this Dan?'

'I did check with her. The name wasn't familiar.' Steve snatched up a paper napkin, started to shred it. 'Another bloody mystery. My whole life is now. I've no idea what to believe about anything. I saw the way that woman looked at me in the hospital, worried and a bit frightened. It really annoyed me, made me feel like a freak.'

'Can you talk about this situation to your cousins in Durham?'

'I barely have any contact with them these days. Two of them work abroad, the others have kids. I've not seen them for so long, I wouldn't be able to recognise them.' He slid paracetamol from his pocket and swallowed two with his tea.

'You OK?'

'I've an awful headache, d'you mind if I head home?'

'Please do, it's a lot to absorb.' Swift would be glad to be relieved of his company. His agitation was draining, made it hard to focus. 'Leave this with me now. Try and take your mind off it with some ironing.'

Steve turned bleary eyes on him. 'Doesn't matter what I do, I can't stop turning it over. Obsessing, really. I have a horrible suspicion that this is never gonna be smoothed out.'

Swift watched him trudge away, head bowed despondently. The napkin was in tiny pieces, sprinkled all over the table. He swept them into his cupped palm and put them in a pile. His untouched tea had a greasy surface film, slightly blueish, like oil in a puddle. His stomach turned and he pushed it away.

His own instincts were that this case was going to deliver canyons of hurt and pain.

CHAPTER FIVE

Two border terriers called Thistle and Heather lay in beds side by side below the window. Swift was keeping a wary eye on them. He'd once had a bad dog-related experience, admittedly with a huge Alsatian, which had left nasty memories as well as bite marks. These dogs were curious and friendly, but well behaved. After a modicum of sniffing and hand-licking, they'd retired to their beds and were both snoozing.

'I got the dogs when I retired,' Alys Tice told him. 'They're good company and they make sure I get daily exercise. Not sure who walks who! Do you have pets?'

'No, my job doesn't lend itself to them. I wouldn't have time for the responsibility. I have visits from Nigel, the cat next door.'

'Very sensible. That was my view, before I gave up work.'

She was a short, matronly woman with hands like spades. Her name sounded Edwardian and she dressed the part, in a longish, buttoned skirt and a high-necked blouse with lace trimmings on the bodice and sleeves. On her wrist was a delicate beaded bracelet in finely wrought silver. Her faded flaxen hair was coiled in a bun on top of her head. She'd rested her solid legs on a small stool, crossing her tartan slippers at the ankles.

41

'What was your job?'

'Sales rep for a duvet company. That's how I met Corinne. I was visiting the bedding section at Easton's, the shop where she worked. I got to travel all around London and the Home Counties. There's nothing I can't tell you about tog ratings, types of filling, weight and warmth, natural and synthetic fabrics, anti-allergy products. I'm all about a comfortable sleep!'

Her living room indicated a pleasure in cosiness too. The chairs were deep and upholstered in blue velvet, the thick pile carpet was cherry red, and there were several tins of sweets and chocolates on the coffee table.

Swift smiled politely. 'I'll come to you for advice if I'm buying new bedding.'

'I can still get you a discount! You're so tall, you'd need an extra-long duvet.' She recrossed her ankles, wagged a foot. 'What is it you want to ask about Corinne? She died a while ago.'

Swift had decided to be judicious with details about Zac Buckley for now. He didn't want to raise the alarm with anyone who might have been involved in a possible deception when the boy allegedly died.

'Steve, Corinne's oldest son, would like to find out a bit more about how Zac, his brother died. He's received some new information.'

Alys pulled a dubious face and plucked at her bottom lip. 'What information?'

'I can't give you details, it's sensitive.'

'Goodness! Zac had passed away when I met Corinne. She started part-time at Easton's after he died. That's going back a long way.'

'It happens. People go over things in the past, realise they have queries. It was a traumatic event and Steve was just four when his brother died. We don't always ask our parents the questions, we leave it too late and then regret it after they've gone.' He'd experienced that. There were so many conversations he'd have liked to have with his parents, who'd both died comparatively young.

'Right.' She drew the word out slowly. 'I can't see why you've come to me.'

'Did you and Corinne have a close friendship?'

'We'd have lunch, meet for a cuppa, that sort of thing. She wouldn't come out often, and never at weekends or in the evenings. I'd see her during one of her days off work, while Steve was at school. It was hard to get her to be sociable, but then, she'd had two bereavements in quick succession — first her husband and then Zac. That's what we found in common to start with. My husband had died not long before we met, so we were both missing loved ones. Finding someone in the same boat as yourself can be a comfort.'

'I can imagine. How about Steve? Did you spend time with him?'

She shook her head vigorously. 'When we met, Corinne was getting a bit of time away for herself. She said Steve was easy, amused himself, no trouble at all really.'

'And Zac — did she talk about him?'

'Now and again. He had an accident, died of an infection not long after.'

'Fell off his scooter, I understand.'

'Terrible story, makes you realise how fragile life is. I did feel for Corinne — she was so young and she'd been steamrollered by life. Once, she got into a state about Zac, blaming herself for not taking better care of him. I didn't know what to say, just tried to reassure her that she'd done her best. I remember she told me one day that he'd been full of energy, wore her out. She'd had trouble getting him to sleep, and he'd be awake really early. He'd be called hyperactive now.' She added as an afterthought, 'God rest his soul.'

'Did Corinne mention Zac's funeral?'

'I can't recall her saying much about that. I asked one day if she visited his grave — that can be a comfort to some. It was for me. I'd go and sit by my husband's and chat to him. Corinne went into a strange kind of mood, sort of shut down. It seemed best not to push things. It was a while before we met again, and I worried that I'd been insensitive, overstepped the mark.'

43

'Didn't it seem odd, that she didn't want to talk about that?'

'People have their own ways of handling these things and you can never tell how they'll react. My own experience taught me that. I've always found it's best to let the bereaved dictate the terms of engagement.'

That was a sensible attitude, but Corinne's reluctance to discuss Zac's death was intriguing. 'On the Good Friday before he died, Corinne left Zac with someone for the day. Did she ever mention who that was?'

Alys's finely plucked eyebrows shot up. 'No. She never went into details like that.'

This was going nowhere. 'Any idea who her other friends were back then?'

Alys tapped one foot against the other. 'Corinne was quite an introvert. We'd had a few cuppas before she talked about her home life. I couldn't really say about her friends, and she never mentioned any. She had a sister, Tilly, who lived up north somewhere. Corinne mentioned phone calls with her.' Alys reached over to a shelf. 'She spent most of her spare time making these. I suppose it was a sort of therapy.'

Swift examined the large, smooth oval stone she handed him. It was a butterfly painted in acrylic: rich, vivid blues and oranges. It wasn't to his taste, but it was realistic and well executed. He gave it back. 'Did Corinne ever talk about her life before she married?'

She turned away, placing the stone back on the shelf. One of the dogs woke, trotted over to her and jumped on her lap. Alys kissed its nose, fondled its ears.

'She worked at a swanky school near Saffron Walden, lived in there. It sounded like she'd enjoyed it and there'd been loads to do. I've only been around that area once, but it's postcard pretty and there's quite a bit of money there. That's how she met Kev, her husband. He turned up to replace some windows.'

'What about his background? He was Cornish.'

'So she told me. He'd moved to London for work opportunities, like so many others. Oh dear — she used to tear up so when she said his name and then that would start me off. We must have looked a right pair.'

'When did you last see her?'

'It's hard to remember exactly. A couple of months before she died. We didn't see much of each other in later years. I'd suggest meeting up, but she always had some excuse, so I sort of gave up trying. Some friendships fall away, don't they?' She put the dog down. 'Really, Thistle, you're moulting again. You'll need a good grooming session later, and that goes for you too, Heather.' She brushed herself off, catching hairs in her palm. 'These two need walkies soon, if that's everything.'

He suspected that she could tell him more, but she was standing and ushering him to the door, both dogs now snaking around her ankles and barking excitedly.

* * *

'Sliced mango and pineapple. I got you both.' Swift handed Nora the fruit.

'Waitrose — posh! Thanks. I'll put them in the fridge. Want a drink? I've wine or beer . . . unless you're working this evening.'

'A beer would be good.'

Nora brought through two bottles. 'I shouldn't really have this while I'm on meds, but what the hell.'

She was pale around the eyes, her hair cropped short. Her flat in Herne Hill was a modern box, the living room enhanced with large framed posters of Irish landscapes. She'd bought it for its top-floor security, because it was low-maintenance and for the Indian takeaway on the corner, where most of her meals came from. They'd had some great evenings here, feasting on curry, chatting, listening to music. In the main, it had been fine when it had just been the two of them.

She sipped beer. 'How's Branna?'

He was surprised at the enquiry, given that Nora's low boredom threshold with his daughter had been one of the obstacles in their relationship. He assumed that she wanted to steer the conversation away from herself. 'Fine, but not in London these days.'

'How so?'

He explained about the move to Guernsey.

'Ruth tied the knot again, then.'

'She and Marcel want children.'

'Ah. Well, it gets her out of your hair at last. She won't be able to manipulate you so easily.' Nora had always maintained that he still carried a flame for Ruth and was at her beck and call. She'd been resentful of what she saw as his ex's hold over him, through their daughter.

He no longer had to rise to the comment or defend himself. 'That's one way of looking at it.'

'Is it difficult talking to Branna online — how does that work with her hearing?'

'She's had cochlear implants, so her hearing is much improved.'

'That's good. A lot's happened since I last saw you, Ty. Tide of life flows on fast, et cetera.'

'Yes. This beer's good.'

'Just shout if you want another.'

'This is fine.' He tilted the bottle. 'Here's to you.' He'd been trying to put a name to how he was finding her. *Faded*, that was it. Nora had always been sparky, a gym devotee. He could see that her energy levels were low, although she was still quick with a tart comment.

'Well.' She made an effort at a grin. 'We've both been dumped, and more than once. We could form a club.'

'There'd be plenty to join it.' He'd forgotten that Alistair, the man she'd been seeing when they'd first met, had left her. 'It wouldn't be much fun. People sitting around in a glum fog.'

'Yeah, *moan, ain't it awful, yada-yada*. Fitz kissed me good-bye by text. I got it as I finished my second chemo session and needed to throw up.'

'Crap.'

'Yeah, it's all in the timing. Not that I'm asking for your kindness, given how I walked away from you.'

Best to clear the air on this. 'Nora, you did the right thing, albeit in a hurtful way. We didn't gel. It wouldn't have lasted.'

She hesitated. 'Agreed. We had good times, though.'

'The best.'

'Me and Fitz, we'd been doing OK until I got the diagnosis.'

Swift doubted that. Fitz, a womaniser and rover, had probably been waiting for an excuse to bail out, although sending her a text was pretty low, even for him. Was Nora harbouring a hope that if she recovered, he'd come back to her?

'You seeing anyone?' she asked.

'Solo at present. There was a flicker of interest but . . .'

They drank in silence. He wasn't sure what, if anything, he was allowed to ask. If he said the wrong thing, she might throw him out.

'Have any of your family visited from Dublin?'

'Haven't told them. Don't want fuss and alarms. I need to see how this pans out.'

'Righto.' From what she'd revealed about her family, that made sense. They sounded noisy and argumentative, a high-octane tribe of door-slammers.

She settled a cushion behind her head, tucked her feet up. 'Who told you about me?'

'Mary.'

'Ah, yes.' She looked him in the eye. 'Mary doesn't care much for me.'

'She didn't think we were right for each other. She rates you highly as a detective.'

'I'll take that. What are you working on?'

He told her about Steve Buckley. The sun was creeping away to the west in a pale blush of apricot sky, the room dimming.

'That sounds a juicy challenge, and pretty weird too.' She perked up a little. 'What a fuck-up all round, if this guy is Zac.'

'I've nothing much to work with yet, but early days.'

'Why would someone fake their child's death?'

'I've heard of cases where parents have done it to attract attention or sympathy, possibly for financial gain, especially with the reach of social media. But if Steve's mother did lie about the death, she didn't appear to have gained anything from it, either then or in the long term. In 1999, there was no opportunity for Facebook coverage and the like. And she suffered, which isn't much of a pay-off.'

'So, hang on — if this is true, does that mean Ms Buckley knew where her son was over the years? Did she see him?'

'That has to be a possibility.'

'Bit of a head-melter for the remaining son.'

'If his brother is alive and I do find him, it's going to be so overwhelmingly complex, I worry about how Steve will cope. He's not the strongest of personalities. Rock and hard place.' He finished his beer. 'If you want to come out in the boat sometime, just shout.'

'I don't need nursing or therapy,' she said sharply.

'That's not what I was offering. I found this fascinating stretch of the river during my last case. A remote place called Channel sea Island in East London, overgrown and wild. You'd love it, so we should make it a destination sometime. You can check it out online.'

'Maybe, have to see what my energy levels are. I certainly won't be using oars for a while.' She stretched, yawned. 'I was in the middle of a major case when I had to take time off. Bloody annoying.'

'Your health has to come first.'

'So I'm told.' She stared at her hands. Her face had turned a little blueish, but perhaps it was the shadowy light. He recalled her sunlit cheeks in his boat, her laughter, her vitality when she'd rowed. He'd never liked her eruptions of temper, but right now he wouldn't mind if she yelled at him. This was a diminished version of Nora. She yawned again, lifted her beer, put it back down. She'd only had a few mouthfuls.

'Want a takeaway for this evening? I could fetch one for you, unless you've got them on speed dial.'

'No, ta. I can't eat spicy stuff right now. Tastes funny and upsets my stomach.'

She used to dive into the curries with such relish, sighing with pleasure. *And she will again*, he told himself.

She laughed. 'I've started watching early evening game shows. Slippery slope.'

'Like being a student again?'

'A bit.' She rubbed her eyes.

'I'd better make a move.'

'Sure. Thanks for coming. Good to catch up. Sorry I'm not much company.'

'I'll see myself out.' He paused at the door. 'If you need anything, just shout. Or even if you don't need anything.'

She half-smiled, raised a thumb.

He stopped on the pavement outside, fighting a wave of melancholy before walking fast to the station.

* * *

Easton's department store no longer existed. It had undergone a total makeover and was now Easton Inc. Swift could see no sign of kitchen equipment or bedding. Instead, there were coffee and ice cream parlours, a microbrewery, an art gallery, an artisan quarter, a market hall and a pop-up shop called Dribble, devoted exclusively to dogs. The menu offered canine versions of cakes, puddings and various flavoured treats including steak-and-kidney pie and beef casserole. Alys Tice would have loved it.

Lawrie, the manager, was late twenties, bustling, lean and keen. His office was a circular glass pod towards the rear of the ground floor. On the glass were the repeated black-and-pink logos of Dash Properties, now the owners of the site. He had a tiny counter for a desk, on which rested an iMac. A tall stool perched by it. There was no other seating, so Swift stood by the sliding door.

'I'd like to speak to anyone who knew a woman called Corinne Buckley. She worked in the old store, in the kitchen department. We're talking the late 1990s.'

'1990s,' Lawrie echoed, as if referring to a distant century and possibly another planet. 'Big ask. This place has been completely overhauled and redeveloped. It was dead, dreary, on the ropes. We've brought the light and soul back.'

'Did you keep any of the staff from the previous store for your new venture?'

'Possibly, if they understood our concept and wanted to be part of it. We've created a destination, not a shop. The old model of the high street is broken. The future is local, experiential, independent. Dash repurposes buildings and curates spaces to be more human and accessible.'

Swift wasn't finding the pod very human. It was like being in a goldfish bowl, with shoppers staring in as they ambled by. 'If you say so. Is there any way you could check about the staff for me?'

'Difficult, that, because of the number of mini-projects we house.' Lawrie scratched his chin stubble, then snapped his fingers. 'Light-bulb moment! I've seen an older guy working in the market hall.' He popped in an earpiece and pressed a button on his phone. 'Hi, Lawrie here. Yes, got that. Listen, can you fetch that oldish guy with the ponytail who's on charcuterie? His name . . . right, Keith. Yep.' He held up crossed fingers to Swift and gazed at emails on his computer screen, tapped a few replies while he waited. 'Hi, Keith. So, I've got a guy here who'd like to talk to someone who worked at the old shop. That's right. Yeah? Cool, I'll send him up.'

Lawrie beamed at Swift. 'I do love a result. Keith on charcuterie worked here before. First floor, turn left off the escalator, follow your nose.'

Within ten minutes, Swift was sitting with Keith in Camper Café, a pop-up coffee shop inside a huge orange tent. Keith had a pair of rimless glasses propped on top of his bald dome, with the hair that grew at the back of his scalp tied in an elastic band. His heavily lined face was enlivened by humorous blue eyes. He carried a heady scent of aged cheeses and cured meats.

'Lawrie was giving me the hard sell,' Swift told him. 'I'm sure I disappointed him by not wanting to buy into the concept.'

Keith snorted. 'He's an earnest sort, our Lawrie. Had a humour bypass at birth and he evangelises about Dash Properties as if it's a new religion. We call him Saint Lawrie behind his back. I'm not knocking what he does here, mind. You adapt or you wither. I worked at Easton's for years. Reckoned the sky was falling when they announced the place was closing, even though it was gradually getting more depressing. I was in a rut, we all were.'

'Ruts can be a comfort.'

'True. I was terrified about losing my job, got funny turns. But then I applied to be taken on by Dash and it turned out to be a good thing. It rejuvenated me. I've warmed to this new style. There's always something happening in the shop, like this café starting up just two weeks ago. Better than the building standing empty, like a lot of other chain stores that have bitten the dust. So many streets are like ghost towns, full of rough sleepers and charity shops.' He shook his head. 'Rough sleepers in the charity shop doorways.'

'What department did you work in at the old Easton's?'

'Soft furnishings. I sold lots of sofas and curtains. I like the change to charcuterie now, although I get stuff at half price, so I have to try not to eat too many cured meats. The salt's no good for my blood pressure.'

'They're a bit addictive, aren't they? I lived in Lyon for a while and I loved the dried ham and saucisson. Rosette de Lyon was my favourite local delicacy, deliciously peppery.'

'What were you up to in Lyon?'

'I worked for Interpol.'

Keith's eyes widened. 'Wow! I'm impressed. Must have been fascinating, dealing with international crime. Were you involved in big drugs busts with armed cops?'

'Don't be too bowled over. Most of the work was routine, like every other police job, and the sex-trafficking was deeply depressing.' Keith would undoubtedly have been riveted by the story about the time Swift had been stabbed in the thigh, but he didn't want to go there and the man was only on a fifteen-minute break. He showed him a photo of Corinne. 'Did you know this woman, Corinne Buckley? She worked in the kitchen department back then.'

Keith hitched his glasses down to his nose. 'Oh, yes.' He heaped a startling number of brown sugar cubes in his coffee, causing it to spill over the edge of the cup. 'I remember Corinne. Why are you asking about her?'

'Her son's seeking information. A family matter.'

'Well, she was part-time, if I'm right. It was a big store, so we didn't cross paths much. Ever so quiet, frightened of her own shadow.'

'Why do you say that?' Swift tasted his excellent Americano.

'She hardly ever spoke, except for a hello or a comment about the weather. She wasn't unfriendly, just reserved. One of those vague people who blend in with the surroundings. We had a staff room and she'd be in there, head down, reading a magazine. She never joined in the banter. Lovely smile, though.'

'Did she talk about her family?'

'Not much.' He stirred his coffee, slurped from the spoon. 'She was a widow and her little boy had died. Tough, that, on top of losing her hubby. She'd had her share of sadness. Maybe that's why she was so withdrawn.'

'She must have been terribly upset about her son.'

'I suppose. But like I say, she didn't talk about personal stuff.'

'You didn't hear anything about how the boy died, the circumstances?'

'No, just that he'd had an accident.'

'Was she friendly at all with any of her colleagues?'

'I'd say everyone in the store found her pleasant, but no more than that. It was quite a big staff group, so people tended to form little work families and stick with them. I do recall that there was a sales rep she chatted to sometimes, sturdy woman who flogged bedding.'

'I've met her, thanks.' Swift showed him a cropped and enlarged image of the man Steve Buckley thought was Zac. 'Does this guy ring any bells?'

He adjusted his glasses again. 'No.'

'Thanks for your help, anyway.'

'No problem. Corinne had a sad life, really. And then one day she vanished and we heard she'd died, gone to the great department store in the sky.'

Swift passed him his card. 'If you remember anything else, do get in touch.'

He walked back to charcuterie with Keith, tasted a selection of cheeses and bought chorizo, salami and a jar of pickled pine nuts, because life was short and he'd never tried them.

CHAPTER SIX

Swift gave up on trying to trace a Dan Buckley around Falmouth. It was possible the man didn't live anywhere near Kevin's home town. He might be in another country. Swift decided to ask Steve's permission to examine his file of Corinne's papers. For now, he had a date with the Royal Victoria school.

He drove his Mini Cooper, the car Cedric had given him, for an outing to Saffron Walden. It was a still, cool day with high scraps of cloud. Tractors were busy in the fields, throwing up dust and being tailed by swooping, opportunistic crows. Tall, scarlet poppies dotted the hedgerows. It was good to get out of London, have the windows open, breeze tangling his hair.

The Royal Victoria school was a handsome Georgian building set in private parkland a couple of miles outside the town and built of buff-coloured sandstone. Swift drove along an avenue of lime trees to the main entrance, noting signposts to an equestrian centre, fitness suite and swimming pool. The entrance was stunning, with a classical portico of pillars surmounted by statues of the Three Graces. Swift glanced up at the naked figures and bet that they'd caused some sniggering among the pupils over the years.

He had an appointment with the bursar, Celine Fontes. She met him in reception and led him to a pretty wrought-iron conservatory on the south side of the building.

'I thought we'd sit in here as it's such a lovely day. My office is rather dim — it was once part of the scullery.'

The blinds had been drawn down on the roof, making the space a comfortable temperature. There was a tray of coffee and biscuits on the glass table. The wicker chairs were deep, cushioned and comfortable, the plants exotic, colourful and highly scented. A tall plant with waxy, dark green leaves and long, rhubarb-pink flower trumpets stood at his left elbow. Swift regarded it cautiously.

'I hope I don't start sneezing,' he said. 'I'm allergic to some pollen, so excuse me if I do.'

She reacted as if he'd suggested he might expire, her expression aghast. 'Oh, I'm so sorry, I didn't realise — would you prefer to sit elsewhere?'

'No, a few sneezes won't harm me, and this is very beautiful.'

Celine was too — tall, with shining dark hair falling in long ringlets around a sculpted face. Her white trousers and shirt were simple, elegant. But it was her large, conker-brown eyes that were the most riveting.

'If you're sure. Please, just say if it gets too much. I love it in here — I suppose because it reminds me of my parents' garden in São Paulo.'

'How long have you been here?'

'Three years. My husband teaches history. It's a wonderful place to live.' She smiled. 'I've adapted to most English ways — fish and chips, Sunday roast, marmite, and I must confess an embarrassing addiction to mushy peas — but the coffee has to be Brazilian.'

He raised his cup. 'It's good. Have you been able to find anything about Corinne Buckley, maiden name Ellwood?'

She ran a finger through a ringlet, giving it a little pull, in a way he found distracting. 'Very little in the records. *I* ended up having sneezing fits when I went through the dusty old files.' She giggled.

'But there was something?'

'I found her listed as a general teaching assistant from 1994 to 1997.'

'What would that have entailed?'

Celine took a delicate sip of coffee. 'Much as it does now, I would imagine. Helping with class and leisure activities and preparing study aids, chaperoning pupils when needed, escorting prospective parents around the campus. Whatever's required.'

Swift considered this information. It sounded an unlikely role for a woman who was scared of her own shadow and rarely engaged with people. 'Presumably, you'd need to be an outgoing, friendly kind of person for that work?'

Celine nodded, her ringlets rippling. 'Oh yes, someone with energy and enthusiasm. I found one other document, a copy of a reference given to her when she left the school. It was written by the now-retired head of year who managed her. As Ms Buckley has died, I don't see any difficulty in showing it to you.'

She handed Swift a photocopied sheet of paper headed with the school's name and the date, with a few typed lines beneath.

General Reference for Ms Corinne Ellwood

I have worked with Ms Ellwood for three years during her time at our school as a teaching assistant. She has been a reliable, helpful and enthusiastic member of our school community, well liked by staff and pupils and always willing to go the extra mile.

I have no hesitation in recommending her as an honest, outgoing and hard-working person.

Yours sincerely,
Ms H Greer, Head, Year Three.

'It's very favourable,' he commented, handing it back. Most unlike the Corinne who'd isolated herself at home and sat like a shadow in the staff room at Easton's.

Celine reached out and caressed a pale blue blossom. 'You queried if anyone who knew Corinne was still working here. I asked at a staff meeting, sent an email round as well, and unfortunately, the answer is no. All has altered here, you see. There was a change of ownership and a major reorganisation in 2012. Some staff were offered an early retirement package. Sorry I haven't been much help to you.'

'I appreciate what you've done.'

'At least I didn't make you sneeze!'

'True, I got away with it this time.'

Swift was standing by his car, debating whether to have lunch in Saffron Walden, when he noticed that a man loading a jeep was glancing at him. There was a sign on the jeep's side: *Tobias Everitt Tree Care.*

'Hi,' Swift called. 'Do you maintain the trees around here?'

The man pushed back his cap and ambled over. 'That's right. Trees and hedges — some of them are ancient and need specialist care. Would you be the guy who was asking about Corinne? I spotted you with Celine in the conservatory.'

'That's me.'

'My grandad passed this business on to me when he retired. He's Tobias Everitt too, used to manage the trees on this site. One of the cooks here showed me an email that went round from Celine, asking if anyone remembered Corinne. Grandad does.'

His trip hadn't been a waste of time after all. 'I'd very much like to talk to him. Does he live locally?'

'He does, but right now he's in Florida, visiting his brother, driving him round the twist while he suns himself with the snowbirds. All right for some, isn't it?'

'I expect he's earned it.'

Everitt grinned. '*He'd* say he has. I can give you his email address, though Grandad's a law unto himself and kind of unpredictable. He reads his messages now and again, but he doesn't always reply, and when he does, it's brief and usually in capitals. He's convinced that everyone can read what you say online.'

'He's right, to a point. Email is easily hacked.'

'Yeah, although I have tried to explain to him that not many people would be interested in his grumbles about his prostate and rheumatism. Not exactly information that the secret service would get excited about. I sent him a message asking if he remembered Corinne, and yesterday I had an answer, just saying, "YES."'

'When's he due back?'

'Couple of weeks.' Everitt lifted his cap, scratched above an ear. 'I spent a bit of time at the school in my teens — not as a pupil, mind. My parents didn't have that kind of money. Families of people who worked here were allowed to use the swimming pool at weekends. I was a keen swimmer, so I came here quite a bit.'

'Corinne was here from 1994 to 1997.'

'My swims would have been after that.'

'Did you mix with the staff or pupils?'

'Not much. The headmaster was often in the pool, a bit of a fitness fanatic. Liked backstroke. His wife was one of the teachers and a right battleaxe. She told me off once, for not wearing the right kind of swimming gear. I was in briefs and the rule was trunks.' He laughed. 'I expect I gave a cheeky response. Time's wasting, I've got to push on.' Everitt slipped a business card from his back pocket, leaned against the roof of Swift's car and wrote. 'There you go, Grandad's email address. Good luck with him!'

Swift got in his car, started the engine and had a sneezing fit — the pollen taking delayed revenge. He'd give Saffron Walden a miss today. He needed to stretch his muscles, get out on the river, work up a sweat. He stopped at a layby café and bought a sausage roll and an orange juice, then sat in the driver's seat with the car door open, tracing the sun's movement in and out of fleeting clouds and wondering about

Corinne Buckley's apparent change in personality. It could be explained by her husband's death, but he suspected there was more to it and that it was connected to Zac. Her sister had spoken of Corinne having fun at the school, whereas Keith at Easton's had described a woman who hid behind magazines. He was impatient to talk to Tobias Everitt senior and find out more about the engaging young woman who'd worked at Royal Victoria.

When he'd finished eating, he sent Everitt an email, asking if he could phone him. He didn't want to wait several weeks, and he assumed that a face-to-face online conversation might be a bridge too far for a man who responded to emails with one word.

* * *

Swift was ravenous by the time he'd pulled his boat up the slipway and secured it at his club, Tamesas. He'd rowed as far as Syon Reach and back, sniffing autumn's approach on the water, watching swallows and house martins on their migration southwards. He'd taken photos of them for Branna. He wiped his boat down and jogged the ten minutes to his house, keeping warm until he could shower.

An hour later, he was enjoying one of Chand's mother's mild prawn kormas. She bombarded her son with masses of food, and — unknown to her — Swift benefited from her generosity. Chand's marriage had made no difference to Mrs Malla's regular meal supplies, which was fine with Bella, his wife. A drawer of Swift's freezer continued to be filled regularly with foil containers of meals they couldn't cope with.

As he ate, he saw that he'd had an email from Barry Harte.

> *Hi, I was talking to a doctor at the hospital who was at the cricket match. She read my email, and told me that she saw the guy in the photo chatting to the woman who was running the bouncy castle. The symbrachydactyly on his hand snagged*

her attention, because it's a rare condition. The woman we hired, Jan Brockhill, runs an outfit called Bouncy Queen. Hope that helps. Haven't had any other feedback about Mr Anonymous. Cheers, BH.

Swift forked up the last of his meal, found a number for Bouncy Queen and left a message. Then he called Branna on Zoom, looking forward to a chat. He'd tell her about the migrating birds. She liked to pore over the globe he'd bought her and track their flight paths. Ruth answered.

'Hi, Ty. How're you?'

'Fine, thanks. Is Branna around?'

'Sorry, in bed and asleep. She came home from school with an ear infection, poor mite. She's had an antibiotic and painkillers.'

Branna was prone to these infections. 'Give her a kiss from me and tell her I'll call tomorrow.'

'I will. I'm sure she'll have perked up by the morning, but I'll keep her at home. While I've got you, I have some news.' She smiled, put a hand to her abdomen. 'I'm pregnant.'

'Congratulations. Are you well?'

'Very, hardly any morning sickness, unlike with Branna.' She was on good form, her skin tanned, hair piled haphazardly on top of her head.

'Have you told Branna?'

'Yes, we talked to her yesterday. She was excited and demanded a sister. I explained it was pot luck and we'd discover who this little person is once they're here.'

'Well . . . I'm pleased for you all.'

'Thanks, Ty. It's what we planned and hoped for, so we're content. Call around this time tomorrow.'

He cleared up, wandered around the garden, pulling up a few weeds, stooping to sniff Cedric's tea rose. He was glad for Ruth, and it was great that Branna would have a sibling. So why did he feel as if he'd lost something?

CHAPTER SEVEN

Swift was chatting to Jan Brockhill in the garden of her terraced house in Loughton. It was warm enough to sit on the patio under a parasol. She'd sounded cautious when she'd replied to his call, listening silently while he'd explained the context for his contact, but agreeing that he could email her the photo of the man at the park. She'd commented that she was busy and asked if she could think things over, get back to him if she could help. He'd not been optimistic that he'd hear from her again, but she'd phoned a couple of days later, inviting him round.

She had a friendly, open personality, smiling as she popped sweeteners into her coffee. In her fifties with fading ginger hair, her heart-shaped face was sprinkled with freckles. She was dressed in denim, with silver rings on her fingers.

'This is a pretty garden,' Swift told her. It was small, but carefully maintained, the kind that is planned to have year-round colour.

'Thanks. It's south facing, so it does catch the sun for most of the day and the plants thrive. Are you a gardener?'

'After a fashion, but a minimalist. Mainly I hack stuff back. How long have you been on bouncy castle duties?'

'About eight years. I used to work in an office, but I fancied a complete change and starting my own business. I rent out a dozen castles as well as inflatables, but I enjoy taking them to events as well.' She adjusted the parasol in its base. 'How do you reckon I can help you with this photo? I don't know the man in the background — or the other two, come to that.'

'As I indicated on the phone, I'm trying to find him, on behalf of a client. He was at a cricket match in West Ham Park in August, and you pitched your bouncy castle there. Someone saw him speaking to you. I was hoping you could tell me something about him.'

'What's his name?'

If only I knew for certain. 'I can't reveal that. He didn't introduce himself?'

'Didn't get round to that, not enough time.' Jan pursed her mouth. Her lips were full and the palest pink. 'As for being able to tell you anything, the answer's yes and no.'

'Meaning?'

'It was a full-on afternoon, but I do remember a bit about him. He came up to me while I was running the castle. Asked me if it was a good business, how long I'd been doing it, the kinds of places I pitched it, that sort of thing. I was hoping that he wanted to hire from me. I've had some lucrative corporate engagements from that kind of informal networking.'

'Firms hire your bouncy castles?'

'Oh yes. Usually for team building, away days, that sort of nonsense. I've watched drunken executives throw their shoes off and play around like kids.'

'How long were you speaking to him?'

'About ten minutes or so, with lots of interruptions. It was a really busy afternoon with long queues, and I had to keep an eye on the activities. You always get at least one hooligan with each session — the kid who wants to trip others up or deliberately crash into them. Then there are the ones who try to sneak on without paying. Worst is the kid who chucks up, though. I do hate cleaning vomit.'

'My daughter loves a bouncy castle. Last time she was on one, she refused to come off.' Branna had gone into a full meltdown while Swift was surrounded by muttering adults.

In the end, he'd had to climb on, grab her and haul her off because she was holding up the next session. There'd been loud applause, and he'd reflected that you lose all shame once you're a parent.

'Tell me about it. I get a lot of that. I keep a bag of sweets handy. Usually works.'

Swift laughed. 'Before I had a child, I'd have claimed I disapproved of bribery. Now I've learned its value. It sounds as if your conversation with this guy was fragmented.'

'That's right. When I told him I had to concentrate on the job, he mentioned that his company might like to hire me for a staff-and-kids day they were planning. I gave him one of my cards, with my number.' She held her hands out. 'But nothing. Guess he changed his mind or his boss wasn't interested after all. Shame, but there you go.'

This was both a step forward and a step back. The man was eluding him. 'Did he mention where he worked or lived?'

'No, no details. He headed off once he had my card.' Jan shook her head, her hair bouncing merrily. 'Are you after him because he's done something wrong? Have I had a narrow escape?'

'He hasn't done anything wrong as far as I'm aware, no need to worry. My client wants to contact him.'

She finished her coffee. 'Intriguing. How did your client get hold of the photo? Is he one of the chaps in cricket whites?'

'No, he happened to see the photograph and it sparked memories. If this man gets in touch with you, could you ring me? But I'd appreciate it if you don't mention me to him.'

Jan's eyes narrowed and her tone cooled. 'What is he, a runaway? Does he owe someone money?'

'It's confidential, delicate.'

'I'm getting more and more fascinated. I hope he does call me, so I get to hear the story. Is it a sad one or would it have a happy ending?'

Swift recalled Steve's turmoil, put his hands behind his head. 'I can't predict that. I expect all kinds of conflicting emotions might be involved. If you do get a call or email, can I have the number or address?'

She bridled. 'That's a bit too pushy. No, I'm not comfortable with that idea at all. I don't want to frighten off business opportunities.'

'I'd be very careful how I approached him.' Although Swift struggled to envisage how anyone could be circumspect when informing a man that he was supposed to be dead. It would be a stretch of anyone's discretion.

'The answer will still be no. It wouldn't be good for business if I was careless with a customer's private information.' She dabbed a coffee stain from the table. 'I'd better get back to work. I have to say, you've got me hooked. I'll be in touch if I hear from this guy, but I can't promise I won't tell him you're asking about him. Seems a bit underhand.'

'I'd tell you more if I could, but I'd be breaking client privacy. I can only stress that this is a situation that needs to be handled carefully.'

'I'll bear that in mind.'

On the way home, Swift rang Steve Buckley, who picked up immediately.

'Hi, Steve. Can you talk?'

'Yep. Just ironing sheets. Have you got anything? Please say you have.'

He updated Steve on the information from Jan Brockhill. 'We still have no confirmation that this is Zac, but we have some chance that we'll get contact with him.'

'So,' Steve said rapidly, 'with any luck, this man will call Ms Brockhill and then we'll have some details to go on.'

'With luck. Assuming he might live in East London, given he was in West Ham Park, I searched for Zac again, but no result. Of course, he might have a different surname. Did you have any family connection to that part of London?'

'No. My mum grew up in Camberwell and we always lived in Wembley. This Jan Brockhill — what's she like? D'you reckon she'll say if our man contacts her?'

'She seemed straightforward. I hope so, but there's no guarantee. She was more concerned about the business opportunity he might offer than our concerns.'

'Right. What now, then?'

'I keep investigating. Steve, apart from Alys Tice, can you recall anyone your mum was friendly with? Was she a member of any church or other group, or did she ever mention anyone from the job she had at the boarding school before she married? I need to find who she left Zac with on that Good Friday, and Alys insisted it wasn't her.'

There was a pause. 'Mum never talked about the school. She never talked about the past at all. She went to work, she shopped, came home, cooked meals and vanished to her stone painting. Sometimes we'd watch TV together. She liked romcoms and quizzes. Now and again, Aunt Tilly asked us to visit or offered to come to London, but Mum always made an excuse.' He sighed. 'I was keen to see my cousins, but it never happened. Every so often, Mum mentioned that she'd met Alys. That was her life. Sounds so dreary and sad when I say it out loud like that, but when I was growing up, it was just how things were.'

'Children do accept the world their parents offer them, in the main. How about holidays, did you go away?'

'Days out to the seaside: Southend, Brighton, Margate. If this is Zac and he was interested in hiring the bouncy castle, he must live in London.'

'Let's not get ahead of ourselves. Best not to speculate.'

'Oh God, don't use that bloody placating tone of voice to me! Makes me out to be a mental case.'

'Sorry. I'm trying to be pragmatic.'

'Yeah, well . . . easy for you. I can't help it. I get this fizzy sensation in my brain and I just have to go out and walk for miles. I only sleep if I exhaust myself.'

Swift made no comment. He got Steve's permission to check through his mother's things soon and ended the call. Steve would continue to fret and conjecture. How could he not?

A clearer picture of Corinne Buckley was emerging. She'd spent her life in hiding after she reported Zac's death, detaching herself from the past, refusing family visits, spending hours painting inanimate objects instead of seeking company. She'd enjoyed her time at Royal Victoria, yet never alluded to it. The one friendship she'd had, with Alys, had faded. Most people reminisced a little as they crept into their thirties and forties, but not Corinne, who'd locked her life away. Her son didn't even know who this Dan Buckley was. She'd kept the world at bay — through fear, depression, regret, self-punishment? Maybe she'd ticked all the boxes.

Swift turned to the photo album he'd borrowed from Steve, concentrating on Corinne as he turned the pages, trying to read her. Was he imagining that her expression became more closed after Zac died? There weren't many pictures of her and Steve, and in most of them, Corinne's eyes were distant, even if her lips were smiling. He paused at one of her sitting at a desk in a small room with her head bent, brush poised over a large pebble. She was surrounded by shelves of embellished stones. A large box of paint tubes sat by her elbow. There was a radio and a mug, a packet of biscuits. She'd made her own little haven, where she could pass the hours. What had Steve done in the meantime? Had he taken the photo in an attempt to attract his mother's attention? If so, the averted head showed that he'd failed.

* * *

'I'll have the baked ham with mixed vegetables and a sparkling water, please,' Joyce said.

Swift ordered chicken Caesar salad and a glass of Sauvignon. He checked with Joyce. 'Sure you won't have a glass of wine?'

'No thanks, dear. I'm playing bowls later and I need to keep a clear head. It's the tournament final and I don't want to let the side down.'

This was a guilt lunch in the Silver Mermaid, his local pub by the river. Swift had invited Joyce to make up for his frequent lack of consideration. Time to grow up, bite the bullet and stop his usual avoidance manoeuvres. *Frankly, it's a bit childish*, he'd told himself, aware that he did regress in her company. He'd always resented her, but it wasn't Joyce's fault that his father had married her after Swift's beloved mother died. It wasn't her fault that she had a big personality, could be overwhelming and intrusive about his personal life and his job. Nor was it her fault that she liked gaudy, floral dresses. After all, she had loved his father, had been widowed after a brief marriage and had been alone since. She was undoubtedly well-intentioned and kind. He should acknowledge her role as a diplomat concerning Ruth's wedding.

Joyce beamed. 'This is an unexpected treat, Ty.'

'Don't expect too much. It's pub food, but pretty reliable.' That had sounded crass. He rallied. 'I wanted to say a proper thank you for easing the way with Ruth's marriage.'

Joyce had aged in the last year, in the sudden way that older people sometimes did. Spidery lines fanned from the corners of her mouth, she'd lost weight and she was stooping a little. Her dress was her usual bold statement, though — bright blue with red, yellow and orange splashes of daisies.

'Really, it was a pleasure. It was a simple, lovely ceremony, and Branna had a whale of a time. Louis was a little gentleman throughout. He's such a self-contained child.'

'Unlike Branna, who's gregarious and chatty.' He missed her when he babysat Louis. The little boy was quiet, polite and didn't like to get his neat clothes dirty. Last time, Swift had felt like a spare part as Louis got on with his jigsaw, answering any conversational sallies as if he was humouring his guest. It was as if he was the child, Louis the adult in charge. Swift had longed for the trail of chaos his daughter always left in her wake.

'They're chalk and cheese. Like us.'

He sipped his wine, startled. This was an unusually personal note. 'I suppose we are very different personalities.'

'Your father always said you took after your mother.'

'Uh-huh.'

Joyce uncapped her bottle of water, poured half a glass. 'By the way, I hope to go to Guernsey next year. Ruth invited me. I hope you don't mind.' Her eyes searched his face. 'Oh, I can see from your expression that you do. I won't go if you don't want me to.'

He placed a hand on her arm. 'Joyce, it's not that at all. I'm just surprised. I didn't think you liked Ruth much.'

Their food arrived and they waited until the waitress had moved away.

'This is delicious.' Joyce reached for a napkin and smiled gently at him. 'That's true, Ty. I didn't like or approve of Ruth for what she did to you. But time moves on and we have to move with it. I'm so fond of Branna, and Ruth's a good mother. So, the hatchet has been buried and it was kind of Ruth to make the effort, meet me halfway. And if it means I get time with Branna, I would sup with the devil himself.'

Swift was deeply touched. Joyce had no children, and he understood how fond she was of Branna. The affection was reciprocal. 'You must go, Joyce. It's a beautiful place. Ruth's just told me that she's pregnant. Branna's over the moon about having a sibling.'

'How wonderful!' She glanced down at her plate. 'And you, Ty — how do you feel about it?'

'Fine. I was an only child and it made me a tad selfish, encouraged my introspective tendencies. It'll be good for Branna to have her corners knocked off.'

'I agree, it will benefit her.' Joyce cut a slice of ham, cleared her throat. 'Have you been in touch with Nora? Mary told me about her cancer.'

'I went to see her. We had a chat, kept it light.'

'Did she tell you much about her diagnosis?'

'Nothing, and I kept to the brief she gave me — that she didn't want to be questioned.'

'That sounds like Nora. Just as well I haven't contacted her. I find it almost impossible not to quiz people. Once when we met, at that party at Mary's, she told me that I'd have been a good recruit for the Spanish Inquisition.'

Swift coughed on a shred of lettuce. 'Nora's always direct.'

'Hm. To the point of rudeness. Give her my best, please.'

'We caught up when I called round, and I offered a row if she fancies it sometime.'

'That was kind of you.'

'I was glad I visited.'

'Yes, in the end, kindness is all that matters, isn't it? All the rest is noise and distraction.'

Swift chewed his succulent chicken. Joyce was right, and what she'd said applied to their relationship also. A knot that he'd been carrying in his chest for years shifted. 'I've not always been much of a stepson,' he muttered.

She spooned more asparagus from the vegetable dish. 'I realise how much you've always missed your mother. Now you're missing Branna — I can see it in your face. And I realise I can seem pushy.' She sipped water. 'How's your salad?'

'Tasty. The croutons are garlicky.'

'Are you working on anything of interest?'

'I believe I am.' He gave her a brief outline of the case. 'What it might all boil down to is, why would a mother give up her son and fake his death?'

They ordered coffee, and Swift opted for a slice of cheesecake.

'My great-grandmother gave one of her children away. My mother told me about it.' Joyce rearranged the wooden stand holding cutlery and napkins.

'Why was that?'

'It sounds shocking to us now, but I believe it wasn't that unusual then. It was my great-gran's youngest son and she had eight children. The family were poor, scraping a living. Her sister was widowed and childless. She longed to be a mother. So when he was a few months old, my great-gran handed the boy over and the sister raised him as her own.'

'Did he know about the arrangement?'

'I've no idea. I'm sure my great-grandmother missed him, but she was no doubt relieved to have one less mouth to feed, and she'd have been offering the boy a better chance in life. She gave her sister a tremendous gift, someone to love. Can I take a tiny spoon of your cheesecake?'

Swift nudged the plate towards her. 'That's a story of its time. Corinne didn't live in poverty or have a large brood. It's hard to believe she was motivated by generosity.'

'Mm, that cheesecake's so lemony. I won't have any more, though. No, it's hard to fathom why Corinne acted as she did. Make sure you tell me when you find out.'

'*If* I find out.'

Joyce licked her spoon. 'Your track record speaks for itself. You have that intense expression when you talk about it. Bloodhound sniffing the trail. You'll get there.'

'You haven't always approved of my leaving a regular job and taking to private investigation,' Swift teased.

'I still regard it as an odd choice. No pension and no reliable employment, but I can see that it suits you.'

Swift saw Joyce into a cab and walked home. It had all been unusually easy-going. Joyce hadn't banged on about his love life or the riskiness of his work, and he hadn't sounded snappy and defensive. And, best of all, her Christmas at home had slipped her mind.

It had taken over twenty years to turn that corner. Sometimes, you just had to hang on and let time do the work.

CHAPTER EIGHT

One of Swift's tried-and-tested rules was that it was always worth door-knocking neighbours, even if an event was a long time in the past. People's memories might be jogged, things they hadn't considered important at the time may turn out to be significant, the odd crumb of information could prove valuable. He wanted to get a sense of where stay-at-home Corinne Buckley had lived.

The morning after his lunch with Joyce found him in Millfield Road in Wembley, Steve's childhood home. Most of the houses were in need of some TLC: doors missing from electric meters, stained rendering, broken fences, misshapen gutters. Corinne Buckley had rented number forty, and it was now for sale. Swift glanced through the front window. It had been renovated internally, painted white and installed with laminated flooring, but externally, it needed repair and the low front wall was dilapidated.

He got no answer from the houses either side. Further up, a small, timid woman peeped at him and then slammed the door. On the other side of the street, an older man was planting bedding in the narrow strip of front garden. His house was one of the better maintained.

Swift crossed over. 'Pretty pansies.'

'They'll cheer me up in the winter.'

'Do you remember a woman called Corinne Buckley who used to live at number forty?'

The man stood up straight, pressed a hand to his lower back. 'She died.'

'That's right.'

'Used to nod to her. You could ask Sheila Whitehall at number twenty-eight, I saw them chatting sometimes.'

'Would she be at home this time of day?'

'Couldn't say. She's in and out, keeps herself busy.'

Swift got no response at twenty-eight. He walked back towards the Tube, sat in a café drinking coffee and reading a newspaper. He'd had no response to his email to Toby Everitt, so tried again.

Sorry to bother you, but it's really important that I get in touch.

He was in luck when he returned to Sheila Whitehall's. After he'd rung the bell twice he heard a shout, and a couple of minutes later a woman in her early seventies, sporting a turban towel, opened the door. Her forehead glistened with a creamy liquid.

'Yes?' She sounded testy. 'I was just washing my hair.'

'Are you Sheila Whitehall?'

'Yes. Who's asking?'

'I'm so sorry to disturb you. I'm a private investigator and I'm seeking information about Corinne Buckley.' He held out his ID.

'Terrible timing. I've got conditioner on.'

'I'm happy to wait.'

'Fine with me.'

He assumed that she'd invite him in, but she shut the door. He sat on the wall and waited. The brickwork at the front of the house needed repointing, but the windows looked new. After a while, he picked some weeds from around the base of the bay window and threw them at the back of the flowerbed. Then he tore a few browned leaves from a salvia.

Might as well make himself useful. He sat again, did up a button on his shirt, noted that the thread was loose. Maybe she'd forgotten about him.

He had his finger on the bell again when the door opened. Her short hair was still damp, the drying strands a dull copper. She led him into a back room with chintzy furnishings, gas fire on the wall, a couple of pictures hanging crookedly.

'It's an expensive conditioner, has to stay on for ten minutes to moisturise properly.' She lit up a cigarette, flicking her lighter impatiently. 'I wasn't expecting company and I didn't want to waste it. Want one of these?'

'No thanks, don't smoke.'

'Wish I didn't, costs me a fortune, but too late now.'

She had a tobacco addict's parched, furrowed skin, a skinny frame and knobbly bones. Her face could have done with conditioner as well.

She waved smoke from her eyes and squinted at him. 'What d'you want then? Corinne's long gone.'

'Her son Steve is after information. You were friendly with Corinne?'

'We'd have a natter in the street now and then when our paths crossed. I met little Steve when he arrived to live with them — he was Kevin's son. Quiet lad, kept his head down and didn't talk much for a while. Corinne had health problems when she was pregnant with Zac, so she spent a lot of time indoors, resting. High blood pressure, she told me. She wasn't too good after the birth either, it took her ages to get back on her feet. I didn't see the baby until he was quite big and she brought him out in the pushchair. I did her nails for her once, but that was when her husband was still alive. That's how I first met her. I was a manicurist, see. Had my own little business here in the front room.'

'Did you meet Kevin?'

'Just saw him to nod to in the street and the odd few words. He had a van for his window business and he used to complain about the parking sometimes. Didn't bother me, I don't drive. She was head over heels about him, love's young dream. Kev this and Kev that. How he believed it was important for a mum to stay at home with the kids. Just the kind of set-up to send any woman up the wall, if you ask me, but it made her happy. Each to their own and all that jazz. She was in bits when he died. I heard the kerfuffle in the road, so I went out to see what was up. Kevin was lying by the van. Corinne ran out of the house with Zac on her hip, screaming her head off. The things that happen!'

'Very sad.' Swift blinked through the fag smoke. 'Losing her husband must have hit her hard.'

'She was so worn out after Kev went. She'd trudge along the road like the weight of the world was on her shoulders. Steve was a dreamy kid, head in the clouds, but Zac was a dynamo, even before he was walking. He'd be shouting in the pushchair, chucking toys around, and when he bawled, I reckon they heard him at Land's End!'

'I'm particularly interested in the time when Zac died.'

'Little Zac. That was dreadful, just dreadful.' She pulled on her cigarette with deep satisfaction.

'Did you see much of Corinne around then?'

She reached for an ashtray, rolled the cigarette on its rim. 'Word got around, the way it does. I knocked on the door a few times, but she never opened it. I put a card through. Next time I bumped into her was weeks later, and she clearly didn't want to talk about it, so I backed off. I can tell you, all the stuffing had been knocked out of her. After that, it was the odd chat in the street again.' She sat forward, held up a finger. 'She got a job at Easton's. I bought some new kitchen chairs from her. I liked that shop. It was a proper place, sold all kinds of bits and pieces in different sections, so you could work out where to go for what you needed. Now it's full of tat no one wants and funny food I've never heard of. I had a wander round and never went back.'

Swift doubted that Sheila was one of Easton Inc.'s target customers.

'That was a very sad time for Corinne, with her husband and then her son dying.'

'Awful. Some people have rotten luck. At least she still had Steve. He always seemed a nice young lad. Bit nervy, didn't say much when you passed by. He moved away after Corinne died.' She stubbed her cigarette out, went to take another from the packet and slapped her wrist. 'Stop it, bad girl!' She frowned at Swift. 'What's Steve after?'

'Some family business he needs to sort out.'

'Oh. Can't help with that. It's a nice street, I've lived here a long time, but people aren't in and out of one another's houses. That's London for you.'

Swift had never been into any of his neighbour's houses, except to admire Andy Fanning's loft conversion. 'You need your privacy in a city.'

'Tell me about it. I couldn't bear to live in one of those villages, like the ones you see on telly, where everyone's in on your business.' She crossed her legs. 'Little Zac. He had that funny thing with his hand.'

'It's called symbrachydactyly.'

'That's a mouthful. I can see it now, his little finger wasn't there, although it didn't seem to hamper him. He was a bundle of energy the day I had him here, and by the next week, a silly accident and—' she clicked her fingers — 'gone.'

Swift loved it when he tripped across a piece of the puzzle. 'Did you look after Zac that Good Friday?'

'That's right. Corinne knocked on the door and explained that she had to drive Steve to Durham to stay with his aunt. She didn't want to take Zac on such a long journey. I'd never been on my own with him before, so I was a bit reluctant but . . . well . . . it was just one day, so I agreed. She'd had a rough time with Kev dying, after all, and Zac would have been a handful in the car. I was knackered by the evening, but Zac was fine. Corinne made sure he brought his favourite toys with him and a change of clothes in case of accidents. A right little bundle of energy he was, kept me on my toes. I was hoping he'd have a nap after his lunch, but no chance — it just refuelled him!'

'What time did Corinne collect him from you?'

Sheila fingered her hair, sniffed her fingers. 'Smells more like almonds than rosemary, like I've washed my hair with marzipan. Corinne didn't fetch him, because she was going to be late back. Her friend did.'

Swift raised his eyebrows. 'What friend?'

'A woman. Corinne had arranged it, said she'd call for him at five. I'd never met her before. Never saw her again, either.'

'Did you get her name?'

'No. She didn't come in.'

'Can you describe her?'

'Blimey, it's yonks ago. Thirty-something, hair tucked in a hat, pleasant manner. A bit rushed.'

'Did she have a car?'

'Yes, dark blue, quite big and boxy.'

'Can you tell me anything else about her? Was Zac staying the night with her?'

'This is like Mastermind or some kind of memory test!' Sheila lit another cigarette. 'No, I can't, and I've no idea what the arrangement was. She came to the door, we exchanged a few remarks. She collected Zac, headed off. I was pooped by then, glad to hand him over and collapse in front of the telly. What's it matter? It was Corinne's business, her kid. She'd have been making the most of having a little break.'

Swift watched the blue cigarette haze drift upwards. Corinne had arranged for her eldest son to be out of London and for a woman to take charge of Zac. He was fairly sure that Steve wouldn't be able to identify this person. What had been going on and why? He took a breath, focused. 'Did Zac recognise this woman?'

Sheila gave him an odd glance. 'Well, he went with her quite happily, and his mother would hardly have asked me to hand him to a stranger! What are you trying to get at with these questions? What's this all about after twenty or more years?'

'I'm not at all sure,' Swift confessed.

'Well . . . raking stuff up. Ask Steve about it. I expect he'll remember who that was.' She stood. 'I want to make a start on my tea now, if you don't mind.'

'Thanks for your time. Sorry again for interrupting your conditioner.'

Sheila patted her hair. 'It's nice and soft, that's the main thing, although I do smell like a cake shop. Won't buy that one again.' She mellowed at the front door. 'Say hello to Steve for me — if he remembers me, that is.'

'I will.'

'Your nails could do with a proper trim and shaping. If I was still in business, I'd offer.'

He glanced at his hands. They were hardened from rowing. Ruth used to complain about the roughness on her skin. Nora had liked it. They'd lain in bed comparing blisters and calluses. 'If I get a minute, I'll pay them some attention.'

Sheila laughed and blew a jet of smoke after him.

* * *

Swift headed straight to Steve's. He looked blank when Swift asked him about a friend of Corinne's who'd collected Zac from Sheila Whitehall on that Good Friday. He grew distressed in a way that Swift was getting accustomed to, pacing his room, banging into furniture, arms folded tight.

'What the . . . ? This is just unbelievable. I've no clue who that woman was. We knew Sheila, but she wasn't exactly a friend. She was keen on litter-picking in our street, she'd be traipsing up and down with a bin bag, wearing pink rubber gloves. She got me to help her once and it was horrible, clearing up people's rubbish. I used to hide if I saw her out and about, scanning the pavements. Why did Mum leave Zac with her?'

'Convenience, maybe. She was nearby, and it's not as if your mum had a big support network. At least one question's been answered.'

'Yeah, but it raises yet another. How come Sheila handed Zac to a woman whose name she didn't even know?'

'She was doing your mum a favour and following her instructions. By the end of that day, Sheila was exhausted and glad to pass the responsibility of Zac to someone else.'

Steve dug his fingers into the top of the armchair and raked his nails back and forth along the edge. 'Every time I talk to you, there's another bloody horrible bit of news. Can't you find something positive to tell me?'

'If it's too much for you, I can stop any time. I did warn you that this investigation could be upsetting.' Swift was concerned by Steve's short fuse and his ability to deal with this situation. Despite that, he didn't want him to call a halt. But he was annoyed. He understood Steve's anguish, but he could do without the insults.

Steve uttered a cracked laugh. 'Don't be stupid, of course I don't want you to stop. It's just bloody bewildering . . . What was Mum up to? I can't recall that she ever mentioned this woman with a big car, but she knew her well enough to let her collect Zac.' He threw himself down on the chair. 'Maybe Zac was with this woman when he had the accident and cut his leg. Is that why my mum didn't want to discuss it?'

'Except that Zac probably didn't have an accident, or if he did, he didn't need to go to hospital or die as a result.'

'Oh, yes. I keep forgetting stuff, can't get things straight. It's like I've a swarm of bees in my head.'

Swift went to the tiny kitchen, got them both a glass of water, hoping Steve would use the chance to compose himself.

'Here, have a drink. Your mother must have had some other reason for the arrangement with her friend. Could you ring your aunt while I'm here and run it by her?'

Swift balanced on the bed and examined Corinne's papers while Steve talked to Tilly. It was apparent from the conversation that the woman was a mystery to her also. They started to discuss Tilly's visit. If nothing else, this strange business was bringing nephew and aunt closer. There wasn't a great deal in the file, and he had found nothing else on Dan Buckley and no information about Kevin's family. That seemed odd, but then so did many things about this lot. Maybe Corinne had thrown stuff away, or Kevin had travelled light.

After half an hour of fruitless searching, he left Steve plugging in the iron, hoping to find some tranquillity with a pile of creased shirts.

* * *

It transpired that Toby Everitt senior was unfamiliar with Zoom, but his brother in Florida used it regularly and would assist with a call. Swift had arranged to talk at ten thirty in the morning, their time. He made coffee, found a packet of biscuits, opened his laptop and called Florida.

A stocky man, balding, with a freckled, square head and broken veins on his nose was sitting before him. Behind him, with a hand on his shoulder, stood a slimmer, tanned man with close-cropped white hair and sparkling teeth.

'There, all hunky-dory, you don't have to do anything now except talk.' The tanned man smiled. 'Hi, Mr Swift, I'm Toby's brother Jack. Welcome to Clearwater.'

'Thank you and hello from Hammersmith.'

'I'll leave you to it. Holler if you need me.' The man waved and glided from the screen.

'Hi, Mr Everitt. Thanks for agreeing to speak to me.'

He fidgeted, rubbed an eyebrow, twisted in his chair. 'As they constantly say here, you're welcome. How's the weather back home?'

'Warm still, a bit misty in the morning. That hint of autumn.'

Everitt had a stolid, gruff manner, but his lips had a humorous curve. 'Ah, the gentle, rainy air.' He scanned behind him and cupped a hand to his mouth. 'Can't wait to get home.'

Swift gauged that the man wasn't too comfortable talking to a screen and needed time to adjust. 'You miss it?'

He lowered his voice. 'I don't really hold with holidays. Never have. They involve a lot of upheaval and fuss. But I wanted to make the effort before I peg out, or Jack does. It's been great here, fascinating, but tiring too. They all want to live for ever, so it's non-stop activity: swimming, yoga, walking, cycling, pickleball. I'm weary, need to come home for a rest.'

Swift grinned. 'What's pickleball?'

'Oh — sort of tennis for oldies. And don't get me started on vegetable smoothies!' He pulled a face. 'Disgusting, and I'll never love catfish. As for all the salad — that's for rabbits.' He licked his lips. 'I wish you could reach through the screen and hand me a plump pork pie — no, make that two!'

'The technology's smart, but not that smart yet. You just have to put some things down to experience.'

'Yes, and not one to be repeated,' he replied. 'Mind, the climate is kind to my rheumatism, and it's been good to see my brother again after all these years. Nice to reminisce about growing up, some of the scrapes we got into.'

'I was hoping you could cast your mind back for me. Your grandson told me that you remember Corinne Buckley — Ellwood as she was at Royal Victoria.'

He leaned into the screen, his nose almost touching it. 'I do indeed.'

'You're a bit out of focus, Mr Everitt. Best to sit back.'

'Ah, yes. That better?'

'Much.'

'Can't stand this way of talking, seems crazy to me.'

'It is strange when you first do it. Handy, though, when you're on different continents.'

'And it means you can see how handsome I am,' Everitt said slyly.

'Exactly. I'd never have guessed from a phone call.'

Everitt raised an approving thumb. 'How's that reprobate grandson of mine? Working hard, I hope.'

'I'm sure he is,' Swift replied patiently, aware that he was going to have to keep guiding the man back on track. 'I met him when I visited Royal Victoria. He'd been at work in the grounds.'

'I always liked that job. It was a regular, reliable one in lovely surroundings, and they left me to it and paid on time. They've some amazing old beech trees that I had to take a lot of care with. They needed specialist chainsaw work now and again. That's why it was good to pass the business on to Toby. I trained him up about those trees, so at least I left them in good hands.' Regret shadowed his face. 'I didn't want to retire and it's many a day I wish I hadn't, but I had no choice in the matter really. My joints weren't up to the physical work and I wasn't safe up ladders or handling machinery.'

'Did you work around the school for long?'

'Twenty-five years or thereabouts. Corinne used to bring a reading group to sit under the trees on hot days. I'm not sure much work got done. There was a lot of giggling and such.'

'She was a giggler?'

'Good-humoured, got on well with the kids. She wasn't that much older than some of them. They called her by her first name, which I didn't hold much truck with. It didn't seem respectful. She was a pretty girl, nimble, always had a smile. Liked her work, from the way she acted. She'd found herself a niche there. It was a wealthy school, good food and working conditions, no expense spared and the accommodation was top-notch. Heated swimming pool and all that. She was excited that she'd learned to ride. She had a favourite horse, Hercules, and she'd take him apples and celery.'

'Did you see her a fair bit?'

'Not that often. I worked in the grounds once a month in the spring and summer. I'd see her more in the warmer weather. Sometimes she'd lead a group to the swimming pool or the stables. She usually wore her hair on top of her head. She was very trim in her jodhpurs and riding boots.' The old man's eyes crinkled.

He'd had a soft spot for Corinne. 'She left the school to get married.'

'Yes, that's what I heard. Some chap she met when he came to do a job there.' Everitt moved his chair in. 'She was an intelligent girl, interested in the trees, discussed them with me. I miss those beeches, they were like family to me.'

'Any idea if Corinne was particularly friendly with anyone at the school? The staff have all changed now, so no one could tell me.'

'I couldn't say. I didn't mix with the staff, generally speaking. I heard that the place had been overhauled.'

'Who was the head back then? Your grandson told me he used to see him in the swimming pool.'

'Ah, I remember that because his name used to be stamped on my paid invoices. Mr Utley. R.T. Utley. Tall chap, quite an air to him, fond of himself.'

'Thanks for your time, Mr Everitt. You've got my email if you recall anything else.'

'I've no idea how I switch you off now.' His hands hovered around the screen.

'I'll end the call here and I'm sure your brother will log off.'

'Righto. Have to say, the fresh orange juice is delicious.'

'So I should hope, as Florida is famed for it. You'll be full of vitamin C by the time you return. It will set you up for the winter.'

They said goodbye. Swift rolled his neck, stood and stretched. He had more evidence of Corinne's cheery personality when she'd worked at the school. She'd had a good life at Royal Victoria, but she'd given up grand grounds and gardens, swimming and riding, for life with Kevin on a drab London street. Within a couple of years, he'd died, leaving her stranded there with young children. Perhaps she'd sat in Easton's dreary staff room and indulged in nostalgia for her job in the leafy, well-resourced school, comparing her life then with what she'd ended up with.

He'd better see if he could trace R.T. Utley.

CHAPTER NINE

It was another balmy September day. The river flowed silkily, dappled with sunlight. Nora had decided she was up to a short trip, so Swift had rowed to Chiswick with her as his passenger.

The Thames often flooded the road on the wide stretch where he moored the boat. They climbed some steps to a quiet pub garden, and he noticed that Nora used the hand-rail. She wouldn't have done that before; she'd have hopped the steps two at a time.

They sat at a table under the shade of a rowan tree. His muscles were warmed and supple, relaxed. He felt an animal glow of health and then guilt immediately snaked through him. He ordered steak pie and she decided on soup with a roll and water with lots of ice.

'I crave cold drinks and ice lollies — I've found a particularly tasty Valencia orange flavour. The freezer's stacked with them. Thanks for this, Ty. It's good to get out. Sorry that you're having to do all the work.'

'My pleasure.'

She leaned back in her chair. A tiny sore had bloomed on her bottom lip and her skin was dingy. She was wearing a striped cotton beanie hat and he guessed that she had hair loss.

'I'm waiting for some results. The chemo was to shrink the tumour. Next, it's an op. So much hanging around.'

'You must be anxious.'

She snapped, 'No, I'm burdened with joy.'

'Sorry. Clumsy.'

'Yeah. Don't tell me how I am.'

'I'll try to avoid doing that.'

She clenched her hands. 'I'm so tired of being around medics. They're lovely, kind and helpful, but I'm nagged to death with advice about diet, hydration, laxatives, nausea, my support network. My life's not my own. Cancer and doctors invading my days. There's one nurse who really gets my goat. She's got this sympathetic, patronising tone. I'd like to smack her.'

'But it wouldn't be wise to bite the hand that's trying to make you better.'

'There's the conundrum. I have to behave nicely, watch my manners like a kid sent to a party. That's what it is — illness infantilises you.' Nora groaned. 'Oh listen to me, boring myself and you.'

Swift sipped his beer, ventured a casual query. 'Is your support network robust?'

She looked away, gestured. 'Isn't the river broad here? There must be tons of wildlife flourishing in those reed beds we saw.'

Their food arrived and he was glad to see her tucking in, although she crumbled most of the bread around her plate.

'I had a card from Fitz. *Get Well Soon*.' She raised a spoonful of soup to her lips.

'Bit insensitive.'

'Conscience salver. I tore it up, chucked it in the bin.'

'Sounds wise.'

She glared at him. 'Stop sitting on the fence and being careful. I did the right thing, yes?'

He put his cutlery down, tired of tiptoeing around. It was too much like the bad times between them. 'Nora, give me a break here. I'm being careful because you've made it clear that lots of things are off limits, and I'm not sure how you feel about Fitz. How can I comment on what's right for you? It's all too easy to say the wrong thing.'

She swirled her spoon through the soup. 'Sorry, Ty. You're so kind, you've come out today, given me a treat and I'm being barbed-wire Nora.'

He went for the light touch. 'At least it's familiar. The good old days!'

'Touché. I'm a cow, ignore me. Don't let your food go cold. I'll just sneak a crumb of pastry. What's happening on your case?'

He brought her up to speed while they finished their meal, glad to be on neutral territory. He ordered coffee and more iced water for Nora while she went to the loo, then checked his phone. He'd had an email from his cousin Faith.

Hello, Ty, and hope you're well. Has Chand moved out yet? He told us it would be sometime in the autumn. Eli and I were wondering if maybe you'd rent the top flat to us. We need something bigger but everything's so expensive. We're not asking for mates' rates, we checked what rent Chand pays and we could match that. If the answer's no, that's fine, maybe you have other plans. But happy to talk it through and kind of hoping you'll say yes. Faith xx

His heart sank. He was fond of Faith, less so of Eli Caldwell, her partner. He'd worked with Eli in the Met years back and the man had turned up on his doorstep in the spring, needing a bed, saying he was broke. He'd lost his job as a tour guide in Vanuatu and been scammed out of his savings. Or so he claimed. He'd met Faith during the week he'd stayed in the basement, and before Swift could blink he'd moved into her tiny one-bedroomed flat.

'Something wrong?' Nora sat back down, shucked her trainers off, hooked a chair out and rested her feet on it. She'd always had a knack of making herself at home.

Swift showed her the email. 'My cousin Faith, putting me in a quandary.'

She read the screen and handed the phone back. 'Faith's the woman who was attacked on the ferry from Ireland, right?'

'Yes. She still suffers some impairment, brain injury and physical frailty, although she's made improvements and has a job again now.'

'Who's Eli?'

'Used to be a copper, a lousy one, then to everyone's relief he left and went to Oceania as a travel rep.' He explained the background. 'Eli has good intentions, but he's chaotic and a freeloader. He left the iron on and set fire to my kitchen, generally created a trail of destruction. He's often rather vague about plans and he talks in bloody Bislama half the time. Faith finds it intriguing.'

'What's that?'

'The *lingua franca* in the islands. A sort of pidgin English, lots of *tangkyu* and *plis*.' He rubbed his face. 'Faith's keen on Eli and he does seem genuinely fond of her, likes to look after her. She was lonely on her own, rather directionless. She's been domesticating him and he's got a job in telesales.'

'Where are they at the moment?'

'Little place in Leytonstone, just about big enough to swing the proverbial cat. He's a huge man, taller than me and broad. It must be very cramped.'

'Sounds as if they're good for each other, despite your concerns.'

'I had grave doubts to start with, worried that Eli was taking advantage of her, but from what I see, they gel well together, and they're happy too.'

Nora wriggled her toes. 'Your wrinkled brow indicates conflict. That's me doing detection and keeping my skills sharp, by the way.'

He smiled. 'I was considering not renting the top flat out again and making it into an area for Branna.'

Nora slipped an ice cube from her glass and sucked on it. 'Would make sense for when she's growing up.'

'Yep. On the other hand, it would be good to help Faith and I wouldn't have to see much of Eli.'

'But you might be aware of his looming presence.'

'And his elephant-like tread. It would mean that I could keep an eye on him, make sure he's not messing Faith about.'

'Hard work, being someone's guardian angel. Your wings can get singed. I'm no good at advice. Sleep on it.' She yawned, covered her mouth.

He saw that she was flagging. 'Let's head back. You can snooze in the boat if you want.'

'Sounds dreamy. I'll get a cab home from Tamesas.'

In the boat, she curled with her head on her arm. 'It's been a tonic, Ty. Tired now.'

He rowed lightly as she slept, keeping the boat smooth and steady, observing the shadows beneath her eyes. Faith had that same worn expression. She'd been through terrible times, battled on with permanent injuries from a dreadful attack. He'd say yes to her about the flat. How could he refuse?

* * *

His phone rang that evening while he was sitting on the swing seat in the garden, drinking red wine and watching the harvest moon emerge.

'Mr Swift, it's Keith from Easton's.'

'Hi, Keith. How are you?'

'Fine, fine. Knackered after a day on fine comestibles.'

'Must be tiring, being on your feet for hours.'

'I've got them up on the sofa now, propped on a cushion. I'm calling because I have something dead interesting for you. Quite a treasure trove!'

'Go on, you've got me hooked.'

'Well, they've been working on the basement area at the store — "repurposing" it, in Lawrie's Dash speak. That means they're converting it into an area for home design advice — how to reconfigure your kitchen or bedroom, et cetera. They've been getting rid of stuff that's been down there since the old shop closed. This morning, they were shifting an ancient set of kitchen cupboards that never sold, or maybe were never collected. Very 1990s, they are — lots of oak. Covered with dust and cobwebs.'

Swift assumed this was going somewhere. He could hear that Keith was relishing the story. 'Sounds like my stepmother's retro kitchen.'

'If it ain't broke, don't fix it?'

'That's her motto.'

'Anyway, Lawrie rang me at lunchtime. Seems one of the blokes opened a cupboard drawer and spotted a large brown envelope. When he checked it, there were quite a few smaller envelopes inside, addressed to Corinne Buckley, at home. He gave the lot to Lawrie, who checked one of the envelopes and saw a letter and a photo of a boy. To cut a long story short, Lawrie's given them to me and asked me to tell you. He just wanted to get rid of them and I realised you'd be interested. They might be something to do with the family matter you mentioned.'

'Have you read any of the letters?'

'I was tempted but no, I didn't like to. They're personal. I did glance in the big envelope. There must be a dozen or so of them. But why would Corinne have left them there?'

'She must have forgotten about them.' Her illness had been rapid. Maybe there had been no time to retrieve them. But why had she taken them to work in the first place? He was eager to see the cache. 'Where do you live? Can I come and collect them now?'

Keith gave him an address in Harlesden. Swift said he'd be there within the hour and found his car keys, glad that he'd had only one small glass of wine.

* * *

By ten o'clock that night, Swift was back home. He closed his front door, realising how much he enjoyed returning to an empty, quiet house nowadays and recollecting what a nightmare it had been when Eli had stayed with him.

He drew the curtains, switched a lamp on and sat at the dining table with another glass of spicy Shiraz and the A4 brown envelope. He eased the letters out, counting fourteen oblong white envelopes, printed with Corinne's address in Wembley and all postmarked 1 December, from 1999 to 2013. They were franked by a company called Daley Mobility. He laid them out in date order, had a deep draught of wine and opened the one from December 1999. A single page, one typed paragraph, no address, no signature.

Zac is well and in good spirits. He had a cold in November. He is happy, settled and attends playgroup.

The photo showed him sitting on a sofa, grinning, holding a toy train, his left hand with missing little finger. His hair was styled differently, longer and with a fringe. The next envelope, from December 2000, contained a similar message, this time with a photo of a taller Zac standing in a paddling pool, wearing swimming shorts. His birthmark was clear.

Zac continues to be well and happy. He's fascinated by dinosaurs and loves reading.

Swift went through them all. Always a couple of bland sentences, no more:

Zac's really taken to football and he's in the school team.
    Zac came top of his class all year and he's an excellent reader. He sprained his ankle in June, but mended fine.
    Zac's specialising in sciences. He came first in long jump on sports day.

Measles and chickenpox were mentioned, and Zac's progress at school was a constant theme. The annual photos showed a laughing, confident boy passing through gap-toothed childhood and developing into a gangly teenager who didn't smile quite as readily for the camera. He'd won a medal for running and was in the Scouts. Braces appeared on his teeth when he was twelve. In his fifteenth year, he was scowling, his shoulders broader, his hair dyed with purple streaks, and he sported an earring. You could see the emerging face of the grown man in the photo taken in West Ham Park.

Swift poured another glass of wine and went through the photos again, trying to see if any location might be identified. But the backgrounds were as bland as the messages — usually the same shrub-lined garden, occasionally a beach with just the sea and sky behind Zac. Some of those seas shimmered with the vibrant blue of the Mediterranean.

He moved to the sofa and lay back against a cushion. Whoever had taken Zac into their keeping had agreed to a yearly communication, timed pre-Christmas. Corinne must have told them of her imminent death, or they had found out, because the correspondence had stopped. She'd have stored the letters at work so that Steve wouldn't find them. After all, they were dynamite and proved she was a liar.

Maybe she'd pored over the photos during tea breaks and lunch hours, yearning for the boy she'd given away, trying to glean everything about him from one annual image. She'd accepted these scant communications and made the most of them. How traumatising, to see your son change from a distance. It was a painful picture and one that brought a lump to his throat.

He frowned. Why would Corinne have parted with her biological son and kept the boy who wasn't her blood relation? It didn't make sense, but then nothing in this case did.

He would have to show Steve these photos and letters. Swift didn't relish the prospect of that visit.

He reached for his iPad and found Daley Mobility. It was a company that manufactured and sold mobility equipment, based near Liverpool Street station. Swift reflected that trains from around Saffron Walden came into that terminus. Might mean something or nothing.

Before he went to bed, he took photos of the notes and images of Zac, clipped the letters in chronological order and replaced them in the large envelope, ready to take to Steve. A small, complex parcel of mystery, hope and misery.

At midnight, unable to sleep, he propped up his pillows and searched online for articles about two-year-olds and memory. Ruth was an educational psychologist, and it was the kind of subject he'd have consulted her about at one time. Not these days.

CHAPTER TEN

Tilly Western was visiting Steve and staying at a hotel nearby. Swift was relieved and reassured that Steve had his aunt's company when he was about to present him with such a massive shock. This was going to be a tough meeting.

Tilly had broad hips, a geometric haircut and a clear, challenging gaze. Steve appeared a little in awe of her, letting her take the lead as they sat side by side on the bed. Swift had to sit in the grip of the armchair again. The ironing board was folded against the wall, laundry bags stacked under the window. The room had been dusted, shelves tidied. Swift suspected Tilly's hand.

When they'd settled down, Tilly sat upright, not an easy feat on that spongy mattress. 'So, Mr Swift, you have new information.'

'I have, and it will be upsetting. Sorry, Steve, I have distressing news for you — but in a way, it's good news too.'

He tensed, his jaw tightening. 'Right. Just tell me.'

'Here goes then,' Swift said. 'We now have proof that Zac didn't die. I've obtained some correspondence that was found at Easton's, the shop where Corinne used to work.' He explained about his visit there and the contact from Keith. 'Corinne had left letters in a kitchen cupboard drawer.' He paused. There was no easy way to do this, so he pressed on. 'The letters contain regular updates about Zac and photos of him over the years.'

'My God. He *is* alive.' Steve put a hand to his forehead, flinched as if he'd been slapped.

Tilly froze, open-mouthed.

'Very much so,' Swift agreed.

Steve bit his knuckles. 'This is mad, isn't it? All the lies about sepsis and a funeral and his ashes. All the years of shitty *lies!*' Tilly attempted to take his hand, but he pulled away from her. 'Go on, then. Show me.'

'I've put the letters in order. They run from the December after Zac was supposed to have died to the one before Corinne passed away.' Swift shook them from the envelope and handed them to Steve.

He sat back and watched as Steve placed them beside him and released the clip. He exhaled a long breath and picked the first one up as if it might explode.

'Take your time, no rush.'

Tilly edged a little closer to him. Steve examined the contents of each envelope before passing it to her. He spent minutes on each photo, trembling with emotion. Now and again, he gave little shuddering breaths and chewed his bottom lip. Tilly touched his shoulder, cast a glance at Swift and continued reading. When he'd scrutinised them all, Steve made a strangled noise and hurried to the bathroom.

Tilly sighed. 'He's an emotional sort, like Corinne was, and the punches keep landing on him at the moment. I'm very worried about him. He's up and down like a yo-yo, hardly sleeping. And this place is such a rabbit hutch, it must get oppressive.' She indicated an area of damaged plaster by the window. 'He punched the wall yesterday and kicked in a kitchen cupboard.'

'He can't be easy company. Maybe he should see his doctor, get something to help.'

'I have suggested that. It didn't go down well and I doubt that he will.'

'My visit today will add to the tension. The letters make emotional reading. For you, as well.'

'Yes, and bizarre.' She pinched her bottom lip. 'The really weird thing that Steve hasn't grasped fully yet is that Corinne parted with her own son, and kept the son who wasn't actually hers biologically.'

'Exactly. It's perplexing.'

'Mad, more like.' Tilly examined the postmark on an envelope. 'Were they all sent from Daley Mobility?'

'Yes. It's a business in the City of London. I'm going to check it out.'

'Corinne hid them, didn't she? She didn't want Steve to see them. She had to maintain the fiction that Zac was dead.'

'I agree. That must be why she stored them at work. You told me her illness was rapid. I suspect that she forgot the letters once she was overwhelmed by the cancer.'

Tilly unscrewed a bottle of water and drank. 'Yuck, this is warm. I'd never, ever have believed that Corinne could deceive us like this. To spin such a story and tell me and Steve so many lies. She just didn't seem to have it in her. I mean, she was an ordinary woman, not at all secretive. Back when we were kids, she was always dying to tell us what she'd bought us for Christmas, could hardly keep it quiet.'

'She must have found herself in extraordinary circumstances.'

'I certainly hope so, although I can't begin to imagine what those can have been. It's terribly mean and cruel, and she never had a nasty streak.'

Steve returned, eyes blotchy. He looked from his aunt to Swift. 'All that time, all those years, Mum knew where Zac was. She was a bitch, a complete bitch! Maybe she even visited him!'

Swift shook his head. 'That's possible, but I'd say that the letters indicate she didn't see Zac. I imagine that there was a deal — she'd get annual updates if she stayed away.'

Steve picked up a photo, ran a finger across it. 'Zac grew up believing that whoever he was with was his parent, or parents.'

'At two years of age, he'd most likely have forgotten your mum and you,' Swift agreed. 'I'm not sure if he'd have had any memories of his previous home. From what I've read, it's unlikely.'

'And he seems to have recognised this woman who picked him up on Good Friday,' Tilly said.

'Ms Whitehall told me that Zac went with her quite happily, suggesting that they'd spent time together. That's why it's so puzzling that neither of you have heard of her. Tilly, did you attend Corinne and Kevin's wedding and Kevin's funeral?'

'Both, yes.'

'Can you recall anyone from Kevin's family at either event? I can't find any trace of Dan Buckley, who sent Corinne his condolences after Kevin's death.'

'Kev didn't appear to have any family. Corinne said his parents were dead. I got the impression his childhood hadn't been too happy, although I can't say why because he never referred to it. Maybe Corinne dropped a hint. The wedding was a very small affair, as was Kev's funeral. I certainly didn't meet a Dan.' She pressed a finger to her forehead. 'I don't understand how this worked. Surely you can't just hand a child over to someone without informing authorities?'

'Zac didn't attend nursery, he was at home with his mum, so fairly anonymous,' Swift replied. 'People assume that the powers that be monitor our lives, but the truth is that it's easy for a small child to slip under the radar. Look at all the migrant children who vanish within the UK every year.'

There was a long silence. Tilly announced that she'd make coffee and headed to the kitchen.

It wasn't a cold day, but Steve switched on the electric fire. 'How could my mum do this? How could she do it to Zac and me? It's mental, all of it.'

'You'll be asking yourself that until I find Zac. *If* I manage to find him. I imagine you might always have that question in your mind now. Steve, did your mum ever take you to Saffron Walden, or anywhere in that area?'

'No. That's where she worked, right? At a school?'

'Yes, Royal Victoria.'

'We never went there.' He placed a hand on the stack of letters. 'Can I keep these?'

'Certainly, they're yours. I'd like to hang on to one for now. I'm going to visit the business where the letters were sent from, see if anyone can shed any light on it.'

'Well, that's something. I mean, whoever wrote them must work there.'

'Not necessarily. Whoever *sent* them presumably worked there and for fourteen years, but that person might not be there now.'

Steve clasped his hands. 'I'd better not get my hopes up, then. Doesn't seem to do any good.'

'Best not to.' Swift flinched at Steve's despondent expression.

'Have you heard anything more from that Jan Brockhill?'

'Afraid not. One thing to consider here, Steve — Zac seems to have had a happy, content childhood. The photos demonstrate that. Apart from when he became a teenage grouch, he's smiling, laughing. Whoever cared for him did a good job, and kept to the agreement to send your mum a photo every year in time for Christmas.' He'd had a happier childhood than Steve did, Swift thought. Perhaps when he looked through the photos again, he'd realise how loved his brother clearly was. While Zac had had holidays abroad, Steve had been left with the depressed mother who'd sank into seclusion and stone painting. Maybe that would strike home at some point and confuse the poor man even more.

'I suppose there is that. I hadn't considered it that way.'

'You haven't had time to absorb it yet. Talk to your aunt, it will help.'

Steve bent forward, checked the kitchen. Tilly had switched the kettle on and gone to the bathroom.

He kept his voice low. 'I've been wondering if she's been in on it all these years. She might have played along with my mum for some reason, kept the lie going. What if *she's* fooling me too?'

Swift could appreciate that if you discovered that your life had been framed by deception, it would make you distrust everyone. 'Steve, I've found nothing to indicate that and I can't see any reason why Tilly would have been involved.'

'You sure?'

'I can't be one-hundred-per-cent sure of anything, but I have no evidence pointing to your aunt. She comes across as a genuine person who's as shocked as you are.'

Steve was impulsive and lacked emotional intelligence, that useful ability to monitor and analyse experiences and responses. Perhaps that was his nature, but Swift couldn't help wondering how much he'd been damaged by past trauma and his mother's withdrawal.

Swift declined coffee. He wanted to give Steve space and he needed to get to his appointment at Daley Mobility. He walked to a bus stop, another concern nudging to the front of his mind. If he found Zac and the man turned out to have a doting mother and father, parentless Steve might feel even more bereft and grieved.

This case had the potential to uncover a pit full of snakes.

* * *

The managing director of Daley Mobility kept him waiting for almost half an hour. Swift passed the time in his office reading a brochure about stairlifts, wheelchairs, aluminium rollators, riser chairs and beds, universal toilet frames, ramps, trolleys and bedrails. With baby boomers reaching old age, this would be a lucrative business.

At last, Stanley Daley rushed through the door and flicked on a kettle.

'I'm so sorry, there was an urgent machine problem I had to deal with. Coffee?' He waved a jar of cheap instant.

Swift was a coffee snob. 'No thanks.'

'Mind if I do? I'm gasping.'

'Go ahead.'

Daley had a distracted air and gave the impression of a man with a thousand things to do. His sleeves were rolled up, his tie tucked into the front of his shirt. He splashed boiling water, cursed, mopped it up and added powdered cream to his drink. Swift was glad he'd refused one.

Daley sat and pushed a pile of papers out of the way. 'What's this about? Some guy who's tracing his family?'

'That's right. It means a lot to him. I'll try not to keep you long. I'm interested in a series of personal letters that were sent from here between 1999 and 2013.' He'd already removed the contents of the envelope he'd kept and passed it across the desk.

Daley examined the envelope. 'To Corinne Buckley, in Wembley. It certainly came from here. Staff aren't supposed to use us as a mail service, but of course, the odd liberty is taken.' He drummed fingers on the desk. 'Any idea who sent this?'

'No. The note inside is typed and unsigned, with no address.'

'How peculiar.'

'It is. Have you ever suspected any particular staff members of taking liberties?'

Daley removed his glasses, flicked his tie from his shirt and rubbed them with the hem. 'No, can't say I have. I've been MD here for over thirty years and I've learned that it's best to cut employees a little slack. There aren't many perks and it keeps them sweet.'

'How many do you have?'

'Around sixty is the usual complement.'

'Do you have much turnover?'

'People come and go, it's the nature of things, although generally speaking, the staff group has been pretty stable. If you're going back to 1999, there'd have been a few people joining and leaving over the years. Whoever sent these might well have left some time ago.'

'Who would have used the franking machine?'

'Anyone could, as various sections might have needed to send mail. It's in a stationery cupboard up the corridor, beside a tray for outgoing post.'

Swift changed tack. 'Do any of your staff travel in from north Essex?'

Daley stirred his coffee. Some globs of powder were glistening on the surface. 'That would be a bit of a trek, but I wouldn't necessarily hear about where they live. I'm only interested in them turning up. Stacey comes in from Ilford — I remember her mentioning that. She joined us last year.'

'The name Corinne Buckley doesn't mean anything to you?'

'Sorry.'

Swift showed him photos of Corinne and the adult Zac. 'How about these people? The woman is Corinne Buckley and the man is called Zac.'

'I don't recognise them. You seem to have had a wasted journey. I've got phone calls to make, so . . .' He shoved his chair back.

'It's a big ask, but would you be able to check your previous staff records for the years when these letters were sent? I'd like to contact the people who worked here at that time, they might be able to help me.'

Daley tapped the desk again with irritation. 'I can't promise anything. Leave me your details and I'll do what I can.'

Swift decided to push his luck. 'Thanks. Also, if I email you these two photos, could you send them to your staff and ask if anyone can help me with information about the people in them?'

'Yes, very well. Can you see yourself out?'

CHAPTER ELEVEN

Swift was walking home, planning to stop at a supermarket, when Sheila Whitehall phoned, apparently wanting to tell him about her daily exercise. He halted outside Sainsbury's, leaned against the wall next to the trolleys and listened to her.

'These days, I try to have a little walk in the local park at least a couple of times a week, take the air, stretch my legs.'

'That sounds sensible.'

'It's not much of a place, a bit scrubby, and for some reason the council decided to install a skate ramp, which attracts all sorts of kids making a racket and being foul-mouthed. But the flowers are pretty and there are plenty of benches to sit on.'

The day was proving treacherous after a sunny start. The air was thick with a fine rain, the aimless kind that soaks you gently but thoroughly, and Swift hadn't bothered with a jacket. 'Ms Whitehall, has this got anything to do with Corinne Buckley?'

'That's it, you see. Now and again, I have a chat with this old chap called Ivor. He must be late eighties but he's hardy, always there, whatever the weather. He sits on a bench and he reads or watches the world go by. I mentioned Corinne to him yesterday, said you'd been asking questions, and he told me he used to see her in the park sometimes with Zac. Another young woman was with them now and then.'

'Did he recognise the woman?'

'Didn't seem to.'

'Where does this Ivor live?'

'No idea, but you'll catch him in Lyham Gardens any morning, rain or shine. He always sits on the bench to the left of the main entrance and he's got a walking stick with a wolf's head on the top. You can't miss him.'

Swift thanked her, grabbed a basket and wandered around the supermarket, stocking up on milk, bread, eggs and cheeses. He selected ground coffee, hoping that Ivor might be able to tell him more about the woman he'd seen with Corinne. By the time he'd paid and exited, the rain had become purposeful, tumbling from a sky heavy with leaden clouds. He ran through the streets to his house, his shirt sticking to his back.

As he pounded up to the door, his heart sank. Eli Caldwell was sitting on the top step, wearing a bright yellow rain cape and holding a huge umbrella with a duck motif.

'Ty, *mi fren*! You look like a drowned rat!'

Water was dripping into his eyes and down his neck. 'Thanks. Let me get the door open.'

He fumbled with his keys. Eli followed him in, dumping the umbrella in the hall. Swift put his carrier bag on the kitchen worktop and grabbed a towel from a hook, drying his face and hair. Eli stood near him, invading his space and spattering him with more water as he shrugged off his cape.

Swift gritted his teeth. 'Maybe you could hang that in the bathroom.'

'Sure, *mi save*. You could have done with some wet-weather gear yourself today.'

Swift covered his face with the towel so that he could growl silently, stripped his sodden shirt off, stuck it in the washing machine and went to fetch a dry T-shirt from his bedroom. He was still rubbing his hair when his phone rang. He sat on the bed to take the call.

'This is Raymond Utley, Mr Swift. You left a message for me.'

'Thanks for getting back to me. I wanted to talk to you about someone who worked at the Royal Victoria school when you were the head.'

'I see. I retired quite some time ago. I'm not sure how I can help you.'

Swift removed his trainers and damp socks, shivered and put his feet on the towel. 'I visited the school, but no one there recalled the person I'm interested in, Corinne Buckley. She was a teaching assistant from 1994 for three years and her name was Ellwood at that time. I was given you as a contact.'

A brief silence. 'Why are you making enquiries about Ms Ellwood?'

'It's on behalf of her son. He's trying to find information about his mother.'

'Why can't he ask her?'

'She died.'

'How sad. What kind of information?'

'It's a family matter, something troubling.' Swift twitched as he heard Eli clomping around and the sound of water running in the kitchen. He hoped his visitor wasn't touching the iron or the cooker, which had been disaster zones during his last stay.

'As far as I'm aware, Corinne was a single woman when she worked at the school. I don't see how I can assist.' The man's caginess was palpable.

Eli loomed in the doorway and mouthed, '*Coffee?*'

Swift raised a thumb. 'It might help to find out a little more about her time at the school, who she mixed with on the staff. Anything you can tell me, to be honest.'

'That's all rather vague. I had very little to do with the young woman.'

'But you do remember her?'

'Indistinctly. I managed a large staff group.'

'Even so, if you could—'

'No, I'm sorry, there's nothing I can tell you. Good day.'

Utley ended the call. Unusual, curt reactions were always of interest.

Swift found socks and padded to the kitchen. Eli handed him a mug of coffee — it smelled good. Swift noticed that he'd put the shopping away and folded the carrier bag. Faith's domestic training was paying off.

'Heard you were on the phone, so I tidied the stuff, it's all in the right slots. That OK?' Eli smiled ingratiatingly.

'Thanks, appreciated.'

'Got any biscuits, *mi fren*? I could do with *samting* to nibble on.'

'In the cupboard, usual place. Shouldn't you be at work?'

'Day off. I'm working the weekend.'

'Right. How's it going?'

'*Gud.* It'll do for now and it's nice to have money in the bank. I can treat Faith to the occasional meal out.'

They sat in the living room, where Eli stacked a pile of ginger biscuits on his massive right knee. He'd lost some weight and was well groomed, clean-shaven and wearing smart, dark chinos. There was a pleasant whiff of aftershave. Certainly, today's manifestation was a big improvement on the pongy, shambling character who'd turned up earlier in the year.

'How is Faith?'

'She's well, and I can't believe my luck in finding such a good woman to put up with me.'

Swift narrowed his eyes. Eli was a dab hand at soft-soaping when he wanted something. 'You're right, she's an excellent woman.'

Eli demolished several biscuits and swigged coffee. 'Er . . . Faith told me she asked you about the flat upstairs.'

Subtlety wasn't Eli's middle name. Swift wasn't minded to give him an easy ride, and his dealings about the flat would be with Faith, not Eli. No way would his name be on the tenancy. 'She has, and I'm mulling it over. I'm not sure what I want to do with it yet.'

'Right.' He gave a little sigh.

'If you've come to persuade me, don't bother, Eli. I'll weigh it up. I told Faith I'd get back to her soon.'

'Sure, *mi fren*.' Eli stared into the middle distance, nibbled another biscuit. 'It's just . . . it'd be a big help to us both and, cross my heart, I wouldn't bother you or get in your way. I realise I was a bit of a pain when I was here before.'

'Yes, I'd say that setting fire to the kitchen did cause some discomfort.'

Eli bit his lip. 'You're entitled to be sarky, but I'd be on my best behaviour. I did try to make amends by helping with that case you were working.'

Eli had redeemed himself somewhat by obtaining information, although Swift had paid him for his services. 'That's true.'

'You wouldn't know I was around upstairs, honestly.' He hunched inwards, twitched his nose. 'I'd be like a little mouse.'

A huge, blundering brown bear was the animal Eli most resembled. Swift observed him gather crumbs carefully into one big paw. Before, they would have been scattered all over the carpet. 'I'll bear that in mind. Leave it with me. Thanks for making the coffee.'

* * *

Lyham Gardens was a couple of streets from where the Buckleys had lived in Wembley. It was a pretty name for a featureless patch of ground surrounded by scuffed railings. A large notice was attached to the entrance gate.

NO ROLLER SKATES, BIKES or SCOOTERS
NO LOUD MUSIC
NO DOGS
SKATEBOARDS TO BE USED ONLY IN
DESIGNATED AREA
NO SLEEPING ON BENCHES

Someone was ignoring the last rule, huddled in a long coat and concealing woolly hat, fast asleep on a bench by a holly bush. There was a small, fenced play area for young children with swings, the see-saw where Zac's ashes had supposedly been scattered, a climbing frame and a tiny roundabout with moulded dragons as the seats. Circular flower beds were separated by gravelled paths, and at the far end stood a graffiti-covered skateboard ramp. It was a municipal area with little heart, not entirely neglected but not much cared for. At least dahlias and chrysanthemums added bold splashes of colour, enlivening the scene.

At ten thirty in the morning, there were just three people present: a teenage girl sitting on the ramp, smoking and listening to her phone, the rough sleeper and one seated elderly man with a walking stick.

The sun was milky, a brisk nip in the air. Swift pulled up his collar and approached the man with the stick. 'Good morning, are you Ivor? Apologies, I don't know your surname.'

He had a long, straggling beard and button eyes and was dressed in quilted layers. On his head was a tweedy fishing hat. 'You have the advantage of me. You are?'

'Tyrone Swift. May I sit down?'

The man was well spoken, his voice faint. 'It's a free country, unless there's been a coup since I left home this morning. I could be sitting here, unaware that martial law had been imposed. I'd be oblivious until the tanks appeared, wouldn't I?'

Swift sat beside him. 'I didn't see any tanks on my way here. Is it something you worry about?'

Ivor folded his arms, his sleeves rustling. 'Worry? Maybe. Shouldn't we all worry about such a possibility?'

'Seems unlikely in London at present. I'm not sure we have enough of an army left to impose a coup.' Swift hoped he wasn't keeping company with a conspiracy lover. They were such hard work.

'Remember that these things can happen like that.' Ivor snapped his fingers. 'That was the case in Prague in sixty-eight when the Soviets rolled in. We didn't see it coming. It was a big surprise. Armed soldiers when you went to buy bread. I still tremble with the shock of it, the way the house shook when the hardware rumbled past. I've seen how quickly events can turn. One minute you're safe, next you're watching your back and obeying a curfew.'

'What were you doing in Prague?'

'Working as a translator for the Foreign Office. I was flown out sharpish. Never been back, which I find terribly sad. Friends died.' He examined Swift. 'I've been coming here for years and that's the first time I've told anyone about it.'

'I've never been to this park and that was the last thing I was expecting to hear.'

Ivor held his feet up, rotated the ankles. 'At my age, you're walking history. Ancient history to a lot of people. You have to take care not to bore your listener. What *were* you expecting when you came through the gate?'

Swift showed him his ID. 'Sheila Whitehall phoned me and said that you recalled a woman called Corinne Buckley and her son Zac. She told me I'd find you here.'

'Sheila!' He pulled a face. 'That woman witters on so. I'm an easy target for people who can't stand being on their own. They assume I'm lonely when I'm enjoying my private thoughts.'

'You always know where you are with your own company,' Swift agreed.

'Indeed. Did Sheila tell you that you need a manicure?'

'She did, yes.'

'She's a one-trick pony. Although recently, she's been waxing on about the skateboarders, saying they're a nuisance. I like watching them, the way they seem to defy gravity. Some of them are highly skilled.'

'Maybe Ms Whitehall's jealous of their youth and flexibility.'

'Incisive point. I like people who appreciate subtext.' He glanced sideways. 'Why are you interested in Corinne Buckley?'

Swift had taken to Ivor's candour and decided to tell him the truth. Somehow, he deserved it. He explained. Ivor gazed straight ahead, expressionless. When Swift finished, the man cradled his walking stick, leaned his gloved hands on it. The wolf's head handle was large and red, with bared fangs.

'Dear, how sad. I met Corinne here, in the park. She used to bring Zac to play on quite a few mornings. We'd say hello, comment on the weather, that sort of thing. He was a lively child, always running and yelling. Never stopped. He always wanted to go on the see-saw.'

'Corinne told her family that she scattered his ashes around there.'

'Most peculiar, given what you've described.'

'What about this woman you saw her with?'

'Yes, that was on three or four occasions. Youngish, hair tucked into a bell-shaped hat — a cloche, I believe they're called. They chatted and the woman played with the boy, helped him on the swings, sat him on her lap.'

'He seemed comfortable with her?'

'I believe so. Wasn't crying or making strange, put it that way.'

'Can you recall when this was?'

Ivor rotated his walking stick. 'The first time was in January 1999. I can be precise about that because it was my sixtieth birthday and I was lunching with a friend, so I had to keep an eye on the time. The two women were here during those early months of the year. Despite the season, we had some pleasantly mild days.'

Swift put his head back, examined the watery clouds. So that might have been the build-up to Zac being handed over. The woman who'd collected him from Sheila had also had her hair tucked into a hat. He turned back to Ivor. 'How did this woman dress?'

'Jeans, sweatshirts, usual clobber.' He raised a finger. 'She had a big cloth bag, multicoloured, one of those patch-work jobs. You're wondering if she was the person who picked Zac up from Sheila's.'

'I am. I'm also wondering if they met at other times as well as here in the park. Did Corinne seem upset?'

'Hard to say, I wasn't sitting that close. Goodness, it's a rum story.' Ivor grinned, baring white dentures. 'I'm quite annoyed with you for topping my Prague invasion.'

The sleeper on the bench opposite had woken and rolled off. He or she walked around the perimeter, poked in the bins, snatched a package from one, ripped it open and started eating as they left the park.

'Cheese and tomato today,' Ivor muttered. 'I leave a sandwich in there every morning.'

'The woman who was with Corinne — did you see if she came here by car?'

'Can't help you there. I never notice cars unless they're very beautiful, like a Jaguar or a Bugatti, say. You wouldn't see those around these streets. Now that my train of thought has been diverted to Corinne, I saw another, middle-aged woman in here with her once. They were walking through with Zac in the pushchair. Now, that day, I *did* wonder if Corinne was upset.'

'Why was that?'

'Just an impression. I saw the back of them. The older woman was taller than Corinne and she had her face close to hers, a hand pressed on her shoulder, as if she was persuading or cajoling her.'

'That was the only time you saw this woman?'

'That's it.'

'Was that before or after you saw Corinne with the younger woman?'

'I'd guess some time before, although I can't be sure. I seem to remember ice on the ground . . . yes, there was. Corinne slipped as she walked and righted herself with the pushchair.' He removed his gloves and rubbed his hands together, massaged the papery skin. 'I've told you what I can.'

'Thanks. You've been visiting here a long time.'

'And with any luck, I'll be on this bench for many more years.' He held out a hand. 'Ivor Tremlett, by the way.'

Swift shook his hand, the brittle bones delicate in his grip.

'I'll be turning all this over and over in my mind now,' Ivor said. 'Strange, to realise that I was watching such a drama unfold. Corinne Buckley must have been in great distress.'

Swift stood. 'I haven't told Sheila Whitehall any of these details, so please keep them to yourself.'

Ivor tapped his nose. 'The secret's safe with me. Anyway, I barely speak to Sheila, not that she notices. She does all the talking. My role is the silent listener.'

CHAPTER TWELVE

'How do you take your tea? Milk?'

'Just a splash.'

Elizabeth Utley smirked, as if it had been a test and Swift had given the correct response. He was sitting with her in a large, austere living room with furnishings and carpet in shades of mushroom. Dark engravings of brooding castles perched on hilltops covered the walls. They resembled the locations used in horror films, and Swift could picture Dracula lurking on one of the battlements. Not for the first time, he marvelled at what people chose for their interior décor.

The Utleys' large, detached house was a couple of miles west of Saffron Walden. The French windows revealed a colourless back garden with a parched, yellowish lawn and pale ornamental grasses. The crazy paving was covered with moss. A tatty wooden bird table tilted like a drunken sailor. It took a particular talent to make a garden depressing. The weather had deteriorated with murmurs of thunder and the room was on the chilly side. Swift's eye was caught by a rapid lightning streak, but Ms Utley misread his glance for tension.

'We won't be disturbed. Raymond isn't due back until this evening. He's gone to London for a sewing exhibition.' She rolled her pouchy eyes. 'Sewing!'

'Is that something your husband's interested in?'

She sipped tea, laughed with no humour. 'So he *claims*. Oh yes, so he claims.'

'I'm not following you.'

She jerked her head sideways and upwards. 'He dabbles with his needles, but it's really one of his ways of meeting women. My husband's a philanderer. You have to hand it to him for thinking outside the box and putting in the effort. He also volunteers at the cat sanctuary — staffed exclusively by lonely women and widows in the main — and the donkey refuge, ditto.'

Swift stared into his tea, reluctant to wander into tricky marital territory. Ms Utley had sent him an email with her address:

> *I can help you about Corinne Buckley, née Ellwood, even if my husband is reluctant. Come and see me at 3 p.m. on Tuesday, when he'll be out.*

He wasn't going to pass up the intriguing invitation and had replied, saying he'd be there.

'Have I embarrassed you?' Elizabeth Utley enquired.

'No. I'm just not sure why you want to tell me that.'

'Because you need to understand that Raymond is a liar and a cheat, interested only in himself and what benefits him. I discovered that soon after we married. It's a way of life for him. He'll always dissemble rather than tell the truth. His brain is wired that way.' She smirked. 'You could say it's his factory setting.'

'You're telling me that he lied when he insisted that he couldn't help me about Corinne Ellwood.'

'Exactly. Do have a brandy snap.'

Swift wasn't hungry, but he selected one from the tin to buy himself time and because they smelled good. Elizabeth Utley adjusted the Alice band on her long, greying, greasy hair. Her ghostly pallor spoke of a woman who spent many hours indoors. She wore a faded navy-blue tea dress, cinched at the waist with a white belt and a brown cardigan draped around her neck. The skin on her bare legs and arms was mottled, with reddened, scabby patches. She was a woman who'd given up bothering with her appearance, which might indicate that no one cared. She radiated simmering anger. When he arrived, she'd been raking leaves on the front lawn, stabbing the grass with the prongs as if exacting punishment.

'Raymond and I have maintained separate lives for years,' she announced. 'We cohabit under the same roof, but otherwise we go our own ways, with agreed time slots for the kitchen. We have our own bathrooms.'

'Do you have children?'

Her eyelids drooped. 'None of your beeswax, but no. Raymond didn't want them.'

'The arrangement you have here suits you?'

'I suppose it must. It's a mutual agreement.'

Yet she kept tabs on her husband, knew where he'd gone for the day. Her eczema told a story of irritation and resentment. Swift found her need to tell a stranger about her fractured marriage sad, but her unhappiness could work to his advantage.

She gave him a sly smile. 'I expect you're wondering how I worked out you'd contacted Raymond and how I got your details.'

He wanted to say, *People with cheating partners are always detectives in their own lives, constantly seeking clues*, but it wouldn't pay to antagonise her. 'I did speculate. I assume you snooped. Takes one to know one, Ms Utley.'

She stiffened, unsure if she'd been insulted, then laughed. 'I like your bluntness. I bet no one pulls the wool over your eyes.'

'You'd be surprised. Sometimes, we don't see what we want to ignore.'

'That was true of me many years ago, but not for a long time. I heard Raymond's weasel voice when he rang you, so I checked his phone and listened to your message. Then I saw that he'd searched for you online, so I looked at your website. I monitor his phone, search history and email daily anyway. He's so fascinated by himself, he has no idea that I observe him closely. I always made it my business to be on top of everything that went on at the school, and I apply the same principle to my dealings with my husband.'

She must have nothing better to do. Evidently, she wasn't into home improvements or gardening. Her consuming interest was spying on her husband. Swift was tempted to suggest that she might get a life, but there was no point in needlessly alienating her. 'What can you tell me about Corinne?' He was half expecting to hear that Utley had been having an affair with the young teaching assistant.

'Oh no, you first, Mr Swift. What exactly is your interest in her?'

'She's dead and her family are seeking information.'

'Such as?'

'Just some matters that need to be clarified.'

She stroked her long jaw. 'And that's all you're going to tell me?'

'That's all I'm permitted to say. Client confidentiality, you understand.'

She sucked her cheeks in, weighed this up. 'Well, there was no chance that Raymond would tell you anything about the sad little scenario that played out here. He hushed all that up very carefully, for the sake of his own reputation and the school's.' The tea was in a tall, stainless-steel thermal jug. She poured another cup, turned the handle in his direction. 'Do help yourself. What have you learned about RV, as we call the school?'

'It's a Georgian building, very handsome, with impressive facilities. I'd guess that it offers an expensive, rounded education.'

'Yes, all of those. I taught French there and the staff are highly qualified, graduates of Oxbridge or redbrick universities. Since the 1930s, when a board of governors decided to expand the school's social conscience, it's had an added purpose to offer two places a year to refugees — either scholarships for students or posts for staff, which include accommodation.'

'That's generous.'

'Sharing the good fortune. It's easy in some ways to be open-handed when you have wealth, but yes, it's to be applauded. Over the years, there have been students and staff from many troubled parts of the world, and they've certainly opened eyes and enriched the community. The people you need to be aware of were a Lebanese couple, Elias and Abila Harb, who arrived in 1995. Lebanon had been blighted by civil war, and although it had ended by then, life was still unpredictable and jobs were difficult to obtain, so they decided to leave. Elias taught chemistry at RV, Abila was a part-time laundry assistant and looked after Leisha, their little girl.'

She scratched absent-mindedly at her arm as she was speaking. *Scritch, scritch.* Swift saw a tiny thread of red on her skin. He felt as if he was breathing in the loneliness in this house, absorbing it in his bloodstream.

'Was Corinne friendly with this couple?'

'Oh yes, they got on well. You'd see her with Abila around the place, walking in the grounds, playing tennis or ping-pong. They'd go shopping in town with the child, that sort of thing. Abila was a couple of years older, but they had a bond. She was very pretty, with long, flowing hair, and she was strong willed, made a bit of a pet of Corinne, I'd say. Corinne was perky but biddable. I imagine that's why Abila asked for her help.'

'Go on.'

Ms Utley sat back, pulling her cardigan closer. 'Abila had a thing going with Raymond. He usually likes them younger, they're easier to impress. She'd told Corinne — it was a girly secret.' She hissed the words as she ran the back of her hand across her lips. 'Abila wanted to spend time with Raymond one May evening, but she needed to distract her husband and she asked Corinne to help. Elias was learning to ride and he'd had a couple of lessons at the stables. Corinne agreed to assist the deception. She did take small groups riding as part of her duties, so she organised an outing for early that evening and invited Elias along. He was keen, so that worked well for the lovers and their little tryst.'

'Did anyone else know about your husband and Abila?'

'I was always aware when he had a side interest on the go, although not necessarily who it was. I guessed he was up to something at that time. I operated a watch-and-wait policy. Raymond's leching was a standing joke among the staff. His affairs usually lasted a couple of months, rarely longer. You could pretty much guarantee that he'd lust after any new female who joined the school, especially a pretty, young one. His strike rate — I believe that's the phrase — was quite high. He expended a lot of time and energy covering his tracks, keeping people sweet.'

'Didn't you find his behaviour mortifying?' She'd have been aware of sniggers and side glances.

'I made my adjustments. One learns to.'

'How come your husband didn't go after Corinne? Or did he?'

She slipped a tissue from her cardigan sleeve, dabbed at the blood on her arm. 'I expect he'd have got round to her, if that night hadn't produced so much fallout. There was a fair intake of staff at the time, so he was spoiled for choice, and although she wasn't bad looking, she was on the skinny side, rather flat-chested. Raymond had other fish to fry. And he preferred well-stacked types. Still does, I expect.'

The storm had broken and rain wept down the French windows. Swift poured more tea to warm himself up. Ms Utley rose and switched two lamps on. As her skirt swished, he saw that she had a knee support on her right leg.

'What went wrong with Corinne's and Abila's plan?' he asked.

'Ah yes, the assignation — one of so many — in Raymond's study. That evening, Abila made sure the child was asleep before joining him in there. Meanwhile, Corinne, Elias and three students set off for a jaunt on horseback. They chose a bridleway through the fields that diverts onto meandering paths. Elias was at the front. Corinne and the students had halted — something to do with a loose stirrup or bridle. I have no experience of horses, they terrify me. When the problem was sorted, Elias was nowhere to be seen. Turned out he'd got fed up waiting — he was an impatient sort — and had gone off down a path. Corinne told the students to stay put and went ahead to find him. The horse had spooked and he'd fallen off, damaging several vertebrae and his pelvis. He was in hospital for a good while.'

'Given the circumstances, Corinne, his wife and your husband must have shouldered some responsibility and guilt.'

'Oh! Raymond wasn't bothered by *guilt*. He was more concerned that the cosy scene in his study with Abila didn't get out. My husband's always been skilled at cultivating women, making them feel special, attended to. He's equally skilled at discarding them and moving on before things get too difficult. He must have coached Abila and Corinne well, because neither of them revealed anything about the background to the accident — not to the authorities, anyway.'

'Meaning?'

'Guilt does play on *some* people's minds, doesn't it? Those with consciences. Abila confessed to Elias about the affair when he came out of hospital. A couple of months later, he vanished back to Lebanon with Leisha without telling her. Upped and left when she was working. They were killed in a car crash a week later. Abila was distraught. She left the school soon after.'

'How did you get to hear about all of this?' Swift asked.

'Corinne told me, after Abila had gone. She was full of misgivings and wanting to apologise to me. Sorry for herself. If she hadn't colluded . . . If she hadn't agreed to take Elias riding — all those questions that nag at us when bad things happen. What could I say to her? She wasn't directly responsible for the awful events that evening, but she played her part. I told her as much. If she hoped that I could help her salve her conscience, she was mistaken.'

Corinne must have been naïve and a bad judge of character if she'd believed that Elizabeth Utley would offer any solace. Even now, her voice was scornful. The young woman had wanted to get things off her chest, but the wronged wife was hardly likely to have proved a source of comfort.

'Where did Abila go?'

'No idea. It's possible that she told Corinne — unless the bosom buddies had fallen out. I suppose she might have returned to Lebanon, although with everything still being in a state of chaos there, it doesn't seem likely.'

'And Corinne left to get married?'

'Yes, to some man with one of those council-estate names.'

'Do people who live on council estates have specific names? He was called Kevin.'

'Yes? There we are, I expect she found her level. Most people do.' She glanced around at the rain. 'Filthy weather! I hope it's not dampening Raymond's romance. I've never understood why my husband is so attractive to women. He's no oil painting and really not a nice person.'

'Is he rich?'

Her eyebrows shot up. 'Enough, but not the generous type — not one to give jewellery or flowers. You'd have to halve the bill if you went out for dinner, although I don't suppose he wines and dines them much. In fact,' she made a rasping noise deep in her throat, 'he has the amazing talent of getting the women to give *him* gifts. I've lost track of the mysterious pens, ties, monogrammed hankies, colognes, desk toys and the like that have turned up over the years. Some of them expensive. I expected him to slow down when he got old. He's eighty-two now but the sap's still rising!'

Swift had a keen desire to get away. He angled his watch. 'What time do you expect your husband home?'

'He always gets the same train back, the 5.15 from Liverpool Street. I told you, he's not about to walk in on us.'

'Can you recall anyone else at the school back then who might be able to tell me where Abila went?'

'Afraid not.' She smiled nastily. 'I suppose you find a lot of dead ends in your line of work.'

'That's true.' Although this house was deader than many of the trails he'd followed.

CHAPTER THIRTEEN

Raymond Utley's train would arrive at Audley End, the nearest station, at 6.20 p.m. Swift waited in the car park, ready to intercept him. He'd found Utley's photo on the local cat sanctuary website. Utley had been pictured in the centre of five women turned in slightly towards him. The moggy rescuer and his harem. His wife was right about the shrewd choice of activities for an ageing libertine. He had luxurious, curly white hair, a large nose set in a lean, tanned face and a glint in his eye. Not a handsome man, but striking. Much better preserved than his wife, but then he hadn't spent years being gnawed away by jealousy and resentment.

The evening had brought late sun, the clouds swept aside by a warm breeze. The train was surprisingly on time, disgorging a hefty number of passengers. Swift got out of his car for a better view.

After a minute, he watched Utley exit the station. The man was sporting black chinos, a long grey tweed jacket, a cream trilby with a dark chocolate trimming and an orange leather shoulder bag. Swift locked his car and followed him. He had to applaud the man's well-maintained longevity and the spring in his step as he aimed for his black Volvo.

'Mr Utley!'

He turned, a balletic swivel. 'Yes?'

'Enjoy your sewing larks?'

'I beg your pardon?' The sun was in his eyes. He shifted sideways, tilted his hat forwards. 'Who are you?'

'My name's Tyrone Swift. We spoke on the phone about Corinne Ellwood.'

A moment's pause. 'We did.'

'I'd appreciate five minutes of your time.'

Utley compressed his lips. 'I informed you that I can't help.' He lifted his key fob. The electronic clunk of the mechanism unlocking joined others in the car park as commuters headed home.

'I believe you can. Abila Harb.'

'Pardon?'

'You worked with Abila Harb.'

He made a dismissive gesture, flashing an onyx-and-silver cufflink. Maybe a gift from an admirer. 'Briefly, many years ago.'

'Same as with Corinne Ellwood. All these brief work episodes.'

Utley was annoyed now. 'Who told you I'd be arriving on this train?'

'I'm a detective, I find out things.' Swift leaned against the car boot, put a foot on the rear fender. 'With Abila Harb, it was more than work. You had extracurricular activities.'

Utley stared pointedly at the fender. Swift didn't shift.

'I don't understand.' Utley's voice was less certain.

'I've heard about you, her and Corinne.'

Utley fell back on the phrase used so often by someone when they'd been rumbled. It was always deeply satisfying to hear it. 'I've no idea what you're talking about.' He turned away again, opened the back door of the car and placed his bag on the seat.

'I've spoken to your wife.' Swift couldn't resist adding, 'We had tea and brandy snaps.'

Utley jerked round, shock crossing his face. 'You've been to see Elizabeth?'

'That's right.'

'How dare you contact my wife! This is outrageous.'

'I didn't contact her.'

'What do you mean?' Utley held tight to the door handle.

Swift observed alarm in his eyes. This wasn't how Utley had expected the day to work out. He'd had a pleasant afternoon in London, mingling with sewing friends — possibly with benefits — chatting about designs, seams, fabrics and zips — maybe undoing a zip — and now he should have been going home to his allotted kitchen time and perhaps a bit of needlework.

'Ms Utley got in touch with me. She wanted to tell me about what happened, give me the full picture. Elias and the accident on the horse, you and Abila, Corinne, the go-between getting caught up in it all, then the husband and child dying in Lebanon. Sad tale.'

'No, Elizabeth wouldn't do that.'

'How long have you been married?'

'What? Almost sixty years.'

'You don't know your wife very well after six decades. She keeps close tabs on you, despite your separate lives, and she was keen to dish the dirt. According to her, you were the Casanova of RV.'

Utley recovered a little. 'I object to these slurs.'

Swift stepped closer. Men like Utley were so predictable and dreary, locked into their lifelong dishonest routines. 'I don't care what you got up to with Abila, or any other women. It wouldn't be so easy to operate like that in a school now — at least, I hope not. Sounds like you caused a load of unhappiness, but that's on your conscience. Answer me one simple question and I'll go away.'

'What is it you want?' Utley croaked.

'Where did Abila go when she left the school?'

He bowed his head, twisted a shoe hard on the tarmac. *Imagining he's grinding my face*, Swift thought. 'London.'

'Whereabouts?'

'Stoke Newington. She rented a room there.'

'Did you see her after she left?'

'No! I had no wish to. I gave her a reference for the tenancy, that's how I had the address she went to. I expect she moved on ages ago. She might have returned to Lebanon.'

Swift wasn't sure that he believed Utley. Lies would come to him as naturally as breathing. As his wife had remarked, deceit was his factory setting. It would have been easy enough to visit Abila in London. She'd have been alone, vulnerable, just up his street. 'Can you tell me the address in Stoke Newington? It would be somewhere to start.'

'Will you go away if I do?'

'Yes.' *For now.*

'Well, I can, in fact, because it was unusual. One, Peach Place. I'd like to get home now.'

Swift couldn't refrain from a last dig. 'You must have been relieved to see the back of Abila, after things didn't go to plan and the fling created so much drama.'

'I'll certainly be glad to see *you* in my rear-view mirror.'

'Understood. Give my best to your wife. She was amazingly helpful.'

Utley got in the car, slammed the door and accelerated away. Swift waved, watching the Volvo vanish. It was such a simple pleasure to irritate some people.

That had been a successful day. He'd head back to the Silver Mermaid for a late supper and a glass of red.

* * *

The pub was quiet, just a low murmur of conversation and a couple of tourists debating the best way to get to Windsor Castle. Swift was finishing chicken casserole when Jan Brockhill phoned him.

'Hi, you had any luck finding your man?'

'Not so far. Have you got news of him?'

'I had an email from him, saw it after work this evening.'

He leaned forward. This was more like it. 'Are you meeting him?'

'Not for now. I'd decided he wasn't going to contact me, so I was hopeful when I saw the mail, but it wasn't anything to get excited about. The message was brief, just saying sorry he's not been in touch but he's had to go away for a while and he'll try to get back to me. So, something and nothing.'

Swift threw his fork down in frustration. 'Did he say where he's gone?'

She sounded flat. 'No. Bit disappointing. I'm not sure why he bothered to send it, but heigh-ho.'

'Does the email identify him?'

'No, it doesn't use his name and the address isn't personalised. He just says that we met at the park and I'd given him my card.'

'Any chance I can have the address?'

'Absolutely not. Like I said last time, I won't stand much chance with potential customers if I randomly hand out their contact details, will I?'

Swift tried another angle. 'Can I read the content of his message?'

'No, you bloody well can't!' she replied sharply. 'I've told you what's in it and it's hardly worth repeating. Anyway, looks as if he isn't going to be around for a while, so you're not going to have much chance of finding him.'

'How frustrating.'

'Will you carry on searching?'

'As long as my client wants me to.'

'Seems like a fool's game to me.'

She rang off. He should have handled that better, kept her sweet in case the man who must surely be Zac did contact her again. This was so nebulous and tantalising. If he could get hold of Zac through her, it would be a great shortcut. Time to eat humble pie. He sent a text.

Hi Jan, apologies, I didn't mean to be rude or intrusive, and it was kind of you to call me. I'd appreciate it if you would tell me if this man contacts you again.

He finished his wine and was paying the bill when she replied.

Whatever.

He'd asked for that. He left the pub and idled by the river for a while. A full, pale moon streamed on the surging Thames, swollen by high tide.

His phone pinged. A short video from Ruth of Branna turning cartwheels on the sand with the caption, *As you can see, she's fully recovered.*

He smiled and walked home.

* * *

Peach Place in Stoke Newington was a delightful cul-de-sac of ten terraced houses, all built of deep red brick but of slightly different design. Some had bay windows, a couple featured porches, one was hung with terracotta panels and another had a narrow balcony at the front top window. It was as if the Victorian builders had constructed the row as an afterthought, using up spare materials and adding flourishes as the fancy took them. Swift stood, admiring their random, pleasing appearance. All the residents had filled their front gardens with well-tended plants, creating the effect of a peaceful green oasis in this city backwater.

Number one had a bay window with bird feeders attached to the side panes and tall ceramic planters in the front garden filled with — aptly — peach roses. The fifty-ish-year-old woman who opened the door wore a bemused smile. Her vivid green shirt had a mandarin collar and was patterned with fire-breathing dragons. A scarf in the same fabric was wound around her head.

'Hi, I'm sorry to bother you. My name's Tyrone Swift. I'm a private investigator. Here's my ID.'

The woman checked it. 'I believe that you can get these made cheaply enough. Have you a driver's licence to back this up?'

He awarded her full marks for vigilance. So many people accepted him at his word, which was handy but also disturbing. 'No problem.' He found his wallet, showed it to her.

She spoke slowly, with precision. 'Fine. And why are you bothering me?' Her tone wasn't unfriendly.

'I'm searching for Abila Harb. I was told she used to live here.'

'Who told you?'

'Raymond Utley, who was the head at Royal Victoria, a school she once worked at.'

The woman became more alert, inching the door forward. 'Is he sniffing around again? Because if you're here at his behest, you can clear off.'

Swift was impressed. He wasn't sure he'd ever heard someone actually say 'behest'. 'I haven't come here on his account. I've met him and his wife and I didn't care for either of them.'

She tapped a foot. 'I'm starting to like you more.'

'I'd like to speak to Abila because I'm trying to trace someone related to a woman called Corinne, who she worked with at the school. Corinne's son has engaged me to do this. It's hugely important to him.'

She bent down, dead-headed a rose in a container and closed her fist around the browning petals, releasing a rich scent. 'You can come in.' She sprinkled the petal fragments around the base of the rose.

'Abila still lives here?' This was unusually lucky.

'Please, come in.'

The kitchen was at the back of the house, a sunny, comfortable room with mustard-and-red wall tiles and a central light-wood table. There was a mingle of aromas: garlic, herbs, a fresher note of citrus. On the cooker was a green-and-blue tagine pot. Steps led down to a long, thin garden, which was lush with flowers, climbers and small trees. A laptop stood open on the table, a notepad and pen beside it.

'I've interrupted your work,' Swift said.

She closed the laptop. 'Yes, but that's OK. I have a desk upstairs, but for some reason I gravitate to working in the kitchen. I was about to have a tea break. Would you like some?'

'Please.'

'Sit, sit.' She laughed, a gurgle. 'You're too tall, blocking my light.' When she'd made tea in an earthenware pot, she pulled out a tray and stood balancing it between her hands. 'I haven't heard Corinne's name in ages. How is she? Where does she live now?'

'She died some years ago in Wembley.'

'She was living in London?'

'Yes, since she married. Did you hear that she was widowed young?'

'I didn't, no. I'm sorry to hear about her death. That's why her son can't ask his mother for information.' Her voice held a note of pain.

'That's right.' She was outwardly calm, but Swift picked up flickers of anxiety. He eyed an unopened letter on the table, addressed to Beryl Charteris. 'It's a delicate matter that I've come about, concerning Corinne's children.'

'Family problems?'

'Of a kind, and unexpected.'

'And the father of these children?'

'Dead also. A long time ago, so no parents left to consult.'

Swift sensed her weighing him up. She gave little away. 'Not easy circumstances, and whatever this is, it needed someone with your skills.'

'Yes.'

She put the tray on the table, poured amber tea into mugs. Her hands were fine-boned, with small, square nails. She sipped tea, fixing him with eyes the colour of set, creamy honey. 'I noticed you glancing at the letter. I'm not Beryl. I'm Abila Harb.'

'Good to meet you. I worried you'd be hard to find, that you might have left the UK or moved on somewhere else.'

'You seem genuine. If I had suspected for one minute that you had anything to do with Utley, you wouldn't have got through the door.'

'I appreciate your trusting me. It's an important issue, otherwise I wouldn't bother you. I've heard that you had a difficult time at Royal Victoria.

'Mainly through my own folly, although Utley ran the school as if it was his personal fiefdom.'

'I'm aware that you had an affair with him.'

She flinched. 'I was disgusted with myself for getting involved with him. It was madness.'

'He pestered you after you left the school?'

Her mouth tightened. 'He came here twice after I moved in. I had to threaten to call the police. He got the message after that.'

'Utley wouldn't talk to me at first. His wife told me what happened at the school concerning you, your husband and Corinne — the affair and the riding accident.'

She closed her eyes for a moment. 'My husband and daughter died after that.'

'So I heard, back in Lebanon.'

'I expect Elizabeth Utley relished telling you about those events.'

Swift rubbed his chin. 'She's a lonely woman. I'd say that she enjoyed my company and describing her husband's misdeeds and the fallout.'

'Elizabeth was one of the nastiest women I've ever met. I'm not defending what I did, but any man married to her who wasn't a saint would have felt trapped. She was haughty, chilly, always interfering in the school. Finding people's weak spots and exploiting them was her forte. That woman reminded me of a scorpion. You didn't see her coming and then—' she pinched forefinger and thumb together — 'you'd been stung.'

'Have you ever seen her again?'

'No!' She shuddered. 'God forbid!'

'What about Corinne? Did you see her after you moved to London?'

'A couple of times, but it became too difficult. We were like survivors from a storm, we clung a bit to each other because we'd shared the trauma. I liked her, but ultimately, seeing her reminded me too much of what had happened and what I had lost. I suspect she felt the same way. Her life moved on. She married. It was for the best.'

'Your life moved on too?'

'Life is inexorable, isn't it? I've rented a room from Beryl over the years. We get on well, I settled here. She was a single parent with two children and a job, so I was a live-in nanny to them for quite a while. Then I studied and became an academic proofreader.'

'You didn't remarry?'

'No, that wasn't for me.' Her reply was tinged with sadness.

'Did you meet Corinne's husband or any of his family?'

He sensed her drawing back, her eyes growing guarded. Her laptop buzzed. She opened it and scanned the screen, typed quickly. Swift looked around, saw two graduation photos of young women on the wall by the door.

No sign of a man who resembled Zac, though. Abila could well have been a player in what had happened to him. She'd lost a child and would have been the right kind of age for the woman Ivor had seen with Corinne in the park. But nothing here suggested her involvement.

She closed her laptop, tapped the lid lightly. 'I'm sorry, but I have a deadline on the document I'm working on, and this is an urgent query. I need to get back to work.'

'I still have questions about Corinne's marriage and her life once she moved to London. Can we talk later?'

She clasped her hands together. 'It was a painful part of my life and dredging it up is hard. I spent many long and difficult years trying to forgive myself, and I'm not sure that I succeeded.'

'I do understand, but if you could help . . .'

She stood, put their mugs in the sink, replaced the milk in the fridge and leaned against the door. Her tone was final. 'This is what I'll do. This evening, I'll send you an email with everything I can tell you about my friendship with Corinne. It won't be a great deal, but I'll be frank.'

He'd been outmanoeuvred, but he'd take what he could for now. 'Thanks, I appreciate that. Are the two women in the graduation photos the ones who grew up here?'

'Yes, they're Beryl's daughters.'

'Where are they now?'

'I'm not sure why that should interest you. They're adults, left home a while ago.' She moved towards the door.

'This is my card, with my contact details.'

She tucked it in her pocket and said in a neutral, businesslike voice, 'You'll hear from me.'

* * *

Abila kept her word and emailed Swift that evening. He was lying in bed, staring at the light fitting, already imagining that he could hear plodding feet overhead and see plaster dust falling like dandruff. He'd just come off the phone to Faith, agreeing that she and Eli could move in next month. She'd been over the moon, saying that Eli was out on an evening shift and she couldn't wait to tell him. Well, it was done. He'd have to hope for the best.

He opened Abila's email and stuffed an extra pillow behind his back.

Mr Swift,

I was so fond of Corinne. She was bubbly and a genuine, sincere person. Young for her age and eager to please. A better person than me. I'm not going to dwell on what happened at the school. I shouldn't have involved Corinne, she was younger than me and it wasn't fair. The events of that evening have cast a long shadow. We both promised Raymond Utley that we wouldn't say anything about the affair and the reason why Corinne invited my husband out riding that evening. It was an easy enough undertaking. Things were bad enough without getting the school bad publicity or exposing ourselves to gossip. At that point, I was hoping that I could mend my marriage, that Elias would

129

forgive me. Corinne wanted to hang on to her job, which she loved.

I saw her three times after I moved to London. On the first two occasions, we met at a café near Liverpool Street station. Raymond hadn't been bothering her, but she told me that Elizabeth Utley had been horrible. Corinne had unwisely told her about the background to that evening. She had found it too much of a guilty burden and had felt the urge to confess. Foolish of her, but understandable. I advised Corinne to stay away from Elizabeth as much as possible and I suggested that it might be a good idea to leave Royal Victoria when the right opportunity came along. I did feel badly for her, because she'd been happy at the school, but I could see that she wasn't comfortable there by that point.

Then the chance for her to leave did turn up, in the form of Kevin Buckley. Corinne told me about him, how they'd met when he was replacing windows at the school. She was very much in love and making plans. They married within six months of meeting. She invited me to the wedding, but I didn't want to attend. At that time, I was still raw and in a very bad place. Any such social occasions were too jarring and sad.

I did have a drink with her and Kevin two weeks before the ceremony. He was cheerful, friendly. There was another man there, a relative of his called Dan. He said very little, kept the drinks coming. I stayed about an hour. I realised that evening that I didn't want to see Corinne again. I envied her happiness and her unsullied life, which she completely deserved. The kind of life I'd stupidly lost for no good reason except a passing fancy, a man who cared nothing for me. She reminded me of a past I wanted to forget.

We had one phone conversation after that and then I didn't call and neither did she. She seemed happy with Kevin. I remember that during our last conversation, she mentioned that they were going to visit Falmouth, a place called something like Haybast. When the contact fizzled out, I was relieved. I assumed that maybe they'd settled in

*Cornwall, where Kevin was from. I'd no idea she was in
Wembley this whole time.*

*I hope you can help to sort out the family issues you're
dealing with.*

AH.

Swift lay back, stretched. The account came across as
candid. He could understand why Abila had wanted the
friendship to end. Perhaps Corinne had had the same motive.
She might not have told Kevin about the incident with Abila
and may have also wanted to relegate it to the past.

Yet Abila's apparent frankness could be a clever veil.
Was it all *too* straightforward and honest? Corinne had played
a part in the loss of Abila's husband and child, even if that
awful outcome had been unpredictable. People did bizarre
things because of grief. What if Abila had kept in touch with
Corinne and found out about Kevin's untimely death? What
if she'd played on Corinne's remorse and pressured her into
handing over Zac as a replacement for the lost little girl?
Evidence pointed to Abila having been the bolder, more
sophisticated partner in the friendship, Corinne always more
yielding and biddable. It was worth exploring further.

He sent a reply to Abila.

*Thank you for this. Please contact me if anything else comes
back to mind regarding Dan or Kevin. I haven't been able
to trace Dan, and even the smallest detail can be helpful.*

He switched off the lamp, wrestled his pillow and settled down. All of Corinne's friendships had drifted away,
leaving her a solitary woman with only a vague affection for
her remaining child.

On that sad contemplation, he slipped into sleep.

CHAPTER FOURTEEN

'Thanks for coming round,' Nora said. 'The agency I'm using for shopping and domestic stuff has so many staff off sick, they couldn't find a replacement. I just couldn't summon the energy to go out.'

'I'm glad you asked me,' Swift told her.

'Really? It must be a chore when you're busy.' She was wearing a cotton kaftan in red and gold that swirled on the floor when she walked.

'Love the robe.'

'Thanks. Therapy purchase online. If I'm going to lie around a lot, I might as well have some desirable lounge-wear.' Nora sank onto the sofa.

'I bought what was on your list and some extra fruit.'

'Ta.' She added defensively, 'You're not the only person I could call on, but you're the one I can rely on not to make any fuss.'

Swift accepted the backhanded compliment. 'Shall I put it away?'

'Please. Can you stick it in the cupboards and then load the washing machine? I managed to get the laundry basket as far as the kitchen, but then I ran out of energy.'

In the kitchen, Swift put cereal, tea and bread in a cupboard and stocked the fridge with cooked chicken, assorted salad bowls, yogurts and sliced fruit. He emptied the contents of the laundry basket into the machine and set it on a fast wash. The worktops were messy, with drips of soup and tea, crumbs, dabs of jam. Nora's home was usually scrupulously clean. He washed up crockery in the sink, tidied and wiped down work surfaces. Hopefully, he wouldn't get blasted for interfering.

He put his head around the door to the living room. Nora was lying down, squinting at a book. She'd put music on, Patti Smith's 'Paths that Cross'.

'Can I get you anything to eat or drink?'

'Cuppa would be good.'

They sat with mugs of tea. Nora was cross-legged, her kaftan forming a tent over her knees.

'You make a good brew, nice and strong.'

'It's the Irish in me.'

She smiled. 'I got a call this morning. Op on the tumour next week. They're hoping to cut the bugger out now they've reduced it.'

'How long will you be in for?'

'If all goes well, couple of days.'

'Want me to come and see you in hospital?'

'Nah, best not. The agency should be back up to snuff for when I get home.'

She was pasty and puffy. He was tempted to ask more about who was helping her, whether she'd told her family yet, but bit his tongue. It was her private business. He wanted her to call on him if she needed help and couldn't risk alienating her.

She rubbed a tube of salve on her lips. 'How's the case going?'

He described his visit to Abila Harb and the house in Peach Place. 'She added to the picture of Corinne as a young woman who was influenced by others, easy to manipulate.'

'You fancy her having a hand in all this?'

'Has to be a possibility, although a long shot. I checked the electoral register and there's only her and this Beryl Charteris at the address. The daughters have left home. No sign of Zac in the house, although I only saw the hall and kitchen.'

'What's your plan, Stan?'

It had come to him while he was cleaning. 'I wondered if you might help me.'

She gulped her tea, perked up slightly. 'Go on.'

'I found the landline phone number. I was trying to come up with an excuse for someone to phone and see if Zac has a connection there.'

'Difficult. People are rightly suspicious of unexpected phone calls.'

'Yeah, but what if you rang? Women always come across as more trustworthy and your Dublin accent is reassuring.'

'First time I've heard that.'

'I'm hoping Beryl will pick up. If it's Abila, end the call. You could say you're ringing from a utility company about a complaint from Zachary Buckley. Beryl will either recognise the name or deny having heard of him. You can do the wrong-number riff if it's no go.'

Nora put her head to one side. 'It's a tad weak, with obvious drawbacks. After all, if Abila's involved in this, Beryl Charteris must surely be in on it too, and they'll be on high alert after your visit. Beryl can just lie.'

'On the other hand, there's nothing to lose. I deliberately didn't mention Steve or Zac or the name Buckley when I visited Abila, and your call would be unexpected, so there's always the chance of catching Beryl off guard. Worth a punt.'

Nora emptied her mug. 'It's not as if I'm busy. No time like the present.' She reached for her phone. 'What's the number? I won't put the call on speaker. Sometimes it creates an echo and we don't want to arouse suspicion.'

Swift leaned back and crossed his ankles as Nora dialled, waited and raised a thumb. She lowered her voice to a warm purr.

'Good afternoon. I'm calling from British Gas. Could I speak to Zachary Buckley, please. Yes, that's right, Zachary. Oh, really? I'm sorry, this is the landline number he gave us. May I ask who I'm speaking to?' She listened, mouthed '*Beryl*' to him. 'How odd, the number must have been recorded wrongly. I'm so sorry.' Another pause. 'Mr Buckley made a complaint about an aspect of our service and I wanted to assure him that we're following up on this. We haven't got this wrong, Ms Charteris? It's not you who's complained?' She waited, nodding. Her voice dripped honey. 'Well, if you're not with British Gas, clearly we have made an error. I'm so sorry. And a Zachary Buckley has never lived there?' She made thumbs down to Swift. 'Well, once again, apologies for taking your time and for disturbing you. Back to the drawing board for me.' She made a winding up gesture. 'Yes, it does happen now and again. I'll keep trying, but of course I'll remove this number from our database to ensure that you don't get any more calls from us. Thank you, bye now.'

She threw her phone down. 'No go. Beryl sounded genuine — puzzled, not suspicious. No Zachary there nor ever has been. She volunteered that her two daughters used to live there.'

'It was a gamble. If Abila's lived there since she moved to London, it's hard to see that she could have been involved with Zac's disappearance.'

Nora wagged a finger. 'Unless she was an intermediary, a facilitator.'

'But for who? There's no link between her and anyone else I've come across that provides a motive for prising a child from his mother.'

'And getting Corinne to go along with it. I'd check out Kevin Buckley. There's a whiff of mystery to him.'

'He does seem a bit of an enigma. Abila mentioned that he and Corinne spent time in Falmouth after they married. I foresee a visit to Cornwall.'

Nora rubbed her eyes. 'Tough gig. I need to throw you out now, sleepy time.'

135

'Thanks for helping.'

'Yeah, and you. Talk soon, Ty.'

* * *

Back home, Swift searched trains to Falmouth from Paddington, noting that he needed to change at Truro. He booked an open return for the following morning and phoned Steve, explaining why he was going to Cornwall.

Steve got excited and wanted to accompany him. 'Tomorrow? Are you driving?'

'No, going by train. Too many roadworks.'

'I could come along, I'd just need to contact a few clients. How long will it take?'

'That's not a good idea, Steve. You get on with your job and let me do mine.'

'I don't see why I can't come,' Steve urged. 'This is about my family, after all. I've a right to. I've never been to Cornwall.'

'I don't take clients with me during investigations. That's my policy.' *And I don't want you with me, bristling with anxiety, being rude and putting people's backs up.*

'I could help out, ask questions.'

'That's what you're paying *me* to do.'

He started shouting. 'You can't stop me going there if I want.'

'True. But you're not going with me. Believe me, I'll be much faster and more efficient alone.'

'This is awful, I'm getting a rotten headache again and I've run out of painkillers. I'm gonna be anxious all the time now, waiting to hear.'

Swift was exasperated. He'd had difficult clients, but none quite like this man, who was a sparking firework. 'Is Tilly still with you?'

'No, she's gone home.'

With relief, no doubt. 'I'll stay in touch while I'm in Falmouth. You have to trust me and let me get on with this. Go and buy some paracetamol for your headache.'

'Yeah. Hang on — have you heard anything more from that Jan Brockhill?'

'Only that the man she spoke to at the cricket event sent her an email, but he's away for a while. He didn't leave a name.'

'What the hell! Can't you get his contact from her?'

'She won't give it to me.'

'Can't you, I dunno, lean on her or something? Like, threaten her?'

'Be sensible, Steve. I've tried to persuade her, but it didn't work.'

He groaned. 'You will keep me in the loop about Falmouth?'

'I will. Goodnight now.'

Swift packed a rucksack. He had a headache himself by the time he sank into bed.

CHAPTER FIFTEEN

Swift caught the 8 a.m. train and used some of the journey to Falmouth to review the case. He'd heard nothing back from Stanley Daley, which was unsurprising as the man hadn't seemed keen to help. Yet the letters to Corinne had been sent from his company, so it was a crucial tie. An idea came to him. He sent an email.

> *Mr Daley,*
> *When you have a chance to inspect your staff records, could you check against this list of names? It's really important, so I hope you can find the time. If it's too much of an ask, I could come and look through your records myself.*

He added a list of the people he'd come across during the investigation and glanced out as the sea appeared, serene under a dazzling sun. He had a group of four seats to himself, so he stretched his legs out, leaned his forehead against the window and watched the waves for a while, letting his mind roam over the list he'd just compiled. He picked up his phone again and scrolled through the photos of Zac that had been enclosed with the letters to Corinne, pinching and enlarging them. Something niggled at him, but he couldn't decide what.

He switched to making a plan for Branna's next visit towards the end of October. She wanted to see the life-size dinosaurs in Crystal Palace Park. He found the website, checked out the opening times and facilities.

He had half an hour to wait for his connection at Truro. In a platform café, he ate a lunch of toasted ham sandwich and coffee. The station was busy and noisy, filled with the rumbling of wheeled suitcases. The long journey south-west, with the countryside growing wilder and the sniff of the coast growing stronger, created the illusion that he was going on holiday.

His phone pinged and he saw a text from Steve.

Are you there yet?

A child's question. He ignored it and stepped up to the counter to buy another coffee and a local newspaper to read on the last leg of his journey.

* * *

Swift walked the fifteen minutes from the station to the town centre in a snapping breeze, glad to stretch his legs. The sea air was a tonic, clearing his sinuses. He'd booked one night in a small hotel, the Grey Seal, and checked in. It seemed clean and reasonably kept, although there was a dazzlingly patterned floral carpet in the hall and on the stairs and a distracting smell of fried food mingled with bleach.

His first-floor single room had a sliver of a view of the harbour. There were two pictures on the blue-and-yellow striped walls, one of St Michael's Mount and, oddly, one of the Eiffel Tower. It was basically equipped, with a kettle, cheap teabags and instant coffee, long-life milk, a TV on the wall and a tiny shower with a stained base. He tested the bed. The mattress was as soft as Steve's.

It wasn't a room to linger in. He opened the window to dispel the smell of cleaning sprays and set off for the tourist office, where he waited in a queue and listened to enquiries about coastal walks, fishing, cruises and restaurants. At last, he spoke to an older man with a helpful manner and wonky teeth.

'I'm searching for any family I might have in town,' Swift said, 'but I have very few details about them.'

The man seemed impressed by the query. 'From London, are you?'

'That's right. Just had a notion to see if I could find them.'

'Have you searched on the internet?'

'Yes, and phone records, but no result. Their name is Buckley.'

'I'm not sure what I can do to assist. The name isn't familiar to me, but then I come from Padstow originally. You could try the library. How far back are you going?'

'Not that far, a generation or two. Does the name Haybast mean anything to you? I've looked at a map of the area, but I can't find it.'

He looked puzzled, then brightened, glad of a question he could answer. 'Oh, you must mean *Hebask*. It's a Cornish word. I can help you there. It's a bed-and-breakfast down by the harbour. A boutique place, opened a few years back.'

'What was it before that?'

'I'm not sure. I expect the owners can tell you. Just a moment.' He leaned over to a carousel of brochures, spun it round and selected one. 'Here you are, this has the details and address. Good luck!'

Swift sat on a bench outside and examined the brochure. Hebask was a traditional stone house with a pink front door, situated on a narrow cobbled street. The interior featured stripped wood, oak floors, leather armchairs, sleek furnishings, state-of-the-art bathrooms and a palette of subdued colours. It was a lot more enticing than his hotel, with a pleasing deficit of floral carpets, but the prices were far higher than he was paying.

He scanned the information inside:

Steffi and Mart extend a warm welcome to you.
We are located right by the harbour in Falmouth. Our charming res-
idence has just five bedrooms, offering a cosy, quiet, personal space for
your relaxing break.
The snug rooms contain original architectural features such as beams,
exposed stone and brick, and wood panelling.
All the bedrooms have contemporary comforts, free Wi-Fi and their own
private bathroom. Two rooms have a luxurious soaking bathtub with
harbour views in addition to a walk-in shower.

And it was just two streets away.

* * *

Steffi and Mart were a pint-sized couple, skinny and smi-
ley, dressed alike in dark blue jeans and black sweatshirts.
Swift quickly established that they were hipsters who'd fled
Hackney and jobs in IT. They both nodded a great deal,
often in unison, reminding him of toys in car windows. They
finished each other's sentences and addressed each other as
'hubs' and 'wifey'.

'We'd dreamed of doing this for yonks, hadn't we, hubs?'

'It was ten years or so in the planning,' Mart agreed
eagerly. We were up and down from London, after the right
place. Definitely a dream come true.'

'We're booked solid,' Steffi said with pride. 'Just as well you
weren't needing a room, we'd have had to turn you down—'

'But we'd have recommended you elsewhere,' Marti
added. 'Where are you staying?'

'The Grey Seal.'

They pulled faces, smirked.

'No comment,' Steffi giggled.

They'd brought Swift into the kitchen, which was modern but cunningly designed to persuade him he'd stepped

into the 1900s: a navy-blue range cooker, free-standing cabinets, antique porcelain sink, pine dresser and open shelving. The table was next to a window that looked onto the harbour. If you leaned out, you might be able to dabble your fingers in the water lapping below. Steffi insisted on giving Swift tea. It was chamomile and rose, which he didn't like much, but he gave it a try so as not to offend.

'As I mentioned, it's information I'm after, on behalf of a client who had a connection to this property.'

Mart added a slice of lemon to his tea. 'This was a captain's house originally — we've seen photos of it in its heyday in 1860. It had been empty for a while when we found it and terribly run-down, with woodworm and penetrating damp. Took ages to get planning permission because we wanted to make rooms in the loft. This is a conservation area, you see. We got it in the end, but we had to abide by lots of regulations—'

'Not that we minded,' Steffi interrupted. 'We wouldn't have wanted to do anything to spoil the line of the street and annoy the locals.'

Their heads bobbed up and down in agreement.

'We did a lot of the work ourselves,' Steffi continued, 'lived in a caravan for two years while we renovated. Then we bought a flat around the corner for us—'

'It's handy and all we need.'

Swift moved his tea to one side. 'What does *Hebask* mean?'

Mart replied, 'It's Cornish for peaceful. We're learning Cornish—'

'It's tricky, but we wanted to make the effort to fit in.'

It might make them stick out like sore thumbs. 'Do many people speak Cornish?'

'Well, no,' Mart admitted, 'but I believe it's a growing number—'

'A revived language.'

'Do you mind telling me who you bought Hebask from? I want to find a family called Buckley and I believe they're linked to the property.'

They looked at each other, both raising an eyebrow.

'Wasn't Buckley,' Mart said. 'You're better than me at this stuff, wifey.'

'It was an old lady who owned it.' Steffi tapped her temple. 'Penrose, that was her name. She was in a care home, so it was all done via her solicitor. It had been a boarding house of some kind for years and students from the university campus had lived here for a while. That accounted for the beer cans and rubbish we found everywhere.' She shuddered. 'One of the beds had mouldering underpants beneath it.'

Mart reached for her hand, threaded his fingers through hers. 'I'm amazed how you remember names, wifey. You have an astonishing brain, like a walking filing system.'

'You've not heard of a Dan Buckley living here?' Swift asked.

This time, they shook their heads in harmony. Watching their mirroring movements, Swift felt himself surrounded by reflections.

'Sorry, never heard of him.' They spoke simultaneously and laughed.

The expanse of water outside was ruffled and milky, the colour of diluted ink. Boats bobbed on the tide and a cruise ship loomed on the horizon. A huge seagull screeched and landed on the window ledge, glaring in with a baleful eye.

'I'd never get anything done if I lived here,' Swift said. 'This fascinating panorama would distract me.'

'It is mesmerising,' Mart agreed. 'I have to tear myself away. I've burned the breakfast sausages a couple of times, because something's caught my eye outside.'

The seagull lifted its wings, uttered a cry and flapped away.

'Your tea's gone cold,' Steffi pointed out. 'Fresh brew? Or I could pop that in the microwave.'

'No thanks, I'd better make a move. Could you give me the name of the solicitor who acted on behalf of your vendor? I'd like to speak to them.'

'Julian Jenner,' Steffi said. 'His office is near the cinema. Our solicitor reckoned he was a bit pompous, so good luck.'

Mart put the cups on a tray. 'Or as we say in Cornish, *chons da*!'

* * *

It was four thirty. Swift wasn't hopeful of seeing Julian Jenner that afternoon, but when he phoned and explained the reason for his visit, the solicitor was enthusiastic.

'I have to stay in town for a tedious dinner tonight and this sounds novel. Come on by.'

He had a rich, comfortable voice. Swift pictured a rotund man who liked more than his fair share of Cornish butter, pasties and saffron buns. He did a double take when he was greeted by an angular figure with sharp features and cropped, bristling hair.

'Thanks for seeing me at such short notice.'

'Do take a seat. Makes a change from conveyancing, leases and neighbour disputes.'

Jenner sat behind his traditional green-topped mahogany desk, twirling a pair of glasses. Swift parked himself in a comfortable upholstered chair and offered his ID. Jenner popped his glasses on his knife of a nose.

'Mind if I photocopy this? Force of habit and a solicitor's natural caution.'

'Not at all.'

The solicitor crossed to the photocopier, which hummed and spat out a sheet of paper. 'So, this is about a man who "died" but may not be dead after all. Quite a conundrum. I'll make a few notes as we go, if you don't mind.' He drew a yellow legal pad towards him.

'The father of the man I'm interested in was called Kevin Buckley. I haven't been able to find any trace of his family. He came from Falmouth, and at some point in the late nineties he visited here with his wife. They may have stayed at Hebask, which is why I called there.'

'Very tasty job they've done on the house, although the prices are astronomical. I wonder if they'll last there? I've seen Londoners come down here before with big plans and then find they're yearning for the city.'

Swift detected a hint of spite. 'No sign of that at present.'

'We'll see. The place certainly needed some attention. Quite a bit of flotsam and jetsam had been passing through there.'

'The owners told me it was once a boarding house.'

'That's correct. Ms Penrose, the owner, lived there and rented out rooms. She was a rough-and-ready soul with a keen sense of humour. I'd say that she enjoyed flouting convention and annoying the neighbours. The place had a certain rackety reputation. Ladies of the night made use of it and the odd couple having an affair — rooms by the hour. People generally turned a blind eye, including the local police, but I'd say that overall, there was a sigh of relief when Ms Penrose went into a home and decided to sell up.'

'Are you a local?'

Jenner ran a finger down his long nose. 'Born and bred. But the name Buckley doesn't ring any bells with me.'

'Given that there might have been a connection with Hebask, can you put me in touch with Ms Penrose?'

Jenner had a way of becoming completely still when not speaking, like a computer switching to sleep mode. He folded his glasses, placed them in a case. 'Sadly, no. Ms Penrose died two years ago now, so that avenue of information is closed.'

'Did she have any family?'

'Never married, no one close. There's a relative, Sal Penrose, runs the shop near the maritime museum. It's called Sal's Sweets. She's a friendly sort, I'm sure she'd chat to you. Think you'll find this Zac?'

'Now and again I get a sniff that makes me hopeful.'

'Best of luck. Are you staying at Hebask?'

'Not at those prices, and anyway, they're full. I'm at the Grey Seal.'

'Middle of the road, and none the worse for that. What you see there is what you get.'

* * *

Sal's Sweets was a hymn to seaside tat, a poky, low-ceilinged mishmash of confectionery, ice cream, buckets and spades, fishing nets, inflatable dinghies, hula hoops, postcards, beach shoes, balloons and piles of cheap toys. It smelled of artificial sweeteners. Just the kind of place that Branna loved to dawdle in, fingering the merchandise in a delighted daze and, having exhaustively reviewed all the goods, usually buying the first thing she'd seen.

The shop was empty, save for a young woman sorting pocket-money toys back into their correct shelf slots.

'Kids! They maul everything and jumble it all up,' she said cheerily enough. 'I have to do this every bloody day.'

'I'm afraid my daughter's one of those culprits. Roaming fingers.'

She glanced behind him. 'She's not with you, then?'

'Not this evening, you can relax!'

She tittered and headed to her perch by the till. 'Can I help?'

On his way to the counter, Swift collided with a bunch of rainbow-coloured plastic fish dangling from a ceiling beam. They danced and slapped together.

'Bingo!' The young woman applauded. 'I was waiting for that to happen.'

Swift smiled. 'I've been attacked by worse.'

'There is a sign over the door, *Duck and Bend*, but no one takes any notice. There's an advantage to only being five foot one.' She gestured good-humouredly at her diminutive stature.

When he enquired after Sal Penrose, the young woman told him that she was at her ballroom dancing this evening. 'She's mad about the tango.'

'Will she be here tomorrow?'

146

'I open up at eight and she'll be in when she's finished her early morning swim at Gyllyngvase Beach.' She shivered dramatically. 'Every day Sal goes there. No idea how she can stand it!'

There was a perilously stacked pyramid of snow globes in front of him. Swift chose one of a bright-red lifeboat in a stormy sea for Branna, lifting it carefully from the top.

'Well done. They fall down about once a week when some kid prods them,' the young woman said.

'Must be a nuisance.'

'Nah. It's funny, especially the parents' faces when they crash all over. I quite like stacking them back up, there's a skill to it.'

It's the small satisfactions in life that get people through, Swift mused, parting with two pounds.

He bought fish and chips and ate them sitting on a harbour seat. The meal was crisp, vinegary. The chilly evening breeze lifted the paper and stung his ears. He had a cold nose, but his hands were toasty from the hot food.

His phone pinged. Another text from Steve.

You in Falmouth? What's happening? Any progress?

He decided he'd better reply and not make Steve's nerves any worse.

Yes, I'm here. Some progress. More tomorrow, I hope.

He ate the last chip and licked his fingers, watching the tide drift out and the mackerel sky fade to damson.

CHAPTER SIXTEEN

At one o'clock in the morning, Swift gave up trying to sleep on the bed and shifted the mattress to the floor, where he twitched fitfully, waking to the din of seagulls at half past six. His bones ached and he got up carefully, aware of a pull in his lower back.

He stretched gently and showered, banging his elbows in the tiny cubicle. Once dressed, he decided to pass on the cheap beverages and the full cooked English breakfast advertised downstairs. He hefted his rucksack, paid his bill and stepped with relief into the salty morning air. There was no sun visible today, but a sky of low, bruised cloud and Swift felt a colder nip about him. In a café along the quays, he enjoyed croissants with raspberry jam and fresh, rich coffee. A text arrived from Steve.

Have you found out anything? It's torture waiting to hear. Hardly slept last night.

That makes two of us, he thought. He took a bite of flaky croissant and replied.

Seeing someone this morning who might be able to give me information about the Buckley family. I'll be in touch when I have anything.

Soon after eight o'clock he was at Gyllyngvase Beach, just south of the town. He made his way along the crescent of soft sand, his hair flying in the slaps of wind. There was little activity: a handful of paddleboarders, a kayaker and two figures swimming near to shore. Swift sat with his back to a stone wall, rucksack in his lap, and waited. He yearned to be out there in his boat, navigating the choppy waves. He flexed his spine against the rough wall, twisting from side to side, using the jutting stones as a massager.

After ten minutes, one of the swimmers emerged, a man who loped along the beach, shaking himself off. The other figure continued to plough up and down. Swift was content, watching the busy sky and the roll of the sea. He raised his arms, bent his neck, got a satisfying click.

The other swimmer walked out of the waves, a short, squat figure in a black costume. Swift tracked her across the sand to a rock, where she picked up a bath towel and dried herself. He got up and set off towards her, waiting until she'd wrapped herself in the towel before he approached.

'Hello. Sal Penrose?'

She was in her fifties, with strong shoulders, a determined mouth and salt-and-pepper hair twisted up in a knot.

'That's me.'

'My name's Tyrone Swift. I'd like to talk to you. Your shop assistant told me I'd find you here.'

She eyed him. 'Couldn't it wait? I don't like being ambushed on the beach.'

'I woke early, didn't sleep well last night. Reckoned I might as well get a walk and see if I could spot you.'

'Well, you have. What's this about?'

'I'm a private investigator from London, working on behalf of a client. I'd like to talk to you about your deceased relative, Ms Penrose.'

'Oh yes? Why so?'

'It's a thorny matter. I'm trying to trace someone called Buckley.'

Sal became very still. 'Haven't heard that name in a long time.'

At last, Buckley had brought a response. Swift forgot his aching spine. 'Can you help me?'

She glanced out to sea, pulled her towel tighter, bent and picked up a canvas bag. 'I need to have a shower. See you in the café over there in fifteen minutes. Mine's a pot of tea and a bacon bap with brown sauce, not ketchup.'

* * *

The café was bustling with schoolchildren, people attending a surfing class, and a clutch of tourists gearing up for a coast walk. The three staff glided around behind the counter in a synchronised mime, pulling chrome levers, flipping toast, pouring foaming milk into jugs. Swift queued behind two boys who were arguing about whose turn it was to buy muffins. They shoved and elbowed each other in what was undoubtedly a daily ritual.

Swift placed Sal's order and added a coffee with a pot of Bircher muesli for himself. He chose a table tucked around a corner, away from the hubbub. Sal soon appeared, scrubbed, in a fleecy blue tracksuit, her complexion pink. She fell on the bap, closing her eyes at the first mouthful.

'Swimming makes me ravenous. I've been dreaming about this. What's that stuff you're eating?'

'Muesli with banana.'

Sal turned up her nose. 'Rather you than me.'

'You swim every day?' Swift savoured his coffee.

'Yep. Love it. Never miss a morning, and if anything stops me — which is rare — I get grumpy.' She downed half her mug of tea. 'I got to fifty and worked out I could either crumble away or defy old age. Mind you, Ma Penrose sat in a chair most of the day and she lived to ninety. She was a big, strong woman, never afraid of anyone or anything.'

'What relation was she to you?'

'Some sort of cousin by marriage.' She finished the bap, licked brown sauce from a fingertip and picked up stray crumbs. 'Who's this client of yours?'

'His name is Steve Buckley. He's trying to clear up a puzzle about his younger brother. Their father was Kevin Buckley.'

'Kev was a nice enough lad, given his start in life.' Sal signalled to the passing waitress with her mug, indicating a refill. 'I liked it when I went to Seattle, the way they came round and filled up your cup gratis. We Brits are stingy like that.'

Swift contained his impatience while she chatted to the waitress, asking about her sister and the new baby, how her mum had got on at the hospital. The café was quietening, the early morning rush almost over. There'd be a lull before parents with babies and toddlers started arriving. He finished his muesli. The banana tasted of the ice lollies he'd relished in childhood.

Once the waitress had departed, he forged on. 'Ms Penrose, I visited Hebask yesterday and the owners mentioned that it belonged to your cousin.'

'Oh yes, Steffi and Mart, the Hackney blow-ins. If Ma P could see what they've done with it, her eyes would be out on stalks. Big improvement and lovely place to stay now, if you've got the right bank account.'

'You're the first person I've come across who recognised the name Buckley. What can you tell me about Kevin and his family? I believe he had a connection to Hebask.'

Sal guffawed. 'You could say that, given that he was born there.'

Swift's heart lifted. 'Who were his parents?'

She inched the zip of her top down a little, revealing crêpey skin at the base of her throat, and folded her arms on the table. 'That's an interesting question. Ma P ran a boarding house for years at Hebask, although my mum always said it should more rightly have been called a bawdy house. The lodgers were all sorts: sailors, seasonal workers, land labourers. She kept one of her rooms for renting to prozzies and adulterers needing a place to have a quickie. Made a good bit of money from it. I inherited from her, so I suppose you could say I've benefited from immoral earnings.' She laughed again, a throaty chuckle, and accepted her refilled tea from the waitress.

Swift prayed that another conversation about hernias and colic wasn't about to ensue, but the waitress hurried away. 'Where did Kevin fit in?'

'Hold your horses, I'm getting there. Kev was the product of Michela Buckley, one of the prozzies who fell for him with one of her passing trade. She was just a teenager, not local. Not sure how I came by that, but I heard she was a runaway from home. She did another flit and vanished when Kev was still a tiny baby, dumped him on Ma P, who raised him as her own. Father unknown — a sailor, most like. Ma P had a good business head, but she had a sentimental side too. She never married and she did her best by Kev. He left to seek his fortune in London when he was in his late teens, hardly ever came back. Hebask had got a bit rackety by then. Ma wasn't as fit as she used to be and the place had started to deteriorate.'

'And neither Ms Penrose nor Kevin ever heard from Michela again?'

'Not to my knowledge.'

'Did Kevin always have his mother's surname?'

'No, he was Penrose when he was growing up, but he started calling himself Buckley in his teens, like he was daring anyone to talk about his origins. Brave of him, really. He got teased at school. Some of the kids heard the story about his mum's being the oldest profession and how he was left with Ma P, who kept company with prostitutes.'

The set-up at Hebask, with Ma Penrose as a part-time madam, suggested a strong likelihood to Swift. 'I don't want to cause offence, but d'you reckon Ms Penrose had her own clients at times?'

Sal winked at him. 'I'm sure she did. My parents kept away from her because of the kind of establishment she ran. She told me once that it was a business like any other and it was never affected by unemployment or recessions!'

'In some ways, it's a secure trade, never a lack of customers.'

'Not sure Kev saw it that way, with his mum leaving him like an unwanted parcel. I can understand him being keen to get away. He was fond of Ma, but it was all a bit painful for him.'

'Did you ever hear that Kevin had a child in Falmouth and the mother died? I believe that the child was looked after by someone here for a while.' Swift wondered if Ma Penrose had been a substitute mother yet again, caring for Steve until Kevin took him to London.

Sal looked dubious. 'Never heard that, no. I'd have thought Ma P would have mentioned it, although she could play her cards close to her chest when it suited. Can't help you.'

Swift was puzzled, but moved on. 'Ms Penrose must have missed Kevin when he left, having raised him as her own.'

'I suppose there were letters. She didn't talk about Kev. She was a realist, was Ma, she'd have seen that he had to strike out for himself. She knew he'd died, so someone must have told her.'

Swift considered this. Buckley had wanted to escape his origins. His enthusiasm for Corinne to be a stay-at-home mother now made sense, given his dubious start in life. It was curious that he'd brought his wife to Hebask after they'd married. Surely he'd have wanted his new relationship to stay on a fresh page, untainted by the context of his having been raised in a part-time brothel. Perhaps he'd loved Ma Penrose, despite his mother's abandonment and his upbringing, and had wanted her to meet Corinne.

'Do you recall Kevin and his wife, Corinne, staying at Hebask around 1997? That was soon after they married.'

Sal rubbed a bloodshot eye. 'I forgot my goggles today, the salt's a killer. Can't say I do. I didn't see him or his wife.

Last time I recall speaking to him was when he was about sixteen.' She checked her watch. 'I'd better get to the shop or they'll worry I've drowned.'

'One more question.'

'Yes, but let me text first.' She sent a message, shielding her eyes to see the screen.

Swift's head was dull now, a combination of poor sleep and the warmth of the café. He suppressed a yawn, circled his shoulders. 'Have you heard of a Dan Buckley?'

'No . . . but hold on, I'm sure Ma mentioned that Kev's mum had a brother. She used to chat to me a bit when she was in the care home. I tried to visit every week and bring her out when I could. She loved the sea air and sunshine, grumbled that the home was gloomy and smelled of wee and cabbage. She was right. Mind, Hebask didn't smell too sweet by the time she left it.'

'And Dan?'

'I'm trying to remember. I'd fetched her from the home one time and we were sitting by the sea. She mentioned Kev, which was unusual. I asked if she'd ever tried to find his mum's family, or if the authorities had. She mentioned there'd been a brother, but that was all. That might have been the Dan you're referring to.'

'You've no idea where I might find him?'

She shrugged, picked up her bag.

'Just before you go, and I realise you need to, did your cousin leave much paperwork — letters and such?'

'Very little. She must have decluttered before she died, like that Japanese woman recommends. I could go through what's left if you like, see if there's anything from a Dan.'

'Please, or from anyone who seems connected to Kevin's past. Also, if there's a birth certificate for him. Here's my card with my contact details. I do appreciate what you've told me, it's important information.'

'My good deed for the day, then. You going back to London today?'

'Yes, there's a train in an hour.'

'Safe travels. Ta-ta for now.'

At the station, Swift composed an email to Steve while he waited for the train. It was odd that Sal Penrose had no knowledge of him being Kevin's child. Perhaps the mother had lived elsewhere in Cornwall. He decided not to touch on that topic for now. Steve would have plenty to absorb.

He wrote a résumé of what he had established. It was hard to tell a man that his grandmother had been a prostitute and Swift deemed it best to put it in writing, so that the information had time to sink in before they spoke. At least, that's what he told himself. A tiny voice in his head suggested that email was the cowardly choice, but he quashed it.

CHAPTER SEVENTEEN

Swift had just reached home and put his rucksack down when he had a text from Ruth.

Branna is about to Zoom you. Heads up — she's been upset, changed her mind about the baby. Not keen at all now and extremely grumpy. ☹

He flicked the kettle on, opened his iPad and accepted the call. Branna was sitting on her bed in the star-patterned sleepsuit he'd bought for her earlier in the year. Her eyebrows were lowered, her face mutinous. She was clutching her elbows, arms crossed, always a sign of distress.

'It's lovely to see you. Is your ear better?'

She signed, *I had medicine.*

'That pink stuff?'

Yes.

'Good. I've just come back from Cornwall. I bought you a little snow globe.'

She stared at him, unblinking. *I want to live with you.*

He sat down, winded. 'That's sudden. You love it there.'

I hate it. Hate it. Hate Mummy. Come and get me, Daddy.

156

He swallowed hard. Why was she not speaking? Should he sign back? He decided to continue talking. 'Branna, you love your mum and she loves you. She tells you you're the moon in her sky.'

Hate her, hate Marcel. Hate school, it's stupid. Want to live with you. Get on a plane now.

'I can't do that. You're visiting me soon, won't be long.'

Then I can stay with you, not come back. I'll bring my stuff.

That floored him. 'Well . . . you live by that beautiful beach now.'

Hate this house.

Panic coursed through him. 'You're very upset, aren't you? Is that why you're signing everything?'

A tear rolled down her cheek. His heart thumped. This distance from her was agony. He wanted to hold her.

'Is Mummy there, is she around?'

In the bathroom.

'What's upset you?'

She stamped a foot. *Don't want a silly baby.*

'Right. It's a big change for you. But . . . well . . . the baby's happening and that's a fact.'

She gave a nasty, sly smile. *I'll make Mummy sick her baby up.*

Alarm filled him. 'How do you mean?'

I'll put sugar in her tea. She hates sugar, she'll get sick.

He could only hope that his daughter never became familiar with poisons. 'It doesn't work like that. Anyway, it would make Mummy very sad.'

Good.

'I reckon that when you see this baby, you'll fall in love with him or her.' He had his fingers crossed in his lap.

No I won't. I'll come and live with you.

'Why don't we wait and see how it pans out?'

She sighed, kicked her legs. *My ear hurts now.*

'I'm sorry. Listen, things are always worse when you're not well. Mummy will give you something for it. Want to see the globe I bought you? It has a lifeboat in it.'

She yawned.

'Hang on a minute.' He went to his rucksack and rummaged in a pocket. 'Here it is.' He shook it and the snow flurried.

She gave a watery grin. *I like you. I don't like Mummy.*

At least she'd downgraded from hate. 'Come on, you're sad, but that won't last. It won't be long before I see you. We'll check out the dinosaurs in Crystal Palace Park.'

She rubbed her eyes.

'You need to get to bed. I'll call you again tomorrow. Can I speak to Mummy now?'

No. Her finger stabbed the screen, ending the call.

He waited for half an hour, giving Ruth time to put Branna to bed. After he'd unpacked his rucksack, he realised that he was ravenous. He chose one of Ms Malla's meals from the freezer, shoved it in the oven and then rang Ruth.

'I guessed you'd be in touch.' She sounded drained.

'That was hard going. Is she asleep?'

'Just about.'

'She said her ear's playing up again.'

'I'll get the nurse to check it, but I suspect that's tiredness and anger.'

'She was very anti the baby, asking to come and live with me. When did this start?'

Ruth was moving around, a sound of dishes clattering. 'Two nights back. Suddenly, from nowhere. Maybe after the initial excitement the penny's dropped, and she doesn't care to share the limelight. It's not uncommon.'

'Isn't it?'

'No. She's been queen bee, the centre of attention. Now she's confused, frustrated, jealous. Hence the behaviour. Just have to ride it out. She's been sulk central, ignoring Marcel completely.'

'The other thing was, she wouldn't speak at all, just signed.'

'Yes, we've been getting a lot of that. I'm not focusing on it while she's getting things off her chest. What did you say when she asked to live with you?'

'Held my ground, sort of ducked it — let's see how it goes, something like that. I wasn't sure how to respond.'

'You do need to be firm and point out that's not an option.'

Easy for Ruth to say, although he understood this was no picnic for her. 'I'll do my best. Branna threatened that she'd put sugar in your tea so you'd get ill and sick up the baby.'

'Crumbs. I'd better watch out, thanks for the warning. This will blow over, Ty. I'll keep explaining and spending time with her. She just needs to ease into this new reality.'

'How's Marcel about it?'

'Very understanding. He bought her a book today about a new baby joining a family. She threw it behind the sofa.'

'Oh dear.'

'Yeah.' She laughed. 'I need a cuppa now, no sugar.'

He told her he'd call again tomorrow and removed his meal from the oven. He plated the chana dal with cauliflower, fetching yogurt, chutney and a bottle of beer from the fridge.

Steve Buckley phoned, shouting down the line just as he was about to take the first mouthful. Swift held the phone away from his ear.

'I can't believe this. My gran a common tart! It's disgusting. I mean, how? Why?'

Swift put his fork down, had a sip of beer. 'I can't answer those questions for now. If it's true that she'd run away from home, maybe it was the only way she could find to make a living.'

'Don't give me that. There are always ways of earning money without stooping that low. I mean, she didn't even know who her baby's father was.'

'She was just a teenager. People find themselves in strange circumstances.'

'Why are you defending her?'

'I'm not. But I'm not accusing her either.'

'Suggesting that I am.'

Swift left a silence, speared some cauliflower, registered how spicy it was.

'Anyway,' Steve whinged, 'my dad knew.'

'Yes. The woman who told me said that's partly why he left Falmouth, to shake off the past.'

'That's something I *can* understand. He must have been so ashamed.'

A car horn blared, someone yelled.

'Where are you, Steve?'

'Out walking. I've been walking the streets for hours. Hang on.'

There were more noises, a throbbing engine, voices in the background. Swift ate some of his meal. It was fierce on his tongue. He swirled in a large dollop of yogurt and licked the spoon to cool his mouth.

'I'm on a bus now,' Steve panted. 'Did my mum know?'

'No idea. Presumably yes, if she visited Falmouth with your dad and met Ma Penrose, who raised him.'

'And you didn't find anything about where my gran was from, or this guy Dan?'

'As I mentioned in my email, I'm waiting to hear from Ms Penrose. I'd like to get on with my supper now, Steve. It's been a long day. Have you told Tilly?'

'Yeah. She was gobsmacked. My mum never revealed any of this.'

'It's not the kind of thing people broadcast.' *Especially when they might get a reaction like yours.* 'I'll talk to you soon.'

He finished his meal and the beer, overcome with weariness. While he cleared up, he pondered Branna's life. She'd had to deal with a lot of upheaval as well as her hearing impairment. His own childhood had been settled, routine, remarkably lacking in incident, until his mother died when he was fifteen. Guilt sat heavy on him. He and Ruth had presented Branna with so many challenges.

He picked up the snow globe, shook it and watched the flakes dance around the lifeboat before sinking to the bottom.

* * *

The following couple of days were frustratingly quiet. Swift rowed his boat in a teasing wind, under louring cinder clouds. The London skyline hunched sulkily beneath biting flurries of rain. He ordered a book to be sent to Branna, *I'm a Big Sister*. The title would appeal to her ego and underpin her position in the pecking order. Or so he hoped. It might be rejected and join Marcel's offering behind the sofa.

In his office, he spent time going through his notes, sifting and listing information and questions.

- The man in the photo is probably Zac. Jan has his email but won't share it. So near, yet so far.
- Who were the two women Ivor saw with Corinne in Lyham Gardens? Was one of these the woman who collected Zac from Sheila Whitehall?
- Where was Michela Buckley from?
- Where is Dan Buckley?
- Who posted the letters from Daley Mobility?

He sat, tapping his fingers on the desk, then emailed Jan Brockhill and Stanley Daley, asking if they had any updates. He didn't want to hassle Sal Penrose and sour her goodwill.

Lassitude overcame him, the autumn gloom dampening his spirits. This case carried a flavour of hopelessness, and Steve Buckley was proving an unpredictable client with his fragility and emotional outbursts.

Gloomy musings took him to Nora. Against his better judgement, he called her.

'Just checking in.'

'As long as you're not checking *up*.'

'Never.'

'I'm slumming it on the sofa, watching *Bergerac*, eating toast and honey. You?'

'Back from Cornwall, which was useful, although I'm no closer to pinning down Zac Buckley right now and it's trying my patience.'

'Hang on, just catching a honey drip . . . When I was a hot-headed child — which I freely admit may be how I am in my adulthood too — my grandad used to say to me, "*Patience is a virtue, possess it if you can; seldom found in woman, never found in man.*" Make what you will of that bit of homespun wisdom.'

'You should run an advice line.'

'Hardly. That's my cleaner arriving, I'd better go.'

'The agency's back on track?'

'Yes, all fine. My op's on Monday. I'll call you when I'm home.'

'Make sure you let—' he started to say, but she'd gone. She and Branna were skilled at pulling off a fast exit.

Swift distracted himself by cleaning the house from top to bottom. He opened the windows in the upstairs flat to air it, paid bills, tidied the garden, did laundry, shopped and stocked the fridge and cupboards, and bought Branna a new duvet cover with a monkey pattern (the previous one having suffered a disastrous spillage of blackcurrant juice).

He'd spoken to her again. She was back to using speech, still adamant that she didn't want a baby in her life, but now appeared more interested in talking about her time with him in October. It occurred to him that she might refuse to go home. She could be very determined. His head swam when he imagined it.

He tackled peeling wallpaper around the front window, gluing it down. While he was doing that, the sun slid out and he saw Branna's handprints all over the window pane, so he set to with cleaner and cloth.

Tilly Western phoned when he was standing back to check his handiwork.

'I'm so worried about Steve. He longs for information, but each new bit sends him into a tizz.'

'It does, yes. He demands updates, and I have to give them.'

'He's been on the phone for hours about this latest stuff from Falmouth. I'm struggling with what to say to him about his grandmother. Clearly it's upsetting, but he takes it all to heart so.'

'At least he can talk to you.'

'Yes,' she replied, reluctance hanging on the word. 'It's just that . . . well . . . my husband has hip problems, so his mobility's restricted, and I have the grandchildren round quite often. I've asked my brood to get in touch with him, but they're all so busy, and they're reluctant, what with the lack of contact over the years.'

'Best to discuss that with Steve. He needs to appreciate that you have family commitments and how much this impacts you.'

'Have you seen him since your trip to Falmouth?'

Swift could guess where this was heading. 'No. I spoke to him on the phone. When I have any new information, I'll ring him again.'

'Could you possibly call round, spend a bit of time with him?'

Swift saw a smudge at the bottom of the window pane and rubbed it. 'Ms Western, I'm not a social service nor a paid companion.'

'I realise that. I did call his ex, Skye, but she's tied up and can't visit him until the end of the week.'

'He can ring you. People have suggested that he see a doctor or a therapist, and he should. That's all I can say. Maybe you could reinforce that with him.'

'Yes. Oh dear, this is so awful, all of it. I wish Steve had never seen that photograph. It's caused so much pain and disruption.'

Aunt Tilly wasn't keen on being burdened. Swift had some sympathy for her position, but it wasn't his job to counsel her nephew, and she'd got off pretty lightly over the years. Time for her to step up. 'You can't turn back the clock. However conflicted his emotions are, Steve wants to see this through.'

'Even so, I can't imagine what my sister was thinking of when she got involved in this . . . Well, I'd better leave you in peace.'

When she rang off, he glanced at the wallpaper. A corner was starting to unpeel again.

CHAPTER EIGHTEEN

Swift struck gold with Sal Penrose early the next morning. He checked his emails when he woke just after seven and saw that she'd sent one at 6.30 a.m. with attachments.

Just getting this to you before I go for my swim. I went through Ma's things late yesterday. Two items that might interest you. One is a letter to her from Dan Buckley, the other is Kevin's birth certificate.
All the best, Sal.

Swift opened the birth certificate. The baby had been registered as Kevin Daniel Buckley, born on 21 February 1973. His mother was Michela Buckley, her address Hebask, his father unnamed. That confirmed Sal's information. He clicked open the letter.

45 Rochester Road
Birchington
Kent

9 January 1997

Dear Ms Penrose,
We've never met, but I hope you might be able to help me. My sister, Michela Buckley, told me that she used to

live with you. After many years, I managed to find her some time ago in Penzance and we had contact. That's when she told me about staying with you and that she'd had a son, who she left in your care. I was so glad to see her after such a long silence. Sadly, Michela has now moved on again and I haven't been able to trace her.

I wondered if she might have been in touch with you, or if you have any idea where I could contact her again.

Thank you,
Dan Buckley

There was a phone number at the bottom of the letter. Swift got out of bed, pulled the curtains back. The sun was big and buttery in a clear sky, bathing him in light. He made coffee, warmed a cinnamon bagel and picked at it while he waited for eight o'clock, which he deemed a reasonable hour to call someone.

He poured a second coffee and carried it to his bedroom, where he stood in the pool of warmth by the window and rang the number — sometimes fortune favoured the detective. It did today. A man answered.

'Hello, am I speaking to Dan Buckley?'

'Yes. Who is this?'

'I'm not trying to sell you anything,' Swift said. 'I'm a private detective, acting on behalf of Steve Buckley, your great nephew. I found your number on a letter you sent some years ago to Ms Penrose of Hebask, enquiring about your sister Michela.'

A stunned silence.

'I'm sorry if this is a shock. I had to speak to you.'

He had a light, husky voice. 'Oh, goodness. After all this time. Have you spoken to Ms Penrose? She must be ancient now.'

'She died. One of her relatives helped me, found the letter you'd sent in 1997.'

'Yes, I remember it.'

'Did Ms Penrose reply to you?'

'She had her dubious networks. She wrote to say that she'd heard of Michela being in Plymouth.' Dan cleared his throat. 'I need to get some water, this is quite a shock . . .'

Swift went through to the kitchen, opened the back door and breathed in the mild air, which was laced with a must of decay. Buckley sounded in his late sixties or seventies, not an age for receiving startling phone calls from strangers.

At last, he was back on the line. 'This is so strange and alarming. Why has Steve employed you?'

Swift explained, trying to keep this tortuous matter simple. He could hear wheezy breaths at the other end.

'I can't really take this in,' Buckley murmured.

'Did you find your sister?'

'Yes, in Plymouth.' A cynical laugh. 'Ports were always good for her line of work and she tended to move around. She was a prostitute, were you aware of that?'

'Yes, I found that out when I visited Falmouth and I've told Steve. He didn't react well. When was the last time you saw her?'

'Then, in 1997. She wasn't happy that I'd found her, told me to go away. I never heard from her again, even though she had my address. She was a sad, lost person, my sister.'

'Did you stay in touch with Kevin and Corinne? I believe you saw them before their wedding. That was the same year you sent the letter to Ms Penrose.'

'I spent some time alone with Kevin and then I had a few drinks with them both. That's the first and last time I saw Kevin. He contacted me out of the blue and invited me to meet up. I wasn't asked to the wedding, mind. Kevin called me later that year and was hostile to me, alleged that I'd never cared about his mother and he didn't want to speak to me again. Next thing I heard, Corinne sent me a note to say he'd died.'

'Were you surprised by Kevin's antagonism?'

'Not really. Disappointed. I wasn't aware of his existence until the late eighties, when I found Michela in Penzance.

She told me about him, and let's face it, he'd had a strange upbringing. Although I was a bit taken aback because he'd been friendly enough when we had that drink.'

'How did Kevin get hold of you — was that through Ms Penrose?'

'Yes, she gave him my details.'

'And you have no idea where Michela is now?'

'No. This is very difficult, and there are other things about Steve and Zac . . . delicate matters. They need to be said face to face. I'd want to tell Steve directly, not through you.'

'No problem. Steve is quite fragile. Would it be OK if I was with him at this meeting, if that's what he wants?'

'Yes, if it's his wish.'

'We could come to you, if that would suit you.'

He hesitated. 'No, no. I'd rather meet in London. Yes, that would be for the best.'

Perhaps he had family who were ignorant of his sister and her branch of the Buckleys and he wanted to keep it that way. 'Leave it with me. I'll speak to Steve and get back to you. At least finding his gran's brother will be good news for him.'

'Before you go . . .'

'Yes?'

'Steve. You see, he's not my great-nephew.'

Swift tried to focus. 'I don't understand. You're his grandmother's brother. He's Kevin's son.'

'I'll explain in person. This is too much now, I'm a bit queasy. I'll go through it all when I meet Steve.'

Swift had a long shower. Buckley's last remarks were baffling. Had someone given him misleading information along the way? But there was Kevin's birth certificate, with Michela recorded as his mother. Was it possible that Kevin had been the child of another transient resident at Hebask and, for some reason, Michela had claimed him as her own? But if that was the case, why dump him not long after? And it would mean that Dan Buckley was a red herring with no blood connection to Steve, and Falmouth had been a trip to chase phantoms.

Swift lathered his hair vigorously. Another question popped into his mind. Why had Kevin bothered to contact Dan before his marriage and invite him for a friendly drink, only to cut him off?

He raised his face to the jet of water. The sooner he and Steve could meet with Dan, the better.

* * *

Swift suggested his office as a meeting place, but Steve insisted on his flat. Skye offered to be present. Swift advised not — best to keep this meeting small and manageable. Four people in that studio would fight for oxygen.

Steve wore his suit to greet Dan. It was even looser on him, as he'd dropped more weight. He'd had his hair clipped short. It didn't do him any favours. His large, exposed ears made him appear more boyish, a bit goofy.

Dan Buckley arrived promptly. He was average height, with thinning, reddish-brown hair heavily flecked with grey, through which his pinkish scalp gleamed. He wore dark glasses and was dressed all in navy, with a cardigan beneath a thin jacket. When he removed his glasses with gnarled, freckled hands, he revealed a startlingly bloodshot left eye. He told them that he'd had a cataract removed recently.

He looked taken aback when Steve hugged him, saying that it was amazing to find unexpected family. Swift could detect no resemblance to Steve and tried not to imagine the meltdown if Dan was about to tell him that they weren't in fact related. The one thing they had in common was nerves — the tension radiating from them both crackled around the room. Steve was wringing his hands and grinning foolishly.

Swift was banking on this meeting providing some further markers on the trail to Zac. He'd heard nothing back from Stanley Daley or Jan Brockhill.

Steve made coffee while Swift and Dan sat awkwardly on the bed and made small talk about the train journey from Kent. The stacks of folded laundry around the room scented the air with cloying fabric conditioner. Swift saw Dan eyeing them and explained Steve's employment. He appeared nonplussed and made no comment. Once they were settled with their drinks, Dan leaned forward.

'I've been giving all of this serious consideration,' he said in his throaty voice. 'Seems to me that it's best if I tell you what I can, and then we take things from there.'

'Thanks, Uncle Dan,' Steve blurted. 'Is it OK if I call you that?'

'Very much so, because it's correct. I'll clear this up at the outset. I'm your uncle, not your great-uncle.'

Steve's shoulders twitched. 'What? What does that mean?'

Swift was reassured, albeit mystified for a moment. Then it dawned on him. 'Do you mean that Michela was Steve's mother?'

'Yes — and Zac's. Mother, not grandmother.'

'Wait, wait!' Steve held both hands up. 'No. How does that work? That means my dad was my *brother*. How fucked up can this get?'

'I'm sorry. I'll do my best to explain—'

'Hang on!' Steve lurched for a piece of paper and a pen, knocking over a tottering pile of magazines. 'I'm gonna do, like, a family tree as you talk.' He drew lines, jotted names, then waved his pen at Dan. 'So, Michela Buckley, Dan Buckley, Kevin, me, Zac. Yeah, go on.'

Dan balanced his coffee precariously on his knee, giving Steve a measuring glance. 'First of all, Michela ran away from home at sixteen. We lived in Deal then, on the Kent coast. She vanished and—'

'Why'd she run away?' Steve interrupted.

'I'm not sure. She and our mum argued a lot, Dad was strict and unbending, Michela went around with a rough crowd, dropped out of school, generally got herself in a pickle. She was always a troubled person, hard to get close to. Next thing—'

'Hold on!' Steve added another section to his family tree. 'What were your parents' names? They're my grandparents, right?'

'Yes. Jenny and Arnold Buckley. They lived all their lives in Birchington.'

'Thanks, got that.'

'One Wednesday morning, Michela had gone. She wasn't there when we got up. It was like that Beatles song, 'She's Leaving Home'. She just left a one-sentence note in the kitchen, telling us not to bother trying to find her. We couldn't trace her. The police searched for a while but they eventually gave up.'

Steve crouched forward. 'And what — you gave up too?'

'Not completely, no. In the early nineties, I decided to look for Michela. I missed her, worried about her. Mum was in nursing care with dementia and Dad had died. It didn't seem right that she hadn't been told. After a lot of searching, I found her in Penzance. She made it clear she wasn't thrilled to see me. She was a sex worker, in her thirties then, but seemed much older. It was so distressing, discovering her living that life. The place she was in was run down.' Dan shifted on the bed, rubbed a knee. 'I'm sorry Steve, this is very hard, but I don't see any point in not telling you.'

'That's all right,' Steve responded stonily. 'I want to hear it all.'

'Well . . . we talked briefly and Michela told me how she'd headed for Cornwall when she left home, landed up at a place called Hebask in Falmouth. I heard about Kevin, how she'd left him there with Ms Penrose — she was just seventeen when he was born. She wasn't regretful. I don't suppose she could afford to be, in her life. She warned me not to tell anyone where she was, and not to bother contacting her again. When I did try, I was told she'd left Penzance.'

'What about Kevin?' Steve demanded. 'Didn't you want to find him, meet him?'

'Michela warned me off doing that. She insisted that she didn't want any interference in her life or have him come looking for her. I'd have liked to meet Kevin but . . . I didn't want to go against her, or make trouble for Ms Penrose.

Maybe I should have been more insistent, but Michela was his mother, so I accepted her decision.'

Steve was rubbing a finger between his eyes. Perspiration slicked his forehead. 'So, my *mum* was a prozzie. Nice.' He studied his diagram, flicked the pen top. 'And hang on — if Kevin wasn't my dad, who was? Who is?'

Dan put his mug on the floor, blew his nose, slipped off his jacket and undid his cardigan, a cable knit with buttons shaped like acorns. 'Michela told me she didn't know.'

'Right, yeah. He was one of her *customers* or whatever she called them. I'll just put a question mark here, then.'

Swift handed Steve his coffee as a distraction. 'Let your uncle finish, then we can discuss it.'

'It's very painful, talking about this,' Dan said.

'Pretty fucking painful listening to it too,' Steve muttered.

Swift attempted to pour oil on troubled waters. 'It's pain all round, no doubt about that. It's good of you, Mr Buckley, to come all this way to explain in person.'

Dan picked up his drink, swirled it in the mug. 'I couldn't give up on Michela. I found her again in 1997, in Plymouth, after I wrote to Ms Penrose. When I saw her, she had you and Zac. You were a toddler, Zac a month-old baby. I'm sorry I can't tell you who your father was. I'm not sure you and Zac had the same fathers. Michela wasn't living with anyone and she wouldn't talk about why she'd decided to have and keep two children, given her age — she was in her early forties by then — and her lifestyle.'

'*Lifestyle!*' Steve snorted. 'That's a posh name for it.'

Dan flinched, lowered his head.

'How did it go with Michela during that visit?' Swift asked.

'Well . . . she was furious that I'd caught up with her again, told me to leave her alone. She was hot-tempered, always had been — she'd really lash out when riled. I gave her some money, bought some toys for you and Zac. I went home. I didn't try to see her again. I regret that, but she was very clear that she'd just leave town again if I persisted, and I didn't want to persecute her or disrupt her life — or yours. Then I heard from Kevin. Ms Penrose had told him about my letter, the one you've read. I was delighted that he'd instigated the contact, and because of that I decided to meet him.'

Steve was trying to process this story, underlining names on the paper. 'I'm one of three brothers.'

'That's right,' Swift confirmed. 'The middle one.'

He sank back, hands over his face.

Dan touched the corner of his bloodshot eye and twiddled a button on his cardigan, clockwise then anti-clockwise. A washing machine was spinning in the flat above, a distant shuddering that stopped suddenly, leaving a profound silence. Swift longed for a bracing, freshly roasted coffee rather than the instant stuff that Steve served.

He prompted Dan. 'So, when you met Kevin, you told him about his two brothers in Plymouth?'

'Yes. It seemed to me that he had a right to that information. We spent an hour or so together. I explained Michela's history, just as I've told you, and advised him that his mother was living in Plymouth and had two young sons, one just a baby.'

'How did he react?'

'It was hard to gauge. He was quiet, didn't say a lot. Then we met up with Corinne. He asked me not to reveal anything to her, so of course I left that to him. There was another woman there too, can't recall her name.'

'She's called Abila,' Swift said.

'If you say so. Anyway, it was a pleasant evening. Corinne was a lovely person. I had every hope that Kevin and I would stay in touch. I called him a few times, left messages, but he didn't get back to me. Then around November that year, he rang and told me that he didn't want to have any further contact with me. I tried to ask why, but he was unwilling to talk.'

Swift assumed that Michela must have played her part in Kevin's change of heart. 'Did he indicate that he'd been in touch with his mother?'

'No, but I didn't get a chance to discuss that. I never heard from him again.' The button he'd been worrying at came off in his hand. He stared at it, put it in a pocket.

Steve threw his family tree on the floor and stood, shook his hands away from his body, then sat back down. 'You had no idea that Kevin and Corinne had me and Zac with them, pretending we were their kids?'

'None. How could I have? Kevin ended contact with me and then Corinne told me he'd died in a brief letter that didn't mention children.'

'And now we understand why,' Swift said. 'For some reason, they had decided to pass off Kevin's brothers as their children. Perhaps it was a private adoption, although I suspect that there were no formal arrangements, just as there hadn't been with Kevin when he was left with Ms Penrose.' No one would have taken much interest in a sex worker's children and local authorities would have been overwhelmed, as usual, barely managing to cope with the kids who did come to their attention.

'This is starting to make sense,' Dan commented. 'I knew the truth of Steve and Zac's parentage, so Kevin didn't want me on the scene.'

Swift nodded. 'I'd guess that Kevin didn't want his mother's history trailing after Steve and Zac, so he had to cut you out of his life.'

'Sense! What sense?' Steve made a strange, unearthly noise. His teeth were chattering, his torso shaking. He stared at Swift, put a hand to his chest. 'Can't breathe . . . God . . . can't breathe.'

'Open the window,' Swift told Dan. He crouched in front of Steve, grasped his clammy hands. 'You're having a panic attack. Focus on your breathing. Breathe in counting five and out counting five. Do it with me. In through your nose, out through your mouth.'

Steve took sharp, ragged breaths, gradually followed Swift's lead and grew calmer, his eyes less wild. He was still trembling. Dan threw the window open and cool air gusted in.

'That's better, isn't it, Steve?' Swift let go of his hands.

'Yeah. Thanks. Came from nowhere.'

'No it didn't, it came from fear and stress. Might be an idea to splash your face with cool water. Keep focusing on your breathing.'

'Poor young man,' Dan said when he'd gone to the bathroom. 'This is all so crushing. How did you know what to do? I'd have had to call an ambulance.'

'Learned it in the Met. Calming techniques are highly useful in police work. Will you stay in touch with Steve? He's going to need you. There's a lot still to unravel here — why Michela gave her sons to Kevin and Corinne, where she is now, why Corinne parted with Zac, the search for him.'

'Just a moment, the light is hurting my eye.' Dan put his dark glasses on. 'I'll do what I can to help Steve if he'll let me. My wife has no idea about my contact with Michela, or any of this part of the family. She's aware that Michela ran away and vanished. I want to keep it that way, but I'll stay in touch with Steve. Best to give him time to absorb all of this.'

He looked away, the dark lenses obscuring his expression. 'He certainly shares his mother's volatile temperament.'

CHAPTER NINETEEN

Swift was back in Alys Tice's house. The weather had turned colder, with a sharp north wind, and she was fiddling with the gas fire. She was wearing another Edwardian-style lacy blouse-and-skirt combo, this time in lilac and grey, with a tiny blue sapphire pendant at her wrinkled neck. The dogs were snoozing in their baskets, one of them snoring softly.

Swift had been summarising what he'd learned about Kevin and Corinne's history. His angle on Corinne's life had been completely altered. Had she felt lumbered after her husband died so unexpectedly? Even if she'd willingly taken on his brothers as her own children and been devoted to Steve and Zac, it would have been an understandable reaction. She hadn't been Zac's birth mother, so perhaps her parting with him wasn't quite so inexplicable, even if it was still shrouded in mystery.

Corinne had gravitated towards slightly older, resilient women: Alys, Abila, Elizabeth Utley. Alys was Corinne's only friend from the years she'd lived in Wembley. Even though the friendship had dwindled with time, they must have exchanged some confidences. Yet he guessed that Alys would reveal nothing she didn't care to and there was no point in trying to schmooze her.

When she was satisfied with the gas flame and had settled her legs on the footstool, Alys linked her hands in her lap. 'Why are you back here, bringing a cold snap?'

'I've made some headway with my enquiries about Zac Buckley.'

'Oh yes? Earning your money, then.'

'Exactly. The main progress has been finding out something very surprising about Corinne and Kevin's children.'

She tightened her jaw. 'And?'

'Steve and Zac weren't their sons. Kevin was their brother.'

'You don't say!'

'I do.'

She centred her pendant in the hollow of her neck. The sapphire gleamed in the fire's glow. 'Tell me more.'

'I reckon you could tell *me* more, a lot more.'

'You can reckon whatever you like.'

'You don't seem too surprised about the boys not being their sons.'

'I don't surprise easily.' She turned steely eyes on him. 'It was never my business and it isn't now.'

'That sounds like an admission that you do know more. I've established that Michela, Kevin Buckley's mother, abandoned him to a woman in Falmouth who ran a boarding house. Michela Buckley was also Steve and Zac's mother. I've sketched out a lot of her background. Now I need to fill in the picture. It's important for Steve Buckley to find out the truth. He's aware now that he and Zac were Kevin's brothers.'

She recrossed her ankles, smoothed the back of one hand with the other. Eventually she murmured, '*Half*-brothers to be precise.'

'Thank you. I've spoken to Dan Buckley, Michela's brother, so I've tracked how Kevin found her. It must have been tough for Corinne after Kevin dropped dead, leaving her a single parent with two young children who weren't even hers.' He spotted a flicker of affirmation in Alys's face, pressed his advantage. 'If you share what Corinne told you, I'll not contact you again.'

'Promise? I don't want her family coming after me, pestering me with questions and whatnot. I have a peaceful life, just the way I like it. I don't bother anyone and I don't need anyone bothering me. I want it to stay that way.'

'You have my word.'

'Let's see, then. Corinne swore me to secrecy, but I suppose that's by the by now, given what you've uncovered. She was in a right state when I first met her. Husband and one kid dead, Steve to look after, working at Easton's. We had lunch one day and she spilled it all out. I don't remember all of the details. She and Kevin got married and then Kevin met his mum years after she'd done a runner. She was a prostitute somewhere in Cornwall, still a working girl when he caught up with her.'

'That was in Plymouth.'

'Sounds right. The mother had been diagnosed with a brain tumour and was struggling with two kids, one a newborn. The upshot was that Kevin and Corinne did a deal with her that they'd take Steve to live with them as their own. They concocted a tale about Steve being Kevin's kid and his mother dead. Michela wanted to keep the baby as long as she could. She died when Zac was about five months old, so then they brought him to live with them as well. They pretended that Zac was theirs, with a fake pregnancy. Corinne stuffed a cushion down her top and stayed in a lot while she was "expecting". Then they pretended that she wasn't well for a long time after the "birth" as a cover story.'

Swift recalled Sheila Whitehall's comment about Corinne's health problems during the pregnancy. 'High blood pressure was her excuse for staying indoors.'

'That would fit. It was all bloody complicated, but Kevin was mortified by his mum's trade and didn't want anyone to find out. He'd had a rackety childhood. The woman who raised him was kind enough, but she ran a knocking shop and entertained gentlemen callers herself. He was keen for his brothers to have a good home. And they were both determined that the boys shouldn't have Michela's past hanging over them. I got it, it made sense — they cleaned up the story to give the two kids a better chance in life. It was Kevin who worked it all out and Corinne went along with it. She was kind-hearted and wanted what was best for him and the kids.'

'Did they want children of their own?'

'That was the plan. They were going to have one when Zac was a bit older. But that wasn't to be.'

The gas flames licked around ceramic logs with a comforting, steady hiss. One of the dogs stretched a paw out and flexed it in his sleep.

'Did you ever get the impression that Corinne resented the boys, felt that being left on her own with them was unfair?'

Alys shoved the stool away and put her feet on the floor, adjusted a slipper. 'I wouldn't say resented — that's too harsh — and it wasn't in her nature. But yes, she struggled. She was very young, only in her early twenties. Kevin left a bit of money, but finances were always a stretch. I'd say that she begrudged having been dealt a poor hand, and who's to blame her?' Alys put her head to one side. 'Why do you ask that?'

Swift was convinced that Alys had no knowledge of Zac's faked death and disappearance. He explained the full story and the discovery of the letters proving Zac's existence.

Alys had a stunned, sour expression. 'That's hard to credit. Corinne was so upset about Zac's death. For goodness sake, she was full of guilt about not getting him to hospital sooner after his accident! You're telling me that was all nonsense?'

'Corinne was definitely remorseful, but I'm afraid that her guilt was related to an entirely different scenario. She never gave any hint of the death being fabricated?'

'Definitely not. My God, what an awful state of affairs! Suppose it explains why she didn't want to see me so much after a while and went into her shell. Once you've got a secret like that, you don't want people questioning you.' She picked up Corinne's painted stone, touched it to her cheek. 'Goodness, I'm a bit shaky now. Hard to credit that a friend would lie like that, and about such a dreadful thing. I used to sit there, crying with her about her loss of her child, and all the time she was spinning me lies.'

'If it helps at all, I'm sure that Corinne was grieving his loss. I believe that she must have been pressured to part with Zac and lie about what had happened to him.'

'Help? I'm not sure it does. I'm winded.'

'I'm sorry for the distress.' Swift could see her eyes watering, and decided that it was time to make himself scarce. 'You've been helpful. Thank you.'

'A means to an end. It's just as well Corinne's dead, because if she wasn't, I'd go round and have this out with her. Leave me in peace now. You can see yourself out. Close the door quietly, please, so you don't wake the dogs.'

'Let sleeping dogs lie,' Swift muttered to himself, as he shut the door behind him. If only Kevin hadn't suffered that stroke, his and Corinne's sleeping dogs might have stayed somnolent for ever.

* * *

Swift hopped on a bus back to Hammersmith, feeling some satisfaction. He'd established what had happened to Michela Buckley and he'd found Dan. He still needed to identify the two women Ivor had seen with Corinne in Lyham Gardens and the person who had posted the letters from Daley Mobility. Jan Brockhill still hadn't responded, despite his leaving another couple of messages.

To his relief, Skye was spending a couple of days with Steve and the young man was in a slightly better frame of mind. He'd sent Swift an email:

To sum up, both my parents lied to me about my origins. Then Corinne — I can't call her my mum anymore

— pretended that Zac was dead. All this crap to wade
through, but still no Zac. Is my real mum still around some-
where in Cornwall? Do prostitutes work in their old age?
Maybe there's a specialist market. What happens now?

Swift considered his reply. A man two seats in front was
eating a toasted sandwich. His stomach rumbled at the smell
of warm cheese. He tapped a response.

I've found out that Michela, your mum, had a brain tumour
when Kevin found her. She was ill, so agreed that Kevin and
Corinne could take you to live with them. Then Michela
died when Zac was still a baby, and your parents decided to
take him into the family. They pretended that Corinne was
pregnant. They acted with the best of intentions, wanting to
give you and Zac a good home.

Corinne must have been coerced to part with Zac. I
have some ideas and a few leads to follow. More later.

He didn't want to tell Steve about the incident at Royal
Victoria, at least not yet. It would be information overload
for his saturated brain.

He bought a takeaway pizza and hurried home with
it. It was mild enough to eat in the garden. While he ate,
he returned to the photos on his phone, scrutinising Zac's
development over the years. He was missing something, but
again, it wouldn't come to him. He stared up at the sky. The
drifting puffs of cloud offered no inspiration and he was glad
to be distracted by a call.

'Stan Daley here. I can't hang about, but I had a quick
search through the records. Found one staff member that
matched that list you sent me. Someone who worked here
part-time for sixteen years or thereabouts, managing orders.'

He barked the name. Swift thanked him, put his head
back again, studied the sky. Well, well — he hadn't expected
that. Now he was cranking up a gear, but this next move
would have to be handled cautiously.

CHAPTER TWENTY

It was a quirky day — sun one moment, a gusty shower the next, rattling the hedgerows, whisking leaves from the trees and blowing them against the windscreen. The weather matched Swift's restless mood. This encounter was going to be a challenge, and one he was keen to get on with. He could take a guess now at who Zac had gone to live with and the reason why, or at least the reason used to encourage Corinne to part with him.

At one point during the drive, a vibrant rainbow arced across the horizon, so dazzling that Swift pulled in to enjoy it and take a photo for Branna. It was going to prove the best thing in a lousy day.

He was glad to see that Utley's black Volvo wasn't on the drive. When he rang the bell, a shadowy figure rippled behind the door's textured glass.

'What are you doing here? If you've come to see Raymond, he's not in.'

'It's you I want. We need to talk.'

Elizabeth Utley grimaced. 'Do we, now? It's not conven-ient and rather presumptuous of you.'

'That's me all over, always conceited. We really do need to have a conversation.'

She sucked her cheeks in. 'About what?'

'Well, for starters, you worked at Daley Mobility and you used the franking machine to send letters to Corinne Buckley.'

She tried a derisive smile. 'Don't be ridiculous!'

'It was you,' he insisted. 'There's no one else it could have been. You worked there. Come on, don't try to lie to me. I've spoken to Stanley Daley.' Sometimes, given that they were made of straw, hectoring a bully worked.

Elizabeth flicked a glance over his shoulders and made a quick flapping gesture with her hand. 'Come in, then.'

He followed her to the stygian gloom of the living room, made even dimmer by half-closed curtains. She was wearing a long, shapeless cardigan over a skirt and blouse. The TV was on, a home makeover show, and the little table by her chair held a plate of crackers, a tub of cream cheese and a packet of biscuits. He'd disturbed her cosy 'me' time. Good.

She flicked the remote and killed the sound, leaving the orange-faced TV presenter conducting a mime. 'Say what you've got to say and be on your way.'

'I'm here to listen, Ms Utley. I've been trying to work out why you did it. Revenge? Spite?'

'Did what?'

'Leaned on Corinne. Got her to part with Zac, her youngest son. She told everyone he'd died, but I've reason to believe that he's very much alive, and Steve, his brother, wants to meet him.'

She picked up a cracker, made an elaborate show of spreading cheese on it, popped the whole thing in her mouth and chewed. Chives and a hint of onion scented the air. Swift crossed his legs, waited.

'How did you find out about the letters?'

'Following traces. I've seen them, read them all, looked at the photos of Zac growing up. Steve has them now.'

'They won't help you that much.' She sounded satisfied.

'The content doesn't. It's all general, the kinds of things that might apply to any child over the years. It's the franking on the envelopes that identified your part in this.'

Elizabeth licked her lips. 'Steve and Zac weren't Corinne's sons, or rather they were in name only.'

'That's right. How did you find out?'

'That would be telling.'

'You might as well say. It's not that important, only a small part of the story. The way I see it, you were a bit player in the overall scheme.' He didn't believe that, but he was hoping it would hoodwink her into spilling the truth.

Unexpectedly, she asked, 'What does Steve Buckley work at?'

'He's self-employed, runs an ironing business from home.'

She raised an eyebrow. 'He does people's laundry? What an impressive way to make his mark on life.'

'He's doing well with it, and he's content. No need to sneer.'

She glanced at her watch, tapped a foot, seemed to come to a decision. Perhaps her husband was due home soon and she didn't want him involved.

'Kevin Buckley came back to the school to replace more windows after he married Corinne. He was friendly with the caretaker, used to have cups of tea with him and confided that he and Corinne were taking in his brothers. The caretaker told me a while later, when he heard that Buckley had died. He went on about how difficult it would be for Corinne, left with young children that weren't hers.'

'You did say, when I first met you, that you always heard about everything that went on at the school.'

'Yes. Very little got past me. Knowledge is power, as the saying goes.'

'Was it your idea that Corinne should give Zac to Abila and make up for her part in the Harb family's tragedy?'

'You've deduced that Abila took him?' Her manner was playful now.

'She seems the likeliest candidate. Wouldn't you agree?'

'You're the detective. I assisted in conducting negotiations and helping bring a satisfactory conclusion to a situation. I make no apology for saying that Corinne did the right thing. She found it hard to cope with two children on her own and it's not as if she was the real mother.'

'It ruined her life, and Steve's, left an awful legacy.'

Elizabeth threw her hands up. 'Oh, please, don't give me that, it's like a line from a soap.' She mimicked a cockney accent. '*She made me give up my baby and I ain't never got over it.* Corinne made decisions. Decisions have consequences. Tough, but true.'

And yours, to stay in a loveless marriage, has turned you into a rancid old bat. 'I suppose you're referring also to Corinne's decision to play decoy for Abila's tryst with your husband.'

'That would be a fair assumption.'

'You met Corinne in the park near her home, talked to her, persuaded her to hand Zac over.'

'She agreed to meet me. We discussed many issues, in great depth.' Elizabeth examined the nails on her left hand, fiddled with a cuticle. 'She wanted my guidance and I gave it. Any decision was hers alone and I made that clear to her.'

He was convinced that she had browbeaten Corinne. The young Tobias Everitt had referred to her as a battle-axe, and Swift recalled the picture Ivor had painted of those meetings in Lyham Gardens. Corinne had been upset and the older woman with her had pressed a constraining hand on her shoulder. Elizabeth Utley was inflexible, forceful and possibly unhinged. It would have been hard for Corinne to withstand her.

He wanted to rattle her. 'Are you aware that I spoke to your husband after my last visit?'

She'd been reaching for another cracker, but froze. 'Where did you see him?'

'Your information-gathering fails at times, then. I waited for him at the station and told him I'd visited you. Did he not mention it? He was helpful, gave me Abila's address. She told me he'd pestered her after she moved there.'

'That doesn't surprise me. I expect the poor lamb felt thwarted because of the unexpected interruption to his pursuit of the fair lady.' The corners of her mouth lifted. 'If you've seen Abila, you won't have found any sign of Zac there.'

He had the sense that she was toying with him. She was the connection between Daley's Mobility and Zac's new family, and the only link she had in this case was to Abila. 'You passed on the letters from Zac's new family, sent them to Corinne.'

'Correct. I do have a heart.'

Possibly, but it must be a rigid, callous organ. 'Why did you take a job at Daley's?'

'I'd retired and I got bored. As you've gathered, Raymond and I weren't going to potter happily together into the sunset. I had no interest in do-gooding, rural rambling, watercolour classes or any of the other retirement activities that the good ladies of the town pursue while they gossip and bitch about one another. I wasn't looking for anything challenging. Daley's was the kind of part-time work I could have done in my sleep and the location was handy for the train. I liked escaping Sleepy Hollow here, travelling into London and spending time in the city. And of course, it proved to be a useful conduit for correspondence.'

Swift was trying unsuccessfully to read her. She must have been acting for Abila. He was about to pursue the subject when the front door opened and banged shut. Raymond Utley glanced into the living room. When he saw Swift, he sidled in and stood behind his wife. He was in country-casual wear today: olive cord trousers, yellow check shirt, waxed gilet.

'What's he doing here?'

'He invited himself.'

'I visited Abila Harb,' Swift told him. 'She didn't have good things to say about either of you. I've found out that your wife was instrumental in persuading Corinne Buckley to part with her youngest son and give him away when he was two years old.'

'Corinne's son?' Utley pulled his head back. 'Elizabeth, what's this about?'

She half turned, put a hand on the back of her chair. 'Since when have you been interested in anything to do with me, dear?'

186

'I expect it was a way of getting back at you,' Swift told him. 'Indirect revenge for your various dalliances. A chance to pull the strings, exercise power. Petty and spiteful, but satisfying, nonetheless. That right, Ms Utley?'

She lifted a shoulder, dropped it.

'I've no idea what you're talking about. We've had nothing to do with Corinne since she left RV.' Utley appealed to his wife. 'Revenge? What does he mean?'

'Ask him, he's the amateur psychiatrist.' She busied herself with another cracker.

'I don't understand,' Utley complained. 'What's this about Corinne's child?'

'It's a nasty tale. Your wife can explain. You two need to talk more. You must forget how many things you haven't told each other, or lied about. Don't you find it exhausting?' Swift got up, eyed Utley. 'I've no idea whether or not you're bothered about your standing in this community. Your wife has indicated that she isn't, but I suspect you are. If the full story about how you were both detrimental forces in Corinne's life ever got out, you might find yourselves pariahs. Ms Utley, I'll ask one more time. Did Abila take Zac?'

She paused with a cracker halfway to her lips. 'Are you threatening me, Mr Swift?'

'Interpret it any way you want.'

Utley said tentatively, 'Elizabeth, what the blazes—'

'I don't give a toss about my reputation around here,' she told him with relish. 'You do though, don't you, dear? Respected ex-headmaster who devotes his time to good causes. It would be awful if your name was trashed.'

Utley tried again. 'Would one of you please explain what this is all about?'

His wife tittered, a bizarre, girlish sound, and opened her packet of biscuits. 'Bourbon to sweeten your journey home, Mr Swift?'

He left them. Utley's mouth was gaping, like a fish yanked from the river. His wife turned up the TV volume.

As he opened the front door, Swift heard a woman extolling the virtues of shiplap ceilings.

* * *

Back in London, Swift went for a row in an attempt to defuse his frustration. His boat furrowed through the dishwater river. The difficulty in dealing with someone like Elizabeth Utley was that she loved playing the game and, from her viewpoint, had nothing to lose. She'd teased him like a cat with a mouse, batting him around to amuse herself, taking warped pleasure from her deployment of smoke and mirrors. He'd afforded her satisfaction, providing interest to another of her empty days. She'd relished her husband's discomfort. No doubt that kept her warm at night.

The early evening river was busy and noisy, a tricky current roughing the water. Traffic hummed at Putney, geese honked overhead, a passing rubbish barge caused a rolling wash. The exercise warmed his muscles but, unusually, did nothing to improve his mood.

He'd have to go back to Abila Harb. Everything pointed to her as Zac's mother, although there was a significant weakness to the hypothesis. Elizabeth would have been doing Abila a favour by assisting in the plan, yet she intensely disliked the woman for having slept with Utley. On the other hand, perhaps the intervention in Corinne's and Abila's lives and the ongoing role she'd played over the years had paid the dividend she'd needed.

He'd stowed his boat at Tamesas, and was cleaning it when his phone pinged with a text from Nora.

Hard news. Cancer has spread to lungs. Waiting for further test results. Fed up of hospital.

He leaned against his boat. What a crap ending to a crap day.

Want me to come and visit?

Nah, as you were.
Depressing place.
I'll text again.

Just say what, where and when.

There was no further reply. He walked home, heavy-hearted. He'd been hungry but his appetite had vanished.

He poured a glass of wine and slumped in front of the TV, watching a programme about the possibility of a multiverse. He warmed to the premise that there might be parallel universes where Nora didn't have cancer, Branna still lived in London and he'd found Zac Buckley.

CHAPTER TWENTY-ONE

Abila Harb was finishing off a triple-decked sponge cake when Swift arrived.

'You'll have to wait a few minutes while I finish this,' she said chirpily. 'It's Beryl's birthday and we're celebrating later.'

He sat at the kitchen table, watching as she spread a final layer of jam and cream and dotted the top with raspberries. Her hands were steady as she concentrated, a pair of glasses perched on the end of her nose. She didn't strike him as a woman with a secret, or one worried that she'd been found out, but she'd have become skilled at concealment if she'd once finessed a deal with Corinne. And if Elizabeth Utley had tipped her off, she'd have been forewarned about his discoveries.

She covered the cake with a tall Perspex dome and manoeuvred it into the fridge. 'There, one job done.'

'Are you having a party?'

'Nothing as grand. Just a cosy little get-together with the family: nibbles, champagne and cake.' She rinsed her hands, removed her glasses and sat opposite him. Her headscarf today was white with a pattern of blackbirds. 'I don't under-stand why you want to see me again. I told you that I can't add anything to my email. I do have a lot to get on with, so could we keep this brief?'

He'd decided to lay all his cards on the table. While he went through the main points of his investigation, she sat very still, a twitch of her mouth the only sign of emotion. He stopped short of accusing her, but saw that she had worked out why he'd returned.

When he'd finished, she lay a hand across her breastbone. 'What Kevin and Corinne did by taking in those boys was selfless, very generous.'

'It was a big commitment, but he wanted to give his brothers a chance in life.'

'And yet they were split up and Corinne was persuaded to concoct a tissue of lies about Zac. Elizabeth Utley is even more cruel than I'd imagined.'

'And takes pleasure from manipulation and deceit.'

Abila gazed out at the garden. 'She conspired with someone to cajole Corinne into parting with Zac, and then sent Corinne annual updates on his childhood from the firm where she worked.'

'In a nutshell, yes.'

'Poor, poor Corinne. She'd have found Elizabeth overwhelming. And Elizabeth's motive for doing this? What drove her?'

'She's such a strange woman, I can only guess that she wanted to pull strings.'

Abila put her elbows on the table, leaned forward. 'I didn't say this before, because I couldn't be sure, but Corinne might have had a thing with Raymond Utley before I arrived at the school. She implied it once, but then closed down the subject. If Elizabeth had discovered that — and I'm sure she would have — she'd have been getting her own back.'

'That would add up,' Swift said. Why was Abila mentioning this now? Was it a scrap of information to divert him? Elizabeth had denied that there had been such a liaison, but that might have been part of her disingenuous agenda. 'I have to ask you, did you take Zac?'

She stared at him. 'I could see that this was where we were heading.'

'You'll appreciate why the path seems to lead to you, given what I've explained. You'd lost your child and Corinne had played some part in the events that led to her death far away from you. I could see Ms Utley relishing the eye-for-an-eye aspect of it and drawing the two of you into the scheme.'

'I will bear undying shame and regret about what happened at the school and the tragedy that followed.'

'I'm not sure Elizabeth has much time for those emotions.'

She winced. 'I hate the way you've come here to my home, resurrecting all these awful bits of history.'

'I'm sorry.'

'Are you? I doubt it. It's just a job to you, money in the bank.'

He opened his mouth to defend himself, but couldn't be bothered. People often got angry with him when he raised spectres from the past.

'You haven't answered my question.'

Abila shoved her chair back so hard it almost toppled over. She righted it, switched the oven on and rested with her back against the door. Her cheeks flared with colour. 'The answer is absolutely not. I had nothing to do with Zac's disappearance. I've never been to this park you mentioned, or colluded with Elizabeth Utley. I would never have been party to such a terrible trade-off. What you've described is so appalling it stuns me. Actually, I'm insulted that you could suggest such a thing — I lost my own child and you accuse me of taking another woman's? A woman who was my friend, who I was fond of—'

High-pitched giggles and voices sounded, and two figures tumbled through the kitchen door, a woman a little older than Abila and one in her twenties. Swift recognised her from the graduation photo on the wall. They looked taken aback at Swift's presence.

Abila rallied. 'Beryl, Grace, this is Mr Swift, the private detective I mentioned before.'

'Oh, yes,' Beryl said. 'It was something about your friend Corinne.'

'That's right, and I told him what I could. He's come back today, a happy, celebratory day for us all, to accuse me of stealing Corinne's son, a boy called Zac Buckley, and raising him as my own. Did either of you notice that I've been hiding a boy in the attic over the years, educating and feeding him? I suppose you might have seen or heard something.'

Beryl gave an astonished laugh. 'What on earth? Stealing a boy? As far as I can remember, this has always been an all-female household.'

A perplexed-looking Grace moved across to Abila. 'Are you OK? That's an awful accusation.'

Abila put a hand over her eyes, bowed her head.

'I'm doing my job,' Swift offered. 'It was a question, not an accusation.'

Beryl stood at Abila's other side. 'I'd like you to go,' she told Swift. 'Abila's done her best to help you and I'm not having her upset.' She stopped, pointed a finger at him. 'Hold on, there was a phone call recently, purportedly from a woman at British Gas, asking for a Zac Buckley. Were *you* behind that? Have you no shame?'

Abila's head snapped up. 'You got someone to ring here? You made that up?'

'I'm sure it was him,' Beryl said. 'The name Zac Buckley meant nothing to me. I didn't mention it to you at the time, just another nuisance call.'

The three women stared at him, their gaze wrathful.

'Get out,' Grace hissed. 'Take your nasty mind somewhere else and don't *ever* come near us again.'

He didn't need persuading.

* * *

That evening, Swift walked for miles by the river towards Chiswick. He had to accept that Abila was telling the truth, but he didn't like where that left him.

A misty moon shone a sickly light on the water below. He paused by a silent stretch of the river and gazed at the dark, rippling surface. Jan Brockhill had a contact for Zac Buckley but wouldn't share it. Elizabeth Utley knew who had raised him but refused to say. She was at the centre of this web, yet he couldn't trace her to anyone else he'd talked to.

He must be overlooking something. Was this case going to end in failure? Some had to, by the law of averages, but he was used to success. Also, Steve worried him. What would it do to him if the search proved fruitless? Swift had seen an email from him, asking for an update, but was as yet unwilling to respond.

He stopped at a pub, bought a pint of beer and went outside to the garden, where he sat by a sycamore. Silver lights were twined through the branches, shifting and blending shadows. A breeze whispered through the tree, shaking yellowing leaves and sending them twirling gracefully to the ground. One fell in his drink and he flicked it out before he sipped the malty beer, ruminating on the truths and lies he'd been told. That elusive idea that had teased him before kept drifting in his head, like a floater crossing his vision, then vanishing.

Halfway down the pint, watching leaves dance and drift, it came to him. He snatched up his phone, scrolled through the photos of Zac. There it was — there it had been all the time, but growing, like Zac. He checked his watch: seven thirty. Not too late for a visit.

He disliked the confinement of the Tube, got nervous when the train stopped in the hot, oppressive dark between stations, but it was the fastest route, so he took it.

* * *

This time, they sat in the cosy living room at the front of the house. There were lots of candles in coloured-glass holders and a striking turquoise wallpaper, patterned with tiny pineapples. Jan Brockhill was finishing a bowl of pasta, yawning between mouthfuls. She wore a tracksuit and had her wiry hair scrunched back in a clip. A bottle of red wine stood on the coffee table, next to a half-full glass.

'I've not been in long, I was working in Wood Green today. Can't wait to have a shower and crash out. Want some wine? If so, I'll get you a glass.'

'I'm OK, I had a pint earlier.'

'Best not to mix grape and grain, I suppose. Is there any truth in that?'

'Haven't a clue.'

She laughed. 'That's funny, coming from a detective. I wasn't expecting to see you. I've no news, I'd have told you if I'd heard anything more from our mystery man.'

'Would you, really?'

Jan forked up the last pasta twists. 'I realise that I was a bit off with you last time, but I'd had a hard day and I don't like being put on the spot.'

'That's a shame, because I'm about to do that to you now.'

'Meaning?' She put the bowl down, picked up her wine.

'I have a shrub to thank. An evergreen Daphne, to be precise. You have one in your garden.'

'So?'

'It's pretty, with those purplish-pink flowers.'

She frowned at him over the rim of her glass. 'You said you weren't into gardening much.'

'I read up about the Daphne on the way here. It's slow growing, with a long flowering season, spring through to autumn.'

'Right. It is a lovely plant. Do you want a cutting or something?'

'No, it's a man I'm after, not a plant. But the shrub confirmed where I needed to come. Living, floral evidence, if you like.'

'You've lost me.'

Swift found his phone. 'Zac is standing by the Daphne in several photos, year on year. There it is, growing behind him, but not keeping up with him.'

The room stilled. Jan put her glass down, knocking it against the edge of the table. Like most ginger-haired people, when her face paled, her freckles took prominence.

'I can show you a couple of photos, ones you sent Corinne over the years, via Elizabeth Utley,' Swift carried on. 'I've had two long chats with Elizabeth, but I'm sure she's been in touch and you're up to speed about that.' He held his phone to her. 'Here.'

'How did you get hold of these?'

'Hasn't Elizabeth given you all the details yet? Through a stroke of luck. Steve Buckley, who's hired me to find his brother Zac, has seen them and read the notes talking about the sibling he believed was dead.'

Jan tightened in on herself. 'This could be any garden. Daphne's a common enough shrub.'

'True, but it's such a coincidence, and I'm not keen on those. I got to considering what a coincidence it was, too, that Zac should have been chatting to you in West Ham Park. Of all the parks in all the world . . . You fabricated a neat little story once I got in touch with you. It must have come as a real shock that you'd been spotted, but I expect that Elizabeth helped out when you told her that you'd been seen talking to Zac. You had to offer me an explanation and that was a good one. It made you seem upfront, honest. But you're not, are you? What was your son doing in the park that day — giving you a hand, popping by to say hello to his mum?'

Jan poured another glass of wine, cradled the bottle in her hands. 'What has Elizabeth told you?'

'She'll have been in regular contact with you, keeping you updated, but I'm not sure she's shared everything. It's a habit of hers to guard her information closely. She's given me quite a lot. She did her bit in persuading Corinne to part with Zac, and she admitted that she'd forwarded the annual letters through Daley Mobility.'

'She confirmed that?'

'Yes. She didn't have much option, given that I'd discovered that she worked there in the years the letters were posted.'

Jan sucked in a long breath. 'Elizabeth has always been rock solid. When she rang the other day, she said you'd talked to her but that you were on the wrong scent completely.'

'I was. It was clever of her to feed me enough information to head off in the wrong direction. She wasn't to know that the letters would turn up, but even then, when she acknowledged sending them, she still did her best to misdirect me. I bet she worked out that tease you did about the email, playing me, handily letting me know that Zac had gone away. I can see now that you maintained contact with me to keep tabs on where I was with my investigation. Jan, where is Zac?'

'Not here.' The blind wasn't fully closed. A couple of passers-by had paused outside the house to chat. Jan rose and snapped the cord, blanking the night. Then she sank to the floor, her back against the radiator. 'He's had a good life with me, a lovely life.'

'I don't doubt it, from the photos. Is Elizabeth related to you?'

'I'm her god-daughter.' She rubbed a finger on the pale carpet. 'What's Steve like?'

'A nervous man. Particularly so at present. He's desperate to find his brother.'

'Did you tell him you were coming here?'

'No.'

The central heating clanked, water gurgling in the system.

'I really liked Corinne. We got on.'

'You met in the park near her home.'

'That's right. Elizabeth arranged it.'

'Let me guess. Elizabeth came up with the whole idea.'

'Yes.'

'Then there had to be a way of explaining Zac's disappearance.'

'Elizabeth helped Corinne work out the details about Zac's death, rehearsed her. I realise how grim it all sounds, but it had to be something final to make sense.'

'Of course Elizabeth helped. She'd have loved orchestrating the whole thing. Corinne must have been distraught, having to lie like that.' Swift's mouth was dry. 'I'll have that glass of wine now.'

Jan got up, lifted a glass from a cupboard and filled it for him. She sat back in her chair. 'You have a poor opinion of me.'

'I'm not sure. My judgement doesn't really matter. But I've learned that Corinne was still recently widowed and grieving at that time, so unguarded. Not a good time to make a life-changing decision about one of her children. No chance for regrets afterwards — how could she go back once all those lies had been planted? She did regret it though. She was depressed and guilty for the rest of her life.'

Jan shuddered. 'You're assuming that!'

'I'm basing it on what I've heard. I've listened to Steve. But let's not get into recriminations. Why and how did you get involved in this set-up?'

Jan lifted her feet onto the chair and circled her arms around her knees. 'I was thirty-three. I couldn't have children and I was on my own. I wanted a child so much. My dad had left me this house and some money, so I had a secure home to offer. I was a legal secretary, with a reasonable, steady income. I was considering donated sperm or adoption — although then, as a single person, that wasn't hopeful. I'd discussed the options with Elizabeth — we talked regularly and always got on well. I admired the way she was always so sure of herself.'

'She suggested another, more direct way for you to have a child.'

'Yes. Elizabeth had never had children and she regretted that. She didn't want me to end up with the same disappointment. She told me she'd been to see Corinne and explained her circumstances to me. It was awful — she was so young and she'd been widowed and left on her own as a stepmum. She was in a rented place, struggling to make ends meet and exhausted. Elizabeth explained that Zac was delightful but a handful, and he wore Corinne out, that I'd be doing Corinne a favour by taking him. I was against the whole idea at first, found it shocking.'

'But after a while, when Elizabeth kept selling it to you, it became more acceptable.'

'Well . . . I suppose . . . I met Corinne and then Zac and it all seemed to click into place. What you said about Corinne's guilt — the situation was more complicated than you realise. She was feeling guilty before she gave me Zac.'

'In what way?'

'When we'd got to know each other a bit, she told me that she'd never really bonded with Zac, not in the way she had with Steve. She'd slapped and shouted at Zac sometimes, because he exhausted her. Once, she'd gone out for a couple of hours and left him alone in his playpen. She'd been desperate for some peace. It played on her mind and she fretted about her relationship with him and whether it might always be difficult.'

'You're saying that you came along and offered her a way out.'

'Yes. I'm not claiming that Corinne wasn't conflicted, but in all honesty, I'm not sure that Zac would have had a good life if he'd stayed with her.'

It was more fuel to the fire, helping to explain Corinne's decision. 'Was Elizabeth aware of this?'

'I'm not sure. I didn't mention it to her, but Corinne might well have.'

An ambulance siren wailed mournfully outside. Swift waited for it to die away. 'So things moved on once you'd got to know Corinne?'

'Yes. Elizabeth was sort of a broker, she eased the way for us.'

The wine was decent, an Italian red. Swift needed it. 'Corinne must have had grave doubts, despite her problems.'

'Yes, and so did I. But after we'd met quite a few times and I'd played with Zac, she agreed that I could take him. He was affectionate and lively. We got on really well, formed a bond. Corinne said he'd ask after me when I'd gone. She used to look so tired, drained. One day, she commented that really, she'd borrowed the children, ended up with them through random chance. It was like she wasn't convinced they were hers to keep.'

'Sounds as if she was full of self-doubt.' *And you and Elizabeth exploited it.*

'She was.'

'Did you find out much about Corinne's time at the Royal Victoria school?'

'Just that she'd worked there, and that's how Elizabeth met her.'

She said this with no guile. Swift deemed that she hadn't understood the complexity of Elizabeth's motives, nor the extent of the coercion that she'd employed. If Corinne had also had a fling with Utley, Elizabeth would have seen the opportunity for revenge. He could imagine how the bitter woman had worked on Corinne's uncertainty and badgered her, making her pay for what she'd done: *You played a part in a terrible deceit that led to tragedy and Abila losing her only child. Now you have a chance to put things right. You're not coping and you have two boys who aren't even yours. It's sheer chance that they're with you, you did nothing to deserve them. My god-daughter desperately wants a child and she can give it a lovely home. It would be fair, the right thing to do.*

'So, you agreed the deal and how it would work, with Elizabeth's guiding hand.'

'I was concerned about details, things like Zac's birth certificate, but Elizabeth got a fake one and he became Zac Brockhill. It was amazingly easy once I had that. Elizabeth arranged that there would be an annual letter and photo sent via her.'

'Who wrote the letters?' He could guess.

'Elizabeth did, and I gave her the photos. She always showed me a copy of what she'd written.'

Jan loosened her hair from its clip. It sprang away from her head and she rubbed her hands through it. 'I wanted to let Corinne visit Zac sometimes, and bring Steve. It did worry me that the brothers were being separated. Elizabeth urged me not to do that and told me that's why adoptions had to be clean breaks. Otherwise, parents and children were confused, conflicted. I could see her point. And Corinne agreed to the arrangement about the letters once a year. She didn't say that she wanted to carry on seeing Zac, so I assumed that was best for her too.' She shot him a pleading glance. 'I do believe that Corinne was relieved when I took Zac, and he's been very happy with me.'

Swift gulped wine. What must it have been like for Corinne, driving hundreds of miles home on that Good Friday night? The house would have been empty, silent. Zac had gone and she'd never see him again. Her agony when describing his death would have sounded genuine — he had vanished from her life and she'd grieved. There was no point in describing her existence with Steve in the ensuing years. Jan might get the full picture in time and then she'd have to re-evaluate the deal.

'Why the handover via Sheila Whitehall?'

Jan shifted, the memory evidently causing discomfort. 'Corinne didn't want to just give Zac to me, said it would be too painful. She got the neighbour to agree to have him that day. Frankly, that made it easier for me too.'

Swift drained his glass. 'Has Elizabeth visited Zac over the years?'

'Oh, yes. He loves her, calls her Nan. She used to come round every week, sometimes more often when she worked at Daley's. He still sees her regularly. Elizabeth's been so generous over the years, paying towards Zac's education and holidays. She's helped fund his higher education. He's never wanted for anything, thanks to her.'

So, after her own fashion, Elizabeth had had a long affair behind her husband's back. She'd stitched him up neatly and, as he'd refused her a child, grabbed herself a grandson. She was a piece of work.

'Zac never went to Saffron Walden? Raymond Utley had no idea about all of this?'

'That's right. Elizabeth always complained that he was a very difficult man, a constant adulterer, and they went days without talking. I've never met him. It was a relief for her to visit us and get away from him. Elizabeth is kind, she's been so good to me. I was very keen on setting up my own business and she helped me get started financially.'

It sounded to Swift as if Elizabeth had bought herself into this little family. 'Where is Zac now?'

'He's away. That wasn't a lie.'

'Where?'

She pressed her temples. 'This is so difficult.'

'You might as well tell me. With the information I have now, it wouldn't take me long to find Zac Brockhill.'

Her expression was resigned. 'Southampton. He's at university, studying engineering. He was home that weekend of the cricket match. He called by the park to say hello and bring me a sandwich.' She turned plaintive eyes on Swift. 'What good can this do? If you tell Steve, all hell's going to break loose.'

'Presumably, Zac has no idea that he has a brother.'

'Of course he doesn't! This will upset him so much. I can't even begin to imagine . . . Please, please don't tell Steve!'

'I have to. He wants — *needs* — to find his brother, and I can't keep that chance from him. If Zac doesn't want to see him, that's his decision. I agree that there's going to be a lot of distress, but in a way, you set that in motion the day you got a vulnerable woman to part with her child. I'd like Zac's phone number, please. You need to tell him about all of this. I'll give you twenty-four hours, then I'm going to inform Steve and let him take things from there.'

She got up, moving tentatively like an old woman, found her phone and sent him the number. 'All of this because of a random photo! We have a good life, a contented one, and now it's all going to be thrown into confusion. We'd have been OK if it wasn't for that picture.'

'Seems to me that your set-up was always hugely risky. You must have worried over the years — that Corinne might turn up, or something else would emerge.'

'Elizabeth always reassured me that everything was watertight. My life with Zac was lovely. He was so bright and affectionate. And then when Elizabeth told me that Corinne had died . . . I was relieved.'

'Handy for you, but Steve was left alone. You've no idea of the damage this has done to him.'

She put her face in her hands and wept. Swift couldn't find much sympathy for her. Elizabeth would have to rally round. Her money wasn't going to be able to fix this situation and her well of compassion would be limited, if not completely dry, so he could only wish Jan luck on that front. He emptied the remaining wine into Jan's glass, carried the bottle, her bowl and his glass to the kitchen and put them on the work surface.

He let himself out and closed the door gently. It was raining, a light, refreshing pattering. He watched it hopping off leaves and darkening the pavement. Soon, he'd have to sit down with Steve and go through this long, tortuous history from beginning to end.

He walked to the Tube, enjoying the cleansing wash of drizzle on his face after the twisted story he'd just heard.

CHAPTER TWENTY-TWO

A fortnight later, Steve called unannounced to see Swift. They sat in his basement office with coffee. Steve had requested decaf, which seemed wise. He didn't need any more stimulation.

'Hope you don't mind me dropping in. I had a delivery to make nearby.'

'How are you?'

He hardly needed to ask. Steve's skin had an oily sheen, there was a crop of fresh spots on his chin, and his eyes were heavy-lidded.

'I met Zac in Southampton last week. Skye came with me. He's got a lovely flat with a little garden in a smart area and a car. I asked, weren't students supposed to struggle to make ends meet? He told me his nan bought the car for him and pays his rent.'

'Generous of her.'

'Yeah, that's what I reckoned. Sounds like she dotes on him.'

There it was, a little worm of jealousy. 'I imagine it was a difficult meeting for both of you.'

'Yeah, pretty awkward. We talked for about an hour. His mum had given him some details and he'd seen his nan.'

'She's not really his nan.'

'Well . . . no, she couldn't be, could she?' Steve grimaced. 'Just like Tilly isn't really my aunt.'

The case had been littered with people who weren't really fathers or mothers, full brothers or grandparents, but assuming roles they'd either wanted or had found themselves taking on.

'It was a challenge, working out who was who in all of this,' Swift said. 'Are you going to meet again?'

'Hope so. We agreed we'd be in touch.' He didn't sound convinced. 'The hour flashed by, only time to skim the surface really. I was hoping we'd go for a drink, chill a bit together, but Zac had a tutorial to get to.'

Steve had been the supplicant, wanting more. Zac had been determined to keep his distance.

'What did Zac make of the deal that had been done with Corinne?'

'He didn't want to talk about that. Something about how it was all in the past. I'm not sure how much he's been told about it.'

'Possibly too painful to contemplate.' And his mother and nan would have given him an edited version.

'Skye said Zac's a snob,' Steve continued.

'What's your opinion?'

'He did seem a bit up himself and he talks posh compared to me. Went on about the clubs he's in at uni and how he goes sailing on the Solent. I sat there thinking that, in the end, our mum was a prostitute, so there's no point in having airs and graces.'

'Is Zac aware of that?'

'Not sure. I didn't mention it. Skye warned me not to bring it up at the first meeting.' Steve blinked in the steam from his coffee, sipped it. 'He didn't ask me much about myself. Said he hoped I wasn't noticing his badly ironed shirt.'

Maybe that had been an unkind dig at Steve's work. Swift wasn't warming to Zac, although he had to concede that a visit from Steve would have been trying and the meeting fraught with tension.

Steve took a shaky breath. 'I'm a bit flat now, disappointed.'

'You have to give it time.' Swift winced at the platitude, but it was all that was left in these circumstances. The trouble was that Steve didn't have the temperament to let things play out, and the situation would test the most forbearing character.

'I hoped there'd be a . . . well, a sort of understanding when we met. Like, *hey, that's my brother!* But it wasn't like that. I told him a bit about our dad and how I used to believe Zac's birthmark would taste of strawberry. Hoped that would get a laugh, lighten things a bit, but he didn't really react. I dunno. It was a funny experience.'

'You remember Zac from your childhood, but he doesn't remember you. You have to factor that in.'

'Yeah. I took him a photo of both of us, one of those ones with him on my lap. He didn't really look at it, just put it on a shelf.'

'I expect it was too much for him to take in. There's a lot of ground to cover.'

Steve rubbed his neck. 'I thought I'd be able to sleep again when I found Zac, but now I lie awake worrying that this won't work out. I keep going over all the stuff you found out. I'm so sorry for Corinne. Wish I hadn't said those awful things about her. I want to meet Jan and Elizabeth soon, find out more about how they made the deal with her.'

Swift had been judicious about what he'd passed on to Steve, keeping details about Elizabeth and Jan to a minimum. He'd explained the background about Utley, Abila and Corinne because it helped explain Corinne's residual guilt and her decision to part with Zac.

'It would be best to focus on your relationship with Zac,' he cautioned. 'What happened is in the past, nothing to be done about that now.'

'It niggles at me, though. Bothers me. Maybe Corinne was manipulated and not sure about what she was doing. I reckon it played on her mind for the rest of her life. I dunno, my brain's on overload some days.'

'Have you spoken to Tilly and your uncle?'

'A bit. Uncle Dan's thrilled that I've seen Zac. He asked me to keep him posted. Tilly keeps advising me to take it slow, not rush things.'

Swift was due to meet Nora soon. 'I have an appointment to keep, Steve. You should talk to a counsellor, someone outside the family. This is a lot to handle.'

'I might do that, yeah. Thanks, anyway, for finding Zac for me. Great job you did.'

Swift saw him out. Had he done a great job? He'd done what had been requested. That wasn't necessarily the same thing.

* * *

Nora had asked him to meet her in the Parterre, her favourite bar near Portobello Road. Swift hadn't been back since they'd parted. Too many memories, including that of Fitz Blackmore gatecrashing one of their evenings there. It hadn't changed, still sporting cracked leather armchairs, scuffed floorboards, distressed-oak tables, multicoloured Turkish throws and lighting so low, you had to squint to see your drink. Nora had altered, though. Before, she'd have been wearing one of her nifty work suits with a string tie, her gym kit in her bag, laptop on the table. This evening, she was slouched in her chair wearing jeans and a sweatshirt, a pink beret on her head. When she greeted him, her skin stretched tight across the blades of her cheekbones.

'I've got you a wine in and there's nuts and olives coming.'

'Great. Sorry I'm a bit late. Steve Buckley called in. I found his brother and he's met him.'

'Who'd taken him? Was it the household I made the bogus call to?'

'I was pretty sure they were involved, but it turned out to be another candidate. By the way, your call got me in trouble with them.'

'Good. I was shocked that you suggested such a ploy.' She gave him a weak smile. 'It worked out for Steve, then.'

'I'm not sure. I'm pessimistic about him and his brother forming any relationship. So much has happened there.'

'Not your responsibility, Ty.'

'No. I tell myself that.' He gulped down some wine. 'The Parterre is reliably shabby.'

'I was dreading that they might have had an overhaul and be all streamlined and gleaming.'

'Glad you're well enough to venture out.'

'I needed a boost. Pretend I'm my old self. Self-deception — the best kind.' She was drinking a large glass of white wine. Blue veins stood out in her hand as she gripped the stem.

He searched around for the right words. 'What happens now, in terms of treatment?'

'More poking and prodding and stuff pumped into my veins.'

'I'm sorry.'

'Yeah. No chance of getting back to work anytime soon.'

'I'll lend a hand with whatever I can.'

'Thanks. One of my sisters is coming, the one who's the least of a fusspot. She's younger than me, so she won't be trying to boss me about.'

'You told your family.'

'Yep. No messing about now the lungs are misbehaving. Masses are being offered throughout Dublin, novenas made, rosaries are clicking, prayers shooting upwards. I wouldn't be surprised if there's a petition on its way to the Pope. An aunt informed me that she's making a special devotion to Saint Peregrine.' She raised an eyebrow at him.

'And he is?'

'Patron saint of cancer. I had to google him. He had leg cancer and was about to have an amputation, so he did a bit of praying. Next day, the doctors pronounced him cured.'

'I can't come up with any response to that,' Swift admitted.

Two bowls of nuts and olives arrived.

'You dig in, I'm not hungry.' Nora asked the waiter for another large Sauvignon. 'Don't give me that look,' she told Swift.

'What?'

'As in, she's not supposed to be knocking the wine back.'

Swift went to speak, checked himself. 'Fill your boots, Nora.'

She lifted her glass. 'There's the reason I like you. *Slainte.*'

He echoed the toast. He'd no appetite himself, but he scooped a handful of macadamia nuts, showing willing. Pretending things were normal.

* * *

Mid-October and Swift was replacing a light bulb in the top flat, generally checking the place over and switching on the heating. Faith and Eli were moving in the next day.

His phone rang on the way back downstairs, a call from Tilly Western.

'Have you seen the news about Steve?'

'No, what?'

'I've just sent you a link. I'm an hour from London. Can I come and see you, say around two o'clock?'

He agreed, then checked the article.

MAN CHARGED WITH ASSAULT IN SAFFRON WALDEN

Steven Buckley, aged twenty-six, from London, has been charged with grievous bodily harm and remanded in custody pending a further appearance at court.

Officers attended an incident on 14 October at a house near Saffron Walden in Essex. A woman in her eighties, named by neighbours as Elizabeth Utley, had been punched and beaten.

Ms Utley was taken to hospital with injuries that are serious, but not life-threatening.

*Mr Buckley was arrested at the scene. It appears that
he made no attempt to escape.*

Swift made a strong coffee. He'd been right to have bad
vibes about the fallout from this case. He waited for Tilly
Western, searching for other accounts of the assault, but finding nothing substantially different. Some tabloids referred to
Elizabeth as an old-age pensioner, others to her as a frail, old
lady. He imagined her displeasure at such descriptions.

When Tilly arrived, she refused a seat or a coffee, slammed
her bag down on the sofa and went straight into attack mode.

'I wish Steve had never started all this. You saw how
agitated he was, you should have put a stop to it.'

Swift was worried, but in no mood to be a punchbag.
'That wasn't my call. You're his family. Why didn't you stop
him? You could have stayed with him, offered him some
proper support at a difficult time.'

'How dare you!'

'Don't give me that. You feel guilty, so you're angry and
taking it out on me. That's OK, but don't try to make me
shoulder any blame. When I told him that I'd found Zac,
Skye was with him and he was going to talk to you.'

Tilly leaned on the table. 'Skye didn't stay around for
long, she couldn't put up with him. He was too intense and
moody.'

Swift noted that Tilly wasn't saying what she'd done to
help Steve. He suspected she'd kept her distance, hence the
remorse now. 'Please, sit down.'

She sat on a chair, gripped the arms. 'Steve's admitted
the assault. He could get up to five years in jail, according to
the solicitor I spoke to. The only slight ray of hope is that they
seem to believe that he didn't plan to attack Ms Utley, that he
acted on the spur of the moment. There'll be a medical report
on him, with some assessment of his mental health.'

Swift sat at the table. 'Have you talked to him? How
did it happen?'

'Can I have some water?'

He brought her a glass, set it beside her. She'd calmed herself.

'When Steve told me the things Elizabeth said, I understood why he lashed out. I'm not condoning what he did, it's terrible, but she insulted him and Corinne. She was so cruel to him, needled him. Why would she do that?'

'It seems to come naturally to her.'

'How horrible.' She drank the water, emptying the glass. 'Steve found Elizabeth Utley's address, decided to go and see her. He wanted more details about what had happened. Zac and Jan Brockhill kept putting off talking to him, so he got frustrated. You've seen how he is — it all swims around in his head. Elizabeth told him that Corinne had cheated with her husband when she worked at the Royal Victoria school and had encouraged her friend, Abila Harb, to do the same. According to Elizabeth, Corinne was a duplicitous bitch and deserved everything that happened to her. She'd been weak-willed and unable to care for two children, especially Zac, who was bright and active. She told Steve that he'd been a lacklustre boy, inoffensive but an introvert, so not much bother in comparison.'

Swift groaned, rubbed his forehead.

'Yes, exactly. Such a venomous woman, no regard for Steve. Then she added that the proof of who'd been the more capable mother was in front of him. He ironed people's clothes and Zac was doing a PhD, taking part in cutting-edge research. He'd be Doctor Brockhill before too long. That's when Steve lost it and went for her.'

'Is she recovering?'

'Yes. She should be home soon.'

Swift had no doubt that the formidable Elizabeth would bounce back. Steve, on the other hand, would have a criminal record.

Tilly retied the silk scarf around her neck. 'Zac heard about the attack and he contacted Steve, saying he never wants to speak to him again. So, you see, this search was in vain. All it's done is vilify people and turn stones that were better left untouched.'

'I did try to warn Steve about the dangers when he first approached me. He was determined. I don't believe that he'd have let it alone if I'd refused to investigate. He'd have gone to someone else. Putting myself in his shoes, I'd have found it hard not to ask questions.'

Tilly sounded defeated. 'I expect you're right. That woman Elizabeth sounds pure poison. My blood boils at how she criticised my sister and how she treated her. Corinne was only trying to do her best in very difficult circumstances. She was misguided and foolish, but I believe she acted with good intentions.'

'I agree. Corinne stood little chance against Elizabeth Utley, who has an iron will and deliberately exploited her grief. And Elizabeth benefited from her exploitation. She got a stake in a "grandson" and the revenge she'd been after.' *And she hoodwinked her husband for years, which must have afforded her enormous satisfaction.*

Tilly went quiet. 'I'm sorry, I didn't mean to go for you. I'm just so upset and worried about Steve.'

'Can I get you more water, or something stronger?'

'No, thank you.' She opened her bag and handed him an envelope. 'Steve asked me to give you this note. I have to go now and sort some things out. I'm staying at Steve's flat for a couple of days and I want to fetch some bits and pieces for him. Then I'm going to pay a visit to Jan Brockhill, see if we can attempt to pick our way through this muddle. I need to get hold of Dan Buckley as well. Steve gave me his number. He might be able to offer some support.'

She left a trace on the air, a powdery scent like talcum. Swift sat at the table, hands cupping his chin. After all this, Steve might have lost the brother he'd yearned for all along.

Swift opened the note. A hesitant hand, uneven lines.

Dear Ty,
I'm sorry about this. I've really messed up. I expect Tilly will be gunning for you, but take no notice. I didn't mean to hurt Ms Utley. Zac and his mum were keeping me at

arm's length and dodging my questions. I started to write it all down, trying to get it sorted in my mind, and the more I wrote, the more I had gaps that I needed to fill in.

Ms Utley was so horrible, taunting me. She said awful things about Michela and Corinne and bragged about Zac and his potential. She claimed that she'd saved him by getting him away from me and Corinne. I just shrivelled up listening to her.

I lashed out and now I've thrown it all away and upset Tilly. Skye won't return my calls. Uncle Dan might come and see me, but after this, he'll regret that he ever got involved with me.

Sorry again after all your hard work.
Steve

Swift paced up and down, sat for a while, then paced again. He reached for his phone. This went against his rules of engagement, but he'd never been involved in circumstances like these, and sometimes, you had to tear up the rule book.

CHAPTER TWENTY-THREE

'I don't drink tea or coffee. I can offer you fruit juice or herbal tea.'

'Nothing for me, thanks.'

Zac's living room was spacious, lined with books, the furniture Nordic and minimalist. He was polite, bland almost, but Swift caught a flicker of curiosity in his eyes. Swift himself was unusually nervous, as if he was picking his way through a minefield. It had taken him three attempts to get hold of the man, who had finally agreed to see him.

Zac's grey T-shirt bore the motto, *YOU CAN'T CONTROL THE WIND BUT YOU CAN ADJUST THE SAILS*.

'I like the logo. What type of boat do you sail?'

His voice was modulated. 'Various. Mainly Fireflies.'

'Handy, studying by the sea.'

'That was one of my reasons for applying to Southampton.'

'You did your first degree here as well?'

He stretched his arms along the back of the sofa. He was so much more confident than Steve, with distinct polish and ease. A little smile played on his lips, which made him appear supercilious, but it might have been tension. 'Yes. I love being by the coast. I might stay here once I've finished my PhD.'

'I have a boat and row as often as I can. Mainly on the Thames and other rivers, but I've done some coastal rowing too. Being on the water's therapeutic.'

'It certainly is.'

'You must have needed that therapy recently.'

'You're right, I have.'

'I was surprised that you finally agreed to meet me.'

'I was going to refuse, but then I decided that I was interested to see what you're like.' That little sneer again. 'I expected you'd be a bit seedy and grubby.'

Ouch. 'I hope I disappoint on that score.'

'Outwardly, yes, but as for what's in here . . .' He tapped his head.

There were times when Swift was happy to trade insults, but this wasn't one of them. 'In case you're interested, I submitted an account of my investigation to Steve's solicitor to help demonstrate the stress he's experienced in recent months. He's out on bail now, and he's gone to Durham to stay with his aunt. How is your nan?'

'Improving all the time. I spoke to her last night. There's no lasting damage, thank goodness, and she's made of strong stuff.'

There was a silence. Swift cleared his throat. 'This is odd and uncomfortable. I've discovered a great deal about your family background and all its complexities.'

Zac tilted his head, pushed a lock of hair back. 'It's quite unpleasant. Some days, it's as if I've been spied on, had someone going through my rubbish bin. Who wants to hear about children being dumped and passed around like unwanted presents? Truth is, I resent you. Whatever story you've uncovered, it's not mine. I can choose for it not to be. Do you understand?'

'Maybe. Refusing to face reality can cause problems.'

'Facing reality doesn't seem to have done Steve much good.'

'I have to concede that, yes.'

'I didn't ask for Steve to start all this.' He was truculent now. 'It was his choice. I need to protect my mum and my nan.'

'You can only ever protect another person up to a point.'

Zac jabbed a finger at him. 'You can put away your homespun wisdom. Maybe Steve got conned by it, but not me. I decide what's my reality. If you've come to plead Steve's case, don't bother. I abhor violence. What he did to Nan was unforgiveable and I won't forget it. I don't wish him ill, but I don't want him in my life and I've told him that.'

'I've come, I suppose, because I worry for both of you young men. You've both been lied to.'

'I'm not condoning the lies, but what's in the past is better left there. I've no memories of Kevin and Corinne Buckley, although I understand that I owe them for taking me to live with them. From what I've been told, Corinne was no saint and found it hard to cope with two kids. I love my mother. She's the one who brought me up. I don't want to listen to negative things about her, or my nan.'

'I understand that,' Swift replied softly, 'but aren't you just a bit excited about having a brother?'

'Excited?' He pondered this. 'I was stunned and interested to start with. Confused. It was a lot to take in. Now, after what's happened . . . I've spent most of my life without a brother and I haven't missed the experience, so I reckon I can carry on without one.' He clasped his hands. 'I'll be frank. If I'd met Steve in any other situation, I wouldn't have wanted to pursue the acquaintance. He's quite alarming, lacks self-control. I didn't warm to him or his girlfriend with the chavvy name, and even before what happened with Nan, I wasn't keen on meeting again.'

'All I can say is that he was thrilled at the prospect of finding you and meeting you after so many years. It meant a great deal to him.'

'I am touched by that, but I don't share the feeling.' Zac tapped a foot, impatient.

Swift didn't buy it. The framework of the young man's life had been blown apart, just as his brother's had, with everything thrown into question. Zac's way of handling it was denial and putting on a protective front. Swift understood that, although he presumed that the emotions would engulf Zac at some time in the future.

He couldn't see any way forward here. One question still bothered him.

'Your nan's husband had no idea that you existed. Did it not seem strange to you that you never visited her home?'

For the first time, Zac showed discomfort. 'Nan explained that she had a tricky marriage and her husband was a serial adulterer. He could be unpleasant and short-tempered. I accepted that she wanted things that way, and she came to see us pretty much every week, brought treats. We went on lots of trips. Mum always told me that Nan liked to have time out from her marriage and it did her good to get away from home.'

And of course, she was the generous source of money and other goodies over the years. Swift checked himself. Maybe he was being too cynical. Zac had grown up with that status quo, and perhaps Elizabeth Utley had, for once in her life, been genuinely fond of someone and wanted the best for them.

'I've met Raymond Utley, and your nan. It's not a happy marriage and not a house I'd want to take a child to visit.'

'I expect you've come here because you're a tad guilty at what you've stirred up.'

'I have concerns — mainly about Steve — but no, that's not true, and I'll tell you why. I've no idea what you've been told by your mother and your nan, but I expect it's a cleaned-up version of how you came to be Zac Brockhill. It's Elizabeth Utley who should carry guilt about this whole situation, because she set it all in motion. But I'm sure she doesn't and never will. She's not the type.'

Zac put a hand up. 'We should stop there.'

'I agree. I've no interest in upsetting you and I'll go now. All I ask is this: please don't write Steve out of your life without considering another conversation with him. Whatever's happened, he was an innocent party, just like you. He may not be on your social register and he shouldn't have attacked Ms Utley, but he moved heaven and earth to find you. Steve didn't do as well as you did out of the deal that was struck. He is your brother. He's actually a blood relative of yours, unlike your mother or your nan.'

Swift detected a flash of emotion then, but Zac quickly buried it, stood and led him to the door. 'Drive carefully,' he said.

Swift hoped that wasn't a hex. He drove to a garage and filled the tank, picked up a coffee. He didn't entertain much hope that Zac would relent. There had been a whiff of conceit about him, and for now, he couldn't see any positives in creating a fraternal bond.

The coffee was acidic, but that was probably the taste the meeting had left in his mouth. He drank half and deposited the rest in a bin.

A text arrived from Nora, making him smile.

My sister's driving me nuts. Lots of advice, intense glances and bloody fussing. I'm on my knees to St Peregrine, beseeching him to work a miracle and magic her back to Dublin.

He drove on and joined the motorway to London. Time to let go of the Buckleys and Brockhills and focus on his own family, which offered plenty of complications closer to home. Branna would be visiting soon, and when he got back he needed to book the return flights to Guernsey.

He wondered if his daughter was still entertaining dark forebodings about the baby and hoped that her stay wouldn't turn his flat into a battleground.

Was there a patron saint of anxious fathers? He'd check it out when he reached Hammersmith.

THE END

Thank you for reading this book.

If you enjoyed it please leave feedback on Amazon or Goodreads, and if there is anything we missed or you have a question about, then please get in touch. We appreciate you choosing our book.

Founded in 2014 in Shoreditch, London, we at Joffe Books pride ourselves on our history of innovative publishing. We were thrilled to be shortlisted for Independent Publisher of the Year at the British Book Awards.

www.joffebooks.com

We're very grateful to eagle-eyed readers who take the time to contact us. Please send any errors you find to corrections@joffebooks.com. We'll get them fixed ASAP.

Lightning Source UK Ltd.
Milton Keynes UK
UKHW011038070223
416609UK00008B/2115

9 781804 055335